# VANDAL

ASHES & EMBERS BOOK 2

CARIAN COLE

carian cole

# COPYRIGHT

ashes & embers series, book two

Copyright © 2015 by Carian Cole
All Rights Reserved.

No part of this book may be reproduced in any form or by any electronic or mechanical means, including information storage and retrieval systems, without written permission from the author, except for the use of brief quotations in a book review.

This is a work of fiction. The names, characters, incidents, and places are products of the author's imagination, and are not to be construed as real except where noted and authorized. Any resemblance to persons, living or dead, or actual events are entirely coincidental. Any trademarks, service marks, product names, or names featured are assumed to be the property of their respective owners, and are used only for reference. There is no implied endorsement if any of these terms are used.

The author acknowledges the trademarked status and trademark owners of various products referenced in this work, which have been used without permission. The publication/use of these trademarks is not authorized, associated with, or sponsored by the trademark owners.

Edited by Lisa Christman of Adept Edits

Originally Edited by: Lauren McKellar

Cover photography by Invicta's Art Photography

Model Ash Armand

Proofreading by Proofreading by the Page

Special thanks to Rudy for da words xo

*This book is intended for mature audiences.*

# dedication

*To everyone who has fallen in love with the damaged, scarred, hurt and lonely.*

*Embrace them. Accept them. Love them.*

*Keep them.*

*"Loving me will not be easy, loving me will be war.*
*You will hold the gun and I will hand you the bullets.*
*So breathe, and embrace the beauty of the massacre that lies ahead."*

***- R. M. Drake***

# a note from *the author*

Dear Reader,

First, my sincerest thanks for reading my books. It means the world to me to have my stories read.

If you've read Storm, or the other books in the Ashes & Embers series, you know those guys are mostly sweet and sexy, and there are quite a few humorous scenes.

Vandal is much different. He's dark; tortured and damaged. He's not very sweet, and he is rarely funny. However, as he learns to give and accept love, he has some fleeting moments that may make you swoon, or at least want to reach through the pages and give him a hug or offer him a smile.

There are what some may consider triggers in this book. It deals with the tragic death of a child and the grief of her family. It shows the self destruction a person dealing with guilt may go through. Our Hero has had a rough past, and his demons still haunt him as he tries to navigate through the blows that life keeps handing him. He has addictions. He occasionally cuts. He can be an asshole. He has control issues and fetishes that involve light BDSM.

This is not a sweet romance. It's the story of two people dealing with grief, despair, and anger in ways that you may not agree with. Please keep reading. Please try not to judge. People behave in very strange ways when they are attempting to cope with circumstances that are tearing them apart. That doesn't make them bad people, that makes them human. None of us are perfect.

I have always been drawn to the dark, raw beauty of damaged people. I want to love them, when usually no one else will.

If this sort of story is not your cup of tea, you can easily skip this book and move to the next in the series. You could read Vandal's story last, or never read it, and you will still be able to enjoy the Ashes & Embers series. I do hope you'll give Vandal a chance, though.

*Thank you!*

# chapter one

VANDAL

I'm balls deep in my latest blonde when my cell phone starts to vibrate, skidding across the nightstand beside my bed. I drive harder into her, her mile-long legs wrapping tighter around my waist, cherry-red nails digging into her palms, chains clanking against the mahogany headboard.

"Ignore it," she hisses when I glance over at the buzzing device.

*I should have gagged her, too.*

I might have ignored the call if I liked her more and if I didn't hate being told what to do, but instead I stop moving, my dick still stuck deep inside her, and reach across her face to pick up my phone.

"What?" I say, holding the phone against my head, disregarding the writhing chick beneath me.

"You're late." Her voice in my ear is bitter and annoyed. *As usual.*

"Uh, I left you a voicemail hours ago saying I'd bring her home tomorrow. She was exhausted and cranky, so I just let her go to bed."

"You know I never check my fucking voicemail. I've been out all day and then fell asleep. I only just realized what time it was."

"She's sleeping. Just let her stay here, and I'll bring her back in the morning."

Things crash and bang on the other end, and I hold the phone away from my ear. "No, Vandal. You know the rules. You bring her back by eight o'clock. You don't get to just extend your time whenever you feel like it. It's after ten already."

I shift my weight, my dick softening. Renee shakes her head at me with annoyance, pulling at her chained hands.

*Join the club, honey.*

"Deb, it's late. She's sleeping. I'm fucking flat-out exhausted. By the time I wake her up, deal with her crying because she doesn't want to leave, and get her packed up and to your place, it will be after midnight."

Her voice is razor-bitch-sharp. "I don't fucking care, Vandal! And don't think I can't hear the chains in the background. I know exactly what you're doing. I'll call my lawyer right now and tell him you're violating the agreement. I want my daughter home. *Now*. You've had her for a week."

I narrow my eyes at the clanking chains and the bitch purposely making sure she was heard making them clink.

There's no way I'm going back to court. Not again.

"So, what's a few more hours? She's asleep in her bed. She had a great day at the zoo, and she's tired. Let her stay. I'll take her for breakfast and have her home by nine. What's the big fucking deal?"

"The *big fucking deal* is you don't get what you want whenever you want it just because you're a rock star. I want her here tonight or I'm calling my lawyer!"

*Click.*

I let out a long, aggravated breath and roll off of Renee.

"Seriously?" she asks as I release her hands from the shackles. "We're kinda in the middle of something."

I swing my legs over the edge of the bed, toss my condom in the trash, and reach for our clothes on the floor, throwing hers over to her.

"I don't have much of a fucking choice, do I? I can't deal with any more lawyer shit. I love seeing my kid; I can't risk Deb getting her tits twisted and trying to take more visitation away from me."

It took me two years to pass enough drug and alcohol tests to get the visitation I have. I'm not fucking it up. "Put your clothes on and mind your own business," I growl.

"Can't I just stay here? I don't feel like driving around with you and your kid all night."

Standing, I pull my jeans up to my hips and zip them, not bothering to button them.

"No. Last time I let a chick stay here alone, she went through my shit. That privilege has been permanently revoked." I pause. "Unless I leave you chained to my bed while I'm gone."

"Asshole," she mutters under her breath as I leave the room. Ignoring her, I pull my boots on as I shuffle down the hallway to my daughter's bedroom.

Katie, the one and only ray of sunshine in my life, is fast asleep in her bed, the pink comforter wrapped snug around her. I sit on the edge of the mattress and turn on the small lamp above it.

I give her a gentle shake. "Wake up, baby girl."

She stirs, hugging her teddy bear to her chest. Her big brown eyes that look just like mine flutter open and stare at me sleepily.

"Come on, sweetheart. I have to take you home."

She scrunches up her face. "Nooo, Daddy. I sleep here with you."

I brush the dark curls off her face. "I know, sweetie, but Mommy misses you a lot and wants you to come home now."

The tears start, cracking my heart in two, and I hate that witch for making me do this. If I had my way, I'd have sole custody and would make sure she never had to go stay at her crazy mother's house. The last thing I ever wanted was to have a kid with some bitch I can't even stand, but a night of drinking, drugs, and big tits resulted in exactly that.

My daughter clutches my hand. "Daddy, I don't want to go."

Gently, I pick her up and hold her close to me, and she immediately wraps her arms around my neck. I breathe in her baby scent, knowing I'm not going to hold her for another two weeks. Every time I see her she's bigger, talking more, playing with different kinds of toys. I hate Deb, but I refuse to let my daughter have a fucked up childhood like I did, with a father who skipped out and never looked back. It's bad enough she's got a selfish bitch for a mother and a recovering addict father who's in a rock band and likes to chain women up. I make sure when she's with me she gets tons of love and attention—no matter what.

"Don't cry, Katie-bug. I'm going to see you real soon. I promise." I wipe her tears with my thumb and smile at her, not wanting her to pick up on my annoyance with her mother. For a five-year-old, she's amazingly in tune with my moods and feelings.

She pushes her favorite teddy bear into my face. "Teddy wants to stay with you, Daddy. He'll take care of you."

I laugh and take Teddy from her. "I'm going to let him sleep in your bed. He'll be right here waiting for you when you come back," I say, tucking Teddy under the comforter.

She gives me her best smile as I kiss her soft cheek. I carry her out to the living room where Renee is perched on the couch, clad in a mini skirt and high heels.

"Can we go so we can get back here and finish what we started?" Renee has a one-track mind, and willingly spreads for me like peanut butter. Any time. Anywhere. That's something I like when I'm getting what I want, but she becomes annoying as all hell when I'm not screwing her.

Balancing Katie on my hip, I grab her duffel bag of clothes and my car keys. "Renee, I'm completely exhausted. I just want to sleep when I get back home. Alone. You can stay in the guest room. Take it or leave it, but I still ain't letting you stay in my house by yourself."

Katie rests her head on my shoulder, already falling asleep again. The past few days have been crazy, with visits to the zoo, a carnival, and two local hospitals, where Katie and I visited sick kids and brought them teddy bears. It's something we started doing last year when a little girl in her daycare program had a long hospital stay. Last night, after putting Katie to bed, I stayed up all night laying tracks for the band's new CD. According to my quick math, I haven't slept in more than twenty-six hours.

"If she wanted her back so damn badly, why couldn't she drive here herself and get her?" Renee whines as she follows me into the garage. I buckle a drowsy Katie into the car seat in the back and motion for Renee to get into the passenger side.

"Let's go. Get in the car."

Yawning, I get behind the wheel of my new Mustang and push the button for the garage door as Renee slides in next to me.

"This fucking blows," she mutters.

"Don't swear in front of my kid. I don't want her growing up thinking women should talk like that. I said you could stay for a few days while your apartment is being painted, but I didn't agree to have you nagging at me non-stop. You know the deal – you're a toy. Nothing else. How you feel about anything doesn't matter to me. So shut it or go stay in a hotel."

Renee shakes her head and slouches in her seat. "Whatever, Van."

I turn to check on Katie once more before I back out of the driveway. She's fast asleep, her head tilted to the side, her lips parted. I can't help but smile. I love that kid.

Fifteen minutes into the drive and Renee is asleep, too. I'm fighting to stay awake myself; the dark, tree-lined roads are almost lulling me. I pop some gum into my mouth, hoping the sugar will give me some energy, and turn the radio up a tiny bit more, eyeing Katie in the rearview mirror to make sure it doesn't wake her. She's used to loud music, but I don't want to risk her waking and having a meltdown.

Fingers strumming on the steering wheel, I start making a mental list of what I need to do tomorrow. Sleep late. Drink a gallon of coffee. Pick up Lukas. Drive to the studio and practice. Ignore Ash and his shit. Maybe go to dinner with Lukas and try to be all fuckin' brotherly. Go home, chill with some good movies, and …

## Vandal

A faraway voice is saying my name. It's echoing, as if it's coming down a long tunnel. I try to shut it out, but it keeps breaking through, rousing me from the deep, quiet space I'm floating in.

"He's awake. Vandal, we're here." Lukas is leaning over me, and he looks pretty fucked up, as if he's wasted. But I know he's not. One thing I know about the brother I don't know, is that he doesn't party.

"Can you hear me?" Concern rips across his face.

"What the fuck?" I try to sit up. "Where am I?" A mix of severe confusion and pain slams into my skull as I try to figure out how I got where I am.

Another face peers over me. "Vandal, just relax. You're in the hospital. We're here." Aria. My aunt. She's clutching my hand at the side of the bed.

*I'm in a hospital bed.*

"What the fuck is going on?" I yank my hand out of hers.

"You were in an accident. You're going to be all right." Aria's voice is calm, as it always is, but her eyes darting over to Lukas tell a different story. She glances over to Lukas again and then flicks her gaze towards the door. "Go and find the doctor," she tells him. He looks at me for a moment and then nods at her before disappearing from my view.

I turn back to my aunt. She looks so distraught I almost feel bad for wrenching my hand away from her. *Almost.*

"What the fuck's going on?" I ask her. Behind her, white blinds cover the window, but the sun is visible through the slats. The sun seems out of place to me. Like it shouldn't be there right now, because just a few minutes ago, I was driving Katie home in the dark. My head snaps back to Aria.

"Katie . . . where's Katie?"

Tears start to pool and shimmer in her eyes as she grabs ahold of my hand again. I notice her eyes shift to the door and then back to me.

"Vandal . . . honey . . ." Her voice cracks, and she covers her mouth with her hand, struggling to compose herself. Aria is a woman that reeks of elegance and class. A famed romance author, she is never at a loss for words and always knows the right thing to say at the right time. I secretly admire her, and envy her sons for having such an amazing woman for a mother. Unlike the crack-whore who spat me out.

"Aria, where the fuck is my daughter?" The fear building in me is so intense that I can actually hear it. It's a roar in my ears and in my brain, attempting to drown my own thoughts out of my head. "Where the fuck is she?"

She shakes her head, tears falling down her cheeks. "She didn't make it," she whispers.

No.

*No. No. No.*

"You tell me where my daughter is." My voice comes out in a raspy, nasty whisper. My chest is heaving in and out uncontrollably, yet I feel as if I can't breathe.

Lukas comes back into the room with a doctor and a nurse following him. I reach for my younger brother and grab his arm hard. "Lukas, where's Katie? She's in the waiting room, right? Out there? Can you bring her in here?"

The doctor steps forward. "Mr. Dawson, I'm so sorry—"

I interrupt him before he can finish. "I'm talking to my fucking brother." I turn back to Lukas, and he's slowly shaking his head. His hair falls into his face, but not before I see that he's crying.

"Please, just bring her to me, Lukas . . . she's gotta be scared . . . she's okay, right?" My head is spinning and I grip the sheets, trying to ground myself. She can't be gone. This is just like that time she wandered off at the mall and was lost for ten minutes. I felt this same exact fear then, but she came back. She'll come back again.

"Vandal, she's gone."

"Shut the fuck up, Lukas!" I turn to the doctor, my pulse racing. The machines I'm hooked up to start beeping and flashing like a 1980s arcade game. "Just bring me my fucking daughter, please."

"Mr. Dawson, you had a collision with another car. Your daughter, female passenger, and the passenger of the other car didn't make it. There was another driver who sustained serious injuries. I'm very sorry for your loss. We did everything we could, but unfortunately, your daughter's injuries were too severe. You've suffered a head injury and several cracked ribs, as well as many bruises and lacerations over most of your body. I know this is very tragic news, but it's important that you remain calm for your own well-being."

"Fuck you!" I lurch up in the bed and a stabbing pain knifes through my ribs and across my skull. "All of you. Get away from me. Deb put you up to this, right? To take Katie away from me? I'll kill that fucking bitch!"

Lukas puts his hand on my shoulder. "No, Van, you gotta rest, okay? I'm gonna stay right here. I won't leave you."

I shove his hand off me. "Fuck off. All of you, just fuck off!" Sitting up, I swing my legs over the edge of the bed, but a wave of dizziness and nausea comes over me. I grab onto the edge of the bed as the doctor and nurse rush over to grab my arms, pushing my brother aside.

"Mr. Dawson, we're going to give you a sedative to help you calm down." Before I realize what's happening, the nurse is injecting the medication into my IV drip. Within seconds, my head starts to swim, and I feel even more nauseous. Katie . . . she can't be gone. Not my baby girl. My only light. They must be wrong. There's no way she could be gone.

"We'll have the toxicology report in a few hours." The doctor's voice sounds fuzzy and far away.

"Thank you, Doctor," Aria replies. "We appreciate your discretion, and for your help with maintaining privacy. My husband will be here soon to help with the arrangements."

"Wait," Lukas says. "What toxicology report? He's totally clean."

"It's standard procedure in cases like this. It's part of the accident investigation," the doctor advises.

My head aches even more as I try to think back to the previous night. I remember being tired, trying to stay awake as I was driving. I remember watching Katie in the mirror. And then nothing. It's blank. *Holy fuck.* Did I fall asleep while I was driving? Did I kill my baby? And Renee? Fuck. *Fuck.*

My chest heaves uncontrollably. "Lukas . . . I think I fell asleep. Fucking shit. Katie . . . please tell me this isn't happening . . . please, Lukas . . ." Every muscle in my body trembles, my skin crawling with intense fear.

Lukas and Aria appear above me again, and my aunt talks to me very softly. "Honey, it was an accident. A horrible accident. It's not your fault. We're going to get through this together, okay? We're all going to be here for you. You're not alone, I promise you. We all know it was an accident." *An accident.*

"The other car may have hit you. That road is dark at night; there are barely any lights. We don't know what happened. We'll find out soon," Lukas adds.

My head throbs. I can't remember anything about what happened, no matter how hard I try. I can only remember feeling tired. I reach up to touch my head and find bandages there.

Lukas pulls one of the visitor chairs closer to the bed and falls into it. He turns to our aunt, his eyes swollen and red.

"Aria, why don't you go talk to the guys, give them an update and maybe go home and get some rest? I'm going to stay here with him."

"Are you sure? Maybe I should stay . . ." Her voice trails off. I can't listen anymore. I don't want to hear anything else. I want all words to stop.

My vision blurs and my eyes droop. I blink repeatedly and stare at the ceiling, but all I can see is Katie. *This isn't real.* None of this is fucking happening. I let my eyelids fall and allow the drugs to take me under. It's been a long time since I felt the pull into the numbness that I used to crave so much. I go willingly, as if meeting an old friend.

# chapter three

V A N D A L

There's no escape from this nightmare. Sleep brings no relief. I see her in my dreams, smiling at me, reaching for my hand. I can hear her childish, sweet voice, her innocent giggle. Then I wake and reality rushes into my veins, washing her away, taking her from me over and over again.

"Maybe you should stay at my place for a few days?" Lukas suggests, watching me cram my stuff into the plastic bag the nurse gave me for my things. My clothes are covered in blood, and I can't help but wonder if it's mine, Katie's, or Renee's. Today I leave the hospital, and tomorrow I bury my five-year-old daughter and will never, ever see her or be close to her again. She's gone, forever, because of me and my fucked up lifestyle. Why did I have to try to do so much in one weekend? Why didn't I just sleep instead of staying up all night? Why did Deb have to be such an unreasonable bitch and force me into a corner? If she wasn't constantly trying to make me miserable, this never would have happened. *Katie would still be here.* All I want to do is find a scalpel in this hospital and hide in the bathroom and cut myself until I'm numb again, letting all feelings and emotions seep out of me into a dark puddle.

"No," I say.

"You can come stay with us," Storm offers, putting his arm around his fiancée, Evie. I smirk at my cousin. Like I really want to stay with these two disgustingly happy people who can't keep their hands off each other and smile fucking non-stop. That scalpel is calling my name.

"We'd love to have you stay with us, Vandal. I've got homemade chili cooking in the crockpot. Storm said it's one of your favorites." Evie smiles up at me, but shrinks back from my cold stare. I step closer to her and she sinks into Storm's side a little.

"I hafta bury my fuckin' kid tomorrow. You think I want to sit around with you two fucks and eat chili?"

I morbidly enjoy watching the smile disappear from her face and the way she looks down at the floor. *That's right, honey, don't even look at me. I will fucking eat your soul.* Storm glares at me, torn between saving his girl from the big bad wolf and letting me expel my rage a little. Someday he'll learn he can't love everybody.

Lukas touches my arm. "Vandal, take it easy. We're all just trying to help."

I shrug him off. "I don't want any help. I don't want anything."

Except my daughter. And if I can't have her, I'll take that scalpel now so I can cut this pain out of my body.

I grab my bag. "Can we go?" Lukas is supposed to drive me home since my new Mustang is now a mangled mess of metal, glass, and death.

"No, we have to wait for the doctor to come back and discharge you, and there's some other stuff that needs to be taken care of. I told you this already, did you forget?"

I roll my eyes and sit on the bed. I need to get home and get away from everybody. They're smothering me with all their good intentions and attention, and I have no idea how to accept either from them, thanks to me coming from the fucked up side of this family—meaning the father I haven't seen since I was five. I only just found out I had a brother and a clan of cousins a little more than five years ago. Needless to say, I am adjusting to the whole family thing a lot slower than they are.

"Get out of my way." A familiar female voice snarls.

I turn toward the commotion at my door to see Deb pushing

her way past Storm into my room. I knew she would show up eventually.

"You," she says, pointing at me, barely standing up straight. I don't know if she's drunk or just mentally distraught. Possibly both. "You killed my daughter," she chokes out. "You're a fucking murderer."

I rise to my feet and step towards the woman who gave birth to the only person I've ever loved.

"You made me do this, Deb. Your fucking selfish, crazy, control-freak tantrum caused this." I punch the wall next to her, and my fist goes through drywall. "She'd be alive right now if you had just let her stay for one more night. Really, Deb? You had to fucking threaten me and force me to drive in the middle of the night when I told you I was fucking exhausted?"

"I hate you! You killed my baby!" she shrieks, and starts to smack and kick me.

Storm grabs her and pulls her off me. "Deb, please. This is not the time or place for this." His voice is low as he holds her back.

"He should be in prison! He's a murderer!"

"No one's going to prison, Deb," Lukas says, stepping between us. "It was an accident. A horrible fucking accident. You should just leave. Nobody needs this. We're all upset."

She glares at me over Lukas's shoulder as Storm tries to drag her out the door. "I'm going to make you suffer for this, Vandal! You fucking baby killer!"

"I've been suffering my whole life, you cunt. Don't ever come near me again. We have nothing more to say to each other." A security guard enters the room and yanks Deb out as my doctor comes in right behind them. "I know this is a stressful situation, but can you people please remember this is a hospital? There are sick people here," he scolds, as if we're all stupid.

I can't hold back my sarcastic laugh. "Yeah, one just got dragged away."

"What happened here?" He points to the hole in the wall. "You're going to have to pay for this damage, Mr. Dawson."

"Fine. Whatever. Can I just go home now?"

The good doctor eyes my hand. "I'm going to have the nurse come in and get your hand cleaned up first. And might I suggest you talk to the psychologist on staff? I think you're going to need some anger and grief counseling, Mr. Dawson."

Lukas nods in agreement. "I think that's a good idea, Van. Someone to talk to . . ."

"Fuck. No. I don't talk." What I really need is to go home and talk to my good friend, Jack Daniels, for a few hours.

"Your brother is right," Doc says to me, and hands Lukas a business card. "This is her information. Maybe when things . . . settle a bit, he can give her a call."

"*He's* still in the room," I say sarcastically. "And he's not talking to a fucking shrink."

I sit impatiently on the bed as the nurse cleans and bandages my bleeding and swollen knuckles. Apparently only one nurse and one doctor are allowed to treat me while I'm here to diminish the chances of hospital staff who could be fans of the band swarming in here. I have a feeling my aunt and uncle somehow paid for that to happen.

"Mr. Dawson, I'm hesitant to give you a prescription for sedatives given your history and your current agitated state, although I do think you need something to help you calm down," the doctor comments. I didn't even hear him come back into the room.

"Don't worry, Doc. I'm not going to take the whole bottle. Been there, done that."

"Vandal . . . come on, man," Storm voices from his corner of the room, his fiancée hanging on to his hand as if she's afraid she might get lost if she lets go.

"What, Storm? You don't want to talk about all the stuff that me, you, and my little bro here have in common?"

I watch him look uneasily at his fiancée, Evie, and I know that he hasn't told her about his own little trip to the psych ward years ago. Of course I wasn't part of the family when that happened, but I know all about it thanks to Google. And my younger brother, who I actually kinda like, has deep, telltale scars on both his wrists that even his tattoos can't hide from my knowing eyes.

Funny how much mutual fucked-upped-ness we all have, how parallel our lives were, even though we didn't grow up together.

Just when I think I can finally leave, Aria; my cousin Asher; my lawyer, Sam; our band manager, Don; and our publicist, Helen, all parade into the room.

"What the fuck now? I want to get out of here."

"Vandal, we have to talk about the incident and damage control so you and the band and your family don't get dragged into all sorts of gossip and bad press," Helen says, taking the chair next to my bed. "For once, one of your fuck-ups has actually helped save your ass. You never changed your birth certificate back to your biological name of Vandal Valentine. So, legally you are still Alex Dawson." Well, at least my adoptive parents did something right – giving me a different name. Helen continues, "Therefore, the accident and medical reports have that name because your identification still has it."

"Vandal, next week I need you to come into my office so we can get all this straightened out with you using your birth name again," Sam says.

"Okay," I reply. I completely forgot about changing my name back legally. Once Gram found me and told me what my real name was, I started using it right away and wasn't worried about filing paperwork. I just wanted a new beginning with the name that was given to me.

"Deb is not doing well emotionally, which is understandable," Aria says. "We've offered her a large sum of money to not speak to the press about Katie's accident, or to mention your name, or the band's, and have had her sign nondisclosure agreements and other legal documents that I'm sure you don't want to be bothered with. The bottom line is, she'll be quiet."

"So that bitch is making money off of our daughter's death? Are you fucking kidding me?"

Aria touches my shoulder. "Vandal, it's fine. If it keeps her quiet, so be it. We can afford it. Don't worry about it or waste time thinking about it, please."

I shake my head in disgust. "All Deb ever cared about was using Katie as a pawn to torture me. She's a fucking whore." I have no idea how such a sweet, beautiful little girl came from two messed up people.

"Thankfully, due to the fact that this is a very small town and your family is so well known and liked, we were also able to pay a few people at the scene to keep quiet and had them sign non-disclosures as well. Also, since the band is made up of family members, there is no worry of any of them talking or selling a story."

"I'd be willing to sell his story for a price," Asher says, half joking.

"Shouldn't you be up on the fourth floor right about now?" I shoot back at him.

"Guys, that's enough," Aria scolds. "Asher, that's not even funny, and Vandal, that was uncalled for and cruel."

My cousin and I glare at each other.

Helen snaps her fingers at us like we're dogs. "The hospital has been wonderful with keeping your visit here discreet. All staff that handled your case, Katie's, and Renee's, have also signed non-disclosure agreements. Renee's only relative that she had any contact with was her older brother, and he showed no interest in you, or her, for that matter. He almost seemed relieved that she was gone. Apparently she'd been in and out of rehab for years."

"Excellent choice in women," Asher comments.

I flip him my middle finger. "At least I'm not jerking off to a corpse every night like you are. Go fuck yourself."

"You two better bury the hatchet." Don stands and paces the room. "We're all tired of it and it's doing nothing to help the band. This is some serious shit happening. You aren't playing in your basement anymore."

Helen continues, "I believe we have covered all of our bases to ensure that no part of this tragedy ends up in the wrong hands. Yesterday we issued a brief press kit stating that there had been a horrible accident, and we ask for sympathy and privacy for everyone involved during this difficult time. I suggest you lie low for a while, Vandal."

"Thanks for all your help with everything," I mumble, my head is spinning thinking about how sick it is that I have to be grateful people aren't talking about my child being killed and some of them even have to be paid off. If anyone tries to exploit what happened to my baby, there'll be hell to pay.

I don't say anything as Lukas drives me home. Time feels fucked to me, as if it's been years since the accident when in fact it was only three days ago.

"I could stay with you for a few days so you're not alone."

"I like being alone. I'm used to it." My voice sounds flat and empty, even to me.

He glances away from the road for a moment to read my face. "You don't have to be. I know what it feels like, Vandal. My life wasn't much different than yours. The difference is, that now I'm trying to make it better."

I stare out the window and into the trees. "I let myself get close to Katie and now she's gone, Lukas. I think it's pretty clear I was never meant to have a family."

"You still have the rest of us. We're not going anywhere."

I know Lukas had a fucked up childhood, as I did. Born six years after me, our father abandoned him when he was just a baby with an eighteen-year-old mother, who gave him to her grandparents to raise until they passed, and he ended up as a teenager in the foster system. When we met for the first time five years ago, he was so excited to have a brother and a bunch of cousins that neither one of us had ever met. Of course, I was a huge disappointment as a brother, being the anti-social asshole that I am. And how could I compare to our perfect Valentine cousins and their equally perfect parents?

The kid didn't give up though. He was determined to be a part of my life, and for us to walk into the welcoming fold of our new family. Slowly, slowly, I've tried to let myself accept these people as family, and they're actually pretty cool. I still struggle with it though.

Lukas pulls into the long driveway of my house and puts the car in park.

"Should I come inside with you?" he asks.

I shake my head. "No. I need to do this alone." I stare out the windshield at the house, which looks lonelier than ever. "Lukas, thanks for being there the past few days. You know I'm not good at this shit and my head is really fucked right now, but I do appreciate you being around."

"Any time. If you need anything, just call, okay? I don't care what it is, day or night . . . anything."

I reach into the back seat and grab my bag. "Thanks, man."

He coughs and hesitates for a second. "Tomorrow . . . I can come and get you; we can go together."

My chest tightens up at the thought of tomorrow. I want to somehow stall time and put off tomorrow for a few years. Fuck, put it off forever. I'm not ready to bury my baby. I will *never* be ready to say goodbye to my Katie.

A lump forms in my throat and my eyes burn as the harsh reality that I will never see my daughter past the age of five crashes into me. I press my fingers against my forehead, wishing I could stop the never-ending pain that keeps getting worse and worse. "Uh, yeah. I think that might be good. I don't think I can . . ." I swallow hard. I can't fucking deal with any of this.

"Vandal, say no more. I'll be here in the morning. I'll have Ivy meet me there. Are you gonna be okay?"

Letting my head fall back onto the seat rest, I shake it back and forth. "Fuck no. I'm never gonna be okay again, Lukas."

"We all loved her. She was a great little kid. But you gotta try to just hang on, ya know? I know all this shit is tearing you apart, but don't let it drag you under."

"Yeah," I say absently. "Be here tomorrow."

I get out of the car before I lose my shit in front of him. No fucking way am I going to break down in front of anyone.

Walking into my house, a burning pain grows in my chest and I can't move past the front foyer. Instead I stand there with my eyes closed, leaning against the door, because I don't think I can take seeing her toys laying where she left them, or her little cartoon cup. I don't want to see her things without her.

The house feels eerie. Too quiet. There's no life here anymore. Just like that, in a moment, everything is gone. I never had a family, I never even *wanted* a family, and then suddenly I had an unplanned child with some crazy bitch that I fucked after a concert and kept around for a little while to party with. Next thing I know, I'm fighting the world just to see my own kid. I lost the first three years of her life because I was too fucked up to be a parent, and now I've lost the rest of her life because her mother just wanted to be a bitch. Katie was an angel and deserved so much better than the two of us as parents. I should have fought harder to keep her safe, and not let my fears of Deb dragging me back to court cloud my judgement. If I had just told Deb no, Katie would be here now. Safe. *Alive.*

I slowly walk down the dark hallway and stop at Katie's doorway. Her pink nightlight is on, illuminating the room. I don't want to go in, but I can't stop myself. The mix of her presence and her void is completely overwhelming, and I fall to my knees in the middle of the room. The pain in my chest is like nothing I've ever felt before, as if my heart is being ripped from my body and sliced into tiny pieces. I want her back so bad. I want to just feel her tiny hand in mine and tuck her into bed.

Lifting my head, my eyes fall on Teddy, Katie's coveted bear that she left here to "take care of me." I crawl to the small bed and lay my head next to the little bear that, just a few days ago, we tucked into her blankets together until she'd be back. Pressing my face against the little bear, I can't hold back my tears anymore.

VANDAL

I'm a shadow at my daughter's funeral. The pain I feel in my heart and soul has turned me into a catatonic zombie. I'm there, but I'm not. Standing next to the tiny, white closed casket, I say nothing as people file by and spill out meaningless words of supposed comfort.

*Closed casket.* Anyone who's ever had a person they love end up in a closed casket knows something horrifying is going on under that lid. I know it. I can't stop thinking about it. I want to pry it open and see my baby. I want to see the damage that I caused so I can torture myself with it for the rest of my life. I want to feel the pain that she must have endured. I want to live in it and suffer in it like I deserve to.

"Vandal?" My grandmother's scratchy voice pulls me from my thoughts.

Turning my head, my eyes drop over a foot to meet Gram's. She squeezes my hand. "Don't turn to dark places, sweetie. Katie will always be watching over you."

"Gram . . ."

She tugs at my hand and I follow because there's no way to deny Gram what she wants. She's five feet of white-haired awesomeness. This is the woman who found me five years ago when she realized her estranged son had two grown children that he'd never told her about. She's the one who insisted Lukas and I get equal shares of my grandfather's millions. Gram changed my life. If only she had found us sooner.

She leads me outside to the porch of the funeral home. The fresh air feels good and helps to clear my head a little bit.

She smiles up at me and smooths my long black hair. She's the only one I let touch my hair. "Losing a child is the worst thing a person can go through," she says, staring off. "A piece of us dies with them."

I nod and wonder which Valentine child she buried and when.

"It won't get better," she continues. "You know all that is crap when people say that. But you learn to move on and carry them in your heart. The pain will never go away. You'll always wonder what they would look like at this age and that age. You'll develop a secret relationship with them, and that's okay." She squeezes my hand harder. "You'll get through this, Vandal. For her, and for you."

"It's my fault, Gram. I never should have gotten in that fucking car." I still blame myself, even though the accident investigation was inconclusive, and I always will.

"Honey, life is a series of mistakes, regrets, bad decisions, tragedies, and occasional good luck. It's not your fault. You loved her. You never would have hurt her."

I rock back and forth on my feet. I hear the words, but I don't know if I will ever believe them.

I stay at Katie's grave until everyone is gone, long after Deb was hauled away by her family, crying hysterically.

"Vandal, we should go now." I almost forgot Lukas was here, leaning against the huge oak tree, watching me.

I can't take my eyes off the mound of fresh dirt I'm sitting next to. My beautiful baby girl, who slept snuggled in a pink down comforter surrounded by teddy bears, is now in a box in the ground. I fight the urge to claw through the dirt and bury myself with her. I want the dirt to slide down my throat and choke me so I can sleep beside her forever.

Lukas's boots appear next to me. "It's getting dark. I'm sorry, Van, but we gotta go."

"I can't leave her."

He shoves his hands into his pockets. "I know. But I have to take you home. And Ivy's waiting for me at my place."

I throw a small rock that I'd been holding. "Must be nice. Does her husband know she's there?" As soon as the words leave my mouth, I regret saying them. I like to hurt people; I always have. I want them to feel the pain that I feel and the disappointments I've been forced to feel. That just seems fair to me. Not fair to Lukas though.

"That was a douche thing to say, Vandal. I know you're hurting, but don't fling your sadistic shit on me. I'm going home. If you want a ride, get up."

I don't look up as he walks away from me to his car, and I have no doubt that he'll leave me here after what I said to him, because I deserve it.

Minutes turn to hours while the sky morphs from blue to fiery orange to gray. I don't want to leave her here, but I know I can't sit in the cemetery all night either. Kissing my fingertips, I press them to the mound of dirt that blankets my daughter.

"Goodnight, sweet girl," I whisper. "I'll be back soon."

When I reach the end of the narrow path and walk through the wrought-iron gates of the cemetery entrance, one lone car remains in the dark parking lot. Trudging over to the black Corvette, I get inside and slam the door. Without a word, Lukas starts the car and pulls out of the lot. I turn to him but his eyes remain on the road, his inked arms taut as he grips the steering wheel, deep in his thoughts.

"Sorry, I'm an asshole," I say after a few minutes of silent driving, and he finally acknowledges me.

"I'm gonna let it slide because I know you're hurting," he says. "But I'll say this: I've tried really fucking hard to get to know you. I thought it was great when we opened the tattoo shop together and got involved in the band together. Unlike you, I was glad to have a family and be around people that understand me and accept me. But you . . . I just don't fuckin' know, man. You act like you hate all of us."

I try to stretch in the cramped front seat. Corvettes must be designed for midgets. All I want to do is get home and be alone so I can drink, pop a few pills, and numb the pain. The last thing I want to do is have a heart-to-heart with my little brother.

"I don't hate you, Lukas. I just don't bond well."

His jaw clenches. "Maybe you should try to *bond*, Vandal. Did it ever occur to you that maybe Katie wasn't the only person that needed you? Or that maybe the people who try to be there for you would like to have some kind of effort back? Not everything is just take, take, take." He glances quickly at me before turning back to the road. "You can be really exhausting, and sometimes I wonder why I bother. If you keep kicking a dog, eventually he's not going to come back. Think about that."

I nod and play with a stray thread on my pants. "I will, Lukas."

We don't say another word for the rest of the drive to my house.

I may be a reckless person, but all the choices I've made in my own self-destruction have been just that: choices. Maybe the path that led me to those choices was out of my control most of the time, but in the end, the decisions have always been mine.

I've been clean and sober for two years, and I chose to do that so I could be a good father to Katie. And as I sit here in bed with a bottle of vodka next to a pile of pills, I choose to go back to my old way of dealing with life.

Sipping the clear, burning liquid while lying in the middle of my bed, my thoughts drift to Renee. I'm pretty sure she's in the ground now, too. *Thanks to me.* Although her death was also ruled to be an unfortunate accident, it's still my fault that she was with me in the car that night. She died trying to be more than she was. She was nothing but a sex toy to me, and an unfortunate victim of my inability to form meaningful relationships with people. I didn't know her well enough to miss her, but I do feel bad that she lost her life. She wanted more than I could give her, even though I'm always honest with the women I fuck. They know there will be no love, no commitment, and no care. There will be fun and there will be fucking. Nothing more. Yet, women always seem to think they will get more, and that they might be the one to change me.

I pop a pill and wash it down with more vodka.

A snake is always a snake.

VANDAL

I'm ripped out of my deep, numbing sleep by someone banging on the front door and ringing the doorbell. Non-fucking-stop. It's obvious after ten minutes of banging that they aren't going away, so I stumble down the hall, holding my sore ribs, wearing nothing but sweatpants, stepping over garbage, empty bottles, and strewn mail on my way.

I swing open the door and Evie is standing there, holding a bunch of grocery bags.

"What the fuck do you want?" I spew at her.

She pushes past me and plops the bags on my cluttered counter, sending a few empty vodka bottles to the floor.

"You've missed the last five practices," she says, looking around in disgust. "No one has seen you in two weeks."

From the fridge, I take out a beer, crack it open, and take a big gulp. "What are you? The fucking band manager now?"

She starts to throw the dirty dishes on the counter into the sink, and then goes after the refrigerator, dragging the garbage can over so she can dump old, rotting food into it.

"This place is disgusting, Vandal."

"No shit. Ask me if I care. Why the fuck are you here?"

"I came to check on you, and bring you some food. And clean, since you apparently need all of the above." She looks me up and down and pokes my stomach. "You look thin."

She completely takes over my kitchen like a tornado, putting groceries in the fridge, rifling through my cabinets, and throwing garbage away.

After listening to the scraping and crashing of her rearranging my kitchen as I once knew it, I take another gulp of beer. "I don't need your fucking help. Does Storm know you're over here, playing maid to his fuck-up of a cousin?"

"Yes, he knows I'm here. You're not a fuck-up, Vandal. Everyone is worried about you. And they need you at practice; the band can't perform without a bass player. You should take a shower, too, you'll feel better."

Chugging the rest of my beer, I toss the empty can onto the counter she just cleaned, and sneer at her. "You can all fuck off."

Evelyn takes a deep breath and looks at me warily. I know she's afraid of me, yet here she is, putting herself right in the line of my fire. I'm not sure if she's determined or just really stupid.

"Thanks for the food. Now get the fuck out of my house." I turn to head back to bed, but she grabs my arm. When I glare at her and rip my arm out of her grasp, she stands there like a lost puppy, bottom lip quivering.

"I know what you're going through, Vandal. I lost both my parents at the same time when I was a teenager. I know how much it hurts."

Lukas's words come back to haunt me: *"If you keep kicking a dog, eventually he's not going to come back."*

I don't know why, but the shimmering tears in her eyes make me lose it. I try to fight crying in front of her, but I can't control the tears that start and the ache that builds in my chest again. I sink to the cold tile floor and she goes down with me, wrapping her arms around me as best she can, holding me close to her.

"It's okay." She whispers those two words over and over. Nothing is okay, but having her close to me makes me feel a little less alone.

I'm not sure how long I cry on the floor with her, but after a while, she takes my hand and leads me to the bedroom, throwing a blanket over me after I fall onto the bed.

When I wake up hours later, she's gone, but my entire house is clean, and my laundry is done and folded. Katie's door is still closed, and I hope Evelyn didn't go in there and touch anything because I want it all exactly how Katie left it. I head to the kitchen to pick at some of the food she left and I find a note taped to the refrigerator.

*"I'll be back next week. I'll keep coming back until I don't have to. ~ Evelyn"*

I crumple the note and toss it in the trash.

I get out my bass and sit on the couch to play, but I just can't get into it. Everything sounds like shit to me. A different fetish is calling my name, and I know it won't shut up until I give in. Laying my bass on the coffee table, I go to the master bathroom. In the back of the closet is a small, painted, black onyx box that I've had since I was twelve years old. I made it myself, not knowing what I would put in it at the time, but it soon housed my most precious items.

I sit the box on the edge of the bathtub and open the lid. Inside are several glistening razor blades, and one very old one, rusty, encrusted with dry blood. My very first blade, which I've kept all these years—a souvenir of sorts.

As I take out one of the blades, my heart beats faster knowing the euphoria that is coming. I push my cut-off sweat pants out of the way and slide the blade down my outer thigh, the trail of red chasing it like a lost lover. Pain has always been my best friend and greatest release. I slide the blade again, a little deeper this time, and close my eyes as the hurt and agony eases from my soul and into my leg, escaping in the drops that slowly drip down my flesh.

The next day I decide to go to the studio and put in some jam time with the rest of the band since I've missed a crazy amount of sessions already.

"Where the hell have you been?" Asher demands the minute I walk into the studio. I drop my bass case and try to focus on him. Hangovers are not my strong point.

"Relax, man, I'm here." My words slur.

My cousin, Talon, puts his guitar down and approaches me, pushing me into the nearest chair. "You're drunk off your ass again. Did you actually drive like this?"

I nod and laugh a little. "I think 'still' is probably more accurate than 'again,' Tal."

He shakes his head at me and looks back at his brothers. "He's a fucking mess, guys. He shouldn't be here."

Storm's huge dog, Niko, trots over and lays his head on my leg. I sink my hands into his long fur. Katie loved this dog and would use him as a pillow, laying her head on him and napping with him on the floor while we practiced for hours. I'd planned to get her a puppy for her next birthday. Leaning over, I rest my head against the dog's big furry one. I want to feel what Katie felt.

"Vandal, for fuck's sake. We know you're hurting, but this shit has to stop. You can't just keep drinking like this; you're ruining your life. Katie wouldn't want you like this. *We* don't want you like this." Storm's voice gets the dog's attention, so he leaves me and goes back to his master's side.

"We have a tour coming up, Van. *Soon,*" Asher reminds me. "There is no way in hell you can play like this. I refuse to let you fuck up my band with your shit. I don't care how fucking good you play. We've all been working our asses off, and we're all trying to help you, but you can't be drunk or high twenty-four seven."

I roll my eyes. "Yeah, I have the two hundred voicemails and text messages you guys have sent me asking me how I'm doing. I get it—you're worried. And I got the fucking gift baskets, and the cards, and the groceries, and the everything else."

Storm steps in front of Asher and puts his hand on his shoulder, always the peacemaker. "Vandal, we've all been talking. You know we've been trying like hell to help you, but you won't even try to help yourself." He takes a deep breath and pets Niko's head before looking up at me again. "We think it's best if you step out of the band for a while, and we have someone else fill in for you for the tour. We just think you need some more time; maybe you should go back into rehab for a while or talk to the doctor. Don't just throw your sobriety away."

"I only straightened out for Katie. It doesn't matter anymore."

"Yeah, it does matter, Van," Asher says. "Your life still matters. But you have to get your shit together."

"Nobody gives a damn about my life."

Storm shakes his head at me. "That's not true. Hopefully next year you'll feel better and can come back. That's what we all want. This isn't just a band. We're family."

I can't believe this shit; they're kicking me out. Katie and the band were my life. Being in Ashes & Embers is like a dream for me. All the years of practicing and playing gigs finally got me somewhere. Ash didn't bring me into the band because he liked me, or because I was family. That fucker hates me. But he loves the way I play bass and my style fits in with them perfectly.

I stand up and look at Storm, swaying a little as the room blurs. "*Feel better?* Is that what I need to do? I didn't realize I was sick."

Storm takes a drag on his stupid e-cig and blows vapor up into the air. "That's not what I meant. I'm trying to be nice."

I flash him an evil grin. "Ya know who's nice, Storm? Your girlfriend. Do you ever wonder why she's at my house every week? Maybe she's bored at home. I think she wants to be tied to my bed."

Storm lunges at me. "You motherfucker!"

Talon grabs him and pulls back Storm's clenched fist that's aimed at my face. "Don't waste your time, Storm," Talon says. "He doesn't even know what he's saying. He's fuckin' wasted."

"As usual," Asher adds. "Just leave and let us know when you can be serious about the band again. We don't have time for all this bullshit. I've got my own issues to deal with."

I grab my bass and turn to him, glaring at him eye to eye and then lower my gaze to his chest. I flick the old skeleton key necklace hanging around his neck that he never takes off.

"You need to deal with reality, cuz," I mumble. "She ain't never coming back."

"Get the fuck out of here," he seethes at me through clenched teeth.

I slam the door on my way out and head for my car. Fuck them. They'll never find a decent bass player to replace me, and the fans will go ballistic. I'm one of the most popular members of the band. They'll be begging me to come back, drunk or not.

Just as I'm about to throw the car in reverse, Talon is banging on my window and trying to open the car door. "Vandal! Get out of the fucking car. You can't drive like this."

"Get off my car," I growl back at him.

"Let me drive you home," He pulls on the locked door handle again. "Open the door!"

I jam the car into reverse and floor it, backing out of the driveway while he's still screaming at me.

I know I shouldn't be driving, but I just don't give a shit anymore. I have nothing left to lose that matters. I want to tempt the hand of fate as much as I can because I should have died in that crash, too, and fate fucked up. Nothing wrong with me giving a helping hand to the powers that be.

# chapter six

## Vandal

The headstone is like a work of art. Now that I'm standing in front of it, I can see why it took three months to fabricate. I think I should apologize to the guy who made it for yelling at him for taking too long. It's a laser-etched scene of a field of flowers, with an image of Katie running, smiling, holding a teddy bear. The detail is absolutely amazing and worth every penny.

Every other Saturday, I visit her grave because every other Saturday was when I would get to see her. I'm just not ready to give up our time yet. I bring a teddy bear with me every time and now her grave is overrun with stuffed toys, as well as various little gifts that other family members must be leaving.

I climb up the huge oak tree that shades this part of the cemetery, get settled on a large, thick branch, and lean back against the trunk. I love the strength of the tree, and I like to think that it's protecting my daughter. Every time I visit, I sit up here and just try to let the quiet seep into me. Maybe it's morbid, but being here calms me and makes me feel grounded to the earth that holds my daughter. It's the only place where I feel like I belong.

My legs begin to feel numb, so I turn to hang them over the branch when I see movement out of the corner of my eye, and slowly turn to see a girl kneeling down in front of a grave not too far away from my tree. This is the first time I've seen another visitor in the cemetery in all the times I've come to sit by Katie. From my perch, I can hear her talking softly to the headstone, placing fresh flowers over the newly-grown grass. *Shit.* I was hoping to leave, but I can't jump out of a tree and scare the hell out of someone in the middle of a cemetery. I put in my ear buds and listen to some tunes as I wait her out, but my attention is soon drawn back to her when I hear her let out a wail like a wounded animal. I pull out my ear buds and squint in her direction. She's kneeling, her head in her hands, rocking back and forth as she sobs uncontrollably. I lower my eyes away from her, knowing all too well what she's feeling. Grief is an evil hungry monster that will eat you alive.

It's almost dusk when the crier finally leaves and I can climb out of my tree. I walk by the grave she mourned over, and sick curiosity leads me to go read the headstone. Nick Bennett. Beloved husband and son. Twenty-seven years old. I'm about to walk off, but something stops me in my tracks. I turn back and stare at the date of death. It's a date that will be engraved in my brain and my heart for the rest of my life because it's the same date that Katie died.

An icy chill spreads through my veins as I stare at the date, and pieces of information slowly come back to me about the accident. I remember Lukas saying the other passenger was young, and his wife was also in the car and got banged up pretty good.

I'm damn sure I'm standing on the grave of another person I may have killed. Just fucking great.

I take the long way home on my bike to try to clear my head of all the thoughts that are jangling around. I never asked for any details about the passengers in the other car, and I'm not even sure if their names were ever mentioned. It was hard enough to deal with the death of Katie, but now, seeing the other side of the accident is even more of a mind-fuck. I can't get that girl's wailing cries out of my head.

I'm not in the house for ten minutes when my doorbell rings. Putting my drink down, I go to the door, not hiding my annoyance as I open it.

"What now?" I demand as Evelyn walks past me, carrying a small pet carrier. I'm utterly confused as I watch her open the little door of the plastic cage.

"What the hell is this?" I ask as she thrusts a small furry animal against my chest.

"It's a kitten."

"What the hell is wrong with it?" I hold it away from me and stare at its tiny face. It's squinting. *A lot.*

"He's blind," she replies simply.

I look closer at the small silver and white cat. "Blind? It has no fucking eyes, Evie." I can't even believe what I'm looking at.

"I know, Vandal. It was tortured as a tiny kitten by some asshole teenagers. He's fine now, but his eyes had to be surgically removed after what was done to him. He's all healed up now and ready for a home. He's been in foster care for three months while he healed and learned how to adapt. He's only about six months old."

*Tortured?* Who the fuck tortures a kitten? I instinctively hold it closer to my chest and it begins to purr violently against me.

I stare at Evie, confused. "Why is it here?"

"You're going to love it. But you're going to have to actually *show* it that you love it. And 'it' has a name; meet Sterling."

Shaking my head, I try to hand the kitten back to her. "No. No, no, and no. I can't take care of a cat, Ev. I've never even owned a cat. Or a dog. Not even a fucking fish, or a plant."

She flashes a sweet but feisty smile at me. "Well, now you're the proud owner of a blind cat, and it's non-negotiable. You need each other. You're both fucked up. He can eat, drink, and use his litter box completely normally. Just put his stuff in a safe place, show him where it all is, and don't move it." She stops for a minute and stares at my leg. "Is that blood on your shorts?"

Fuck. I guess I didn't grab clean shorts when I swapped my jeans for something more comfortable when I got home.

"I cut myself a few days ago," I answer, not looking at her. I focus on the cat, gently rubbing its head, its purr vibrating against my palm.

"Doing what?"

I raise my eyes to meet hers. "Drop it." My tone is no longer friendly. She cringes like a good girl and looks away. I can see her struggling with wanting to say something and knowing better than to poke the monster.

I hold the cat closer, who's rubbing all over my face now, and watch as Evie steps outside the front door and then comes back dragging a large box of cat supplies and leaves it in my foyer.

She looks up at me and gives the cat a quick scratch on the head. "Trust me, Vandal. You'll thank me for this."

I gently put the kitten down on the floor and he promptly arches his little back and rubs against my ankles.

"I don't even like you," I say to Evie. Which is a lie because I do kinda like her. I've slowly gotten used to the fact that even though she can be annoying as hell, she's a good friend and her heart is in the right place, which is more than I can say about most people.

"I don't care if you like me or not," she replies, grinning. "Just like the cat. That's all. Call or text me if you have any questions. If you have to go away or on tour, I'll make sure he's taken care of by either myself or a pet sitter. Make sure he has food and water all the time and don't ever let him outside. Okay?"

"Uh . . . okay?" I can't believe I'm letting her railroad me into being a pet owner.

"Great. Work your charm, Sterling," she says to the cat, then turns and leaves me dumbfounded in the kitchen. I run my hands through my long hair and let out a deep breath. *I really did not need this shit.*

The best thing to do right now is ignore the cat and let it get used to the fact that it's on its own. Life sucks, even for kittens, apparently. He'll be safe and fed and that's obviously better than what he's used to, so he should just be grateful.

I head back into the living room to resume drinking, and the girl from the cemetery creeps into my mind, so I grab my laptop and do a web search for Nick Bennett, his obituary showing up right on the first page of the search results. Sipping my Jack Daniels, I scan the obituary for her name.

*Tabitha.*

I backspace and search for her name and find her social media page. Evidently, Tabitha's not big on privacy because her entire profile is wide open for me to see all her status updates, photos, and friends. I hesitate for a moment before clicking on her profile photo, enlarging it to see blonde hair, tousled around huge, doe-like eyes that a man could easily get lost in. Those eyes are staring right into mine, and something inside me shifts. In her eyes, I see that rare childlike playfulness and sensuality that I've been hungering for longer than I can remember, but never opened myself up enough to find. I curse the irony of seeing it in this woman that I've had a hand in destroying. Closing the photo, I scroll down her status updates. The most recent was two weeks ago.

*I can't do this. Nothing matters to me anymore. I want to go to sleep forever.*

I nod in agreement at the screen. Yup. Been there. *Still there.*

Her post has twenty-four likes. Why the fuck would people like that? There are also a few replies from her friends, saying they're there for her. I wonder how many of them really are there for her. My guess is not too fucking many.

I scroll down further to a post two weeks prior to that.

*I miss you so much. Life is nothing without you :(*

And a few days before that:

*Fuck you, sun. Even you can't brighten my day. The dark is my friend now.*

And a day before:

*I am consumed with pain and loneliness. Please don't call me or tell me things will get better. I died in that car, too.*

*Yes.* Her pain matches mine so perfectly, born together like twins.

And then there is a smattering of pre-tragedy posts:

*Omfg this cookie is amazing #fatass #yum*

*Can't wait for Nick to get home!*

*WTF why can't I get pregnant??*

*Woohoo shopping spree with my bestie!*

*Where the hell do my socks go? Is there a portal in the washing machine?*

*Watching Revenge! #TeamAiden*

A foreign smile spreads across my face as I scroll through her silly and mostly random posts. There are a lot of pictures of her, and him, and them together. All smiles. The perfect, good-looking young couple. I click on another album and it's filled with pictures of butterflies, birds, squirrels, and flowers, and a few of her out in the woods wearing a vintage dress, lying in the leaves, and a few other girls, presumably her friends, in the same setting. It appears to be some kind of themed shoot. Photography and modeling must be some of her hobbies. She has an odd beauty about her that is a mix of cute and sexy with a side of shy innocence. She's petite, maybe five feet, judging from the photos. She possesses the look and aura that my dark side craves to have under me, but I've always refused to let myself give in to. Instead, I stick to the loud, outgoing, easy girls because they make me feel absolutely nothing.

I check my own social media page and there is the usual stuff from fans, mostly chicks, a bunch of them wearing the T-shirts that went on sale a few months ago that say *"Get Vandalized"* on them, the black fabric spread tight across their huge, probably fake, tits. There is nothing about the accident. Sooner or later, someone will start talking about it, or it will be leaked, and I don't even want to know what I will have to deal with then.

I click back over to Tabitha's page, and a strange noise interrupts my continued status stalkfest. Putting the laptop down, I follow the noise, right to the kitchen where the kitten is sitting exactly where I left him—what, an hour ago? *Shit.* I'm gonna fuckin' kill Evie.

Kneeling down, I pet the tiny cat on the head and he leans into my hand. His silvery gray fur feels plush and soft, like a rabbit.

"Okay, little dude, let's get your act together." I pick him up and hold him as I put his food dishes in the kitchen and his litter-box in the mudroom. I set him down in front of each of his things and let him sniff it all, hoping he'll remember where it all is. The last thing I need is a blind kitten destroying my house. I watch him in strange fascination as he navigates around the kitchen, head slightly tilted, as if he's memorizing every step, every smell. He makes his way back to me and rubs on my legs triumphantly. Hmm. Sterling seems to overcome his obstacles. Perhaps there is a lesson to be learned here.

The rest of my night is spent going through all of Tabitha's posts and photos from the most recent to when she opened her social media account four years ago. My newfound obsession with learning about her is a welcome distraction from my usual nightly rituals of self-desecration. A little digging tells me that she quit her job a few weeks ago, and I can tell by her posts since the accident that she's pulling away from her friends and family. A few people have posted on her page, asking where she has been, saying they miss her at work, telling her she should call. She doesn't reply to any of these messages. This girl went from being obviously happy, goofy, and very much in love with life and her husband, to a hater of anything remotely happy. She thinks life betrayed her, but it's actually just the work of some asshole who made a bad decision that in turn destroyed her life.

The ties that bind us each to one another may not always be visible, but they're there like thin, transparent veins. I don't know why, but this is one vein I don't want to slit.

# chapter seven

VANDAL

Every morning for the past two weeks, I've woken up with this vibrating cat either on my chest or curled at my side. Even though he can't see, he's watching me all the time. He follows me from room to room like a furry shadow and sits close to me, sometimes resting with his paw on my leg, or his head leaning against me. He craves closeness, and I let him have it. Somehow he's crept over my walls.

Katie would have loved Sterling. Sometimes when he's playing with a toy—yes, he plays, don't ask me how—or does something unexpected, I catch myself laughing and can almost hear her giggle echoing around me. I've never been one to think about the afterlife, but lately I wonder if maybe she's watching over me.

And not only that, but this house is haunting me with memories of Katie, and I feel as if I'm going mad most of the time. A few days ago, Lukas suggested I get out of here for a while and go up to the small house I have on the lake that Gram talked me into buying two years ago, claiming we all needed a place to "get away sometimes." At first, I'd told her she was fucking crazy. I'd never owned a house in my life—the thought of having two seemed insane to me, and a severe waste of money. I hardly even lived in any houses growing up, being bounced from foster home to foster home until I said "fuck it" when I was sixteen, and then lived on the streets or with friends who were much older than me. I went from sleeping on ratty couches to living in a shitty apartment to owning two houses. Not bad for a tatted-up white boy with long hair.

I call Lukas. "I'm gonna go to the lake for a month. So don't freak the fuck out if you stop by my house down here and I'm not around, okay?" Leaning the phone against my shoulder, I fill the cat's dish, which is empty again. How much does one cat eat?

"Try to get off the shit while you're there." He suggests. "I was thinking, why don't you come back to the shop in about a month? The clients miss you, and I could use the help. I was gonna hire someone else, but I'd rather you were back here."

"Lukas, I don't know if I'm ready for that," I say, watching the cat playing hockey with a ping pong ball.

He continues babbling. "Just hear me out, Van. Even if just for a few months and you go back to playing with A&E, I think it would be good if you were back in the shop for a while. You know, to get out of the house and be around people."

"I don't like people."

"Van, I know . . . but you're an amazing artist. Don't just sit around and rot because you're not playing. You're fuckin' sick at both, so don't give 'em up. You can't be tattooing people wasted though."

"I'm not fucking stupid. I know that. I've been doing this shit way longer than you have—"

"Man, calm the hell down. I had to say it, all right? It's my name on the line here, too. We're partners. This shop is my life, and I can't afford to let anything screw it up."

I start to pace around the living room, annoyed that everyone thinks I'm going to screw up his or her life, or band, or ink shop. Not that they're wrong, but I'm sick to death of hearing it.

I know Lukas is right though. I gotta do *something*. I'm just not ready yet. Jabbing tiny needles into people all day actually might make me feel better. Pretending it doesn't hurt them but knowing it really does, and watching the tiny blood bubbles erupt from the flesh. Yeah, I could get into that again.

"I'll call you," I say after a few moments. "I think you're right though. I do miss it. Who the hell knows if Ash will let me back in the band? Lemme chill for a few weeks and get my head together, and then I'll come back and see how it goes."

"Sounds good, bro. Call if you need anything."

I end the call, still thinking about going back to work at our tattoo shop.

I make another call, this time to Evie.

"Hello?" She answers on the second ring.

"It's me."

"Me, who?"

I roll my eyes because I know this bitch recognizes my voice and just likes to taunt me.

"Fucking *me*."

"That's an interesting way to announce yourself."

"I need a favor. I'm going to the lake for a few weeks. I think I need to get out of the house and the memories here, like everyone keeps saying. It's making me fucking crazy being here."

"I think that's a good idea, Vandal. A change of scenery is good."

"I'm not going up 'til late Saturday afternoon. Can you maybe go up there Saturday morning and clean it, make sure nothing is lying around? You know, like any toys or any of her stuff . . ."

"Of course. I'll bring some food up, too. If any of Katie's things are there, I'll put them in a box in the basement. No worries."

"I'm going to take my bike up, so could you maybe take the fucking cat up there for me?"

"You love *the fucking cat*, don't you?" she teases.

"Yeah, I guess I fucking do. His carrier is in the hall closet. Maybe buy him stuff to keep at the lake? Like a litter box and food dish and all that stuff? So he has things in both places." I wonder what else would keep him busy? "Get him one of those carpeted cat condo things, too. I don't want him scratching the hell out of my furniture. I'll give you some cash when I see you." The kitten jumps on my lap and I pet him absently as he does happy paws on my leg. "He'll be okay in a new place for a few weeks? And you'll come drive him home when I'm ready to come back?" I ask her.

"Of course I will. And he'll be okay; I'll show him where his stuff is when I get there. Give him a day or two to adjust." I gently disengage Sterling's nails from my jeans. "I'm glad you kept him." Her voice lifts in happiness.

"Yeah, yeah, yeah. Your evil plan worked. Thanks for everything, Evie. And tell Storm . . . tell Storm I'm sorry for the things I said to him. I was just fucked up. More than usual."

"He knows that. He's not mad. He just wants you to be okay. They all do." She sneezes and then goes right back to talking. "They're not punishing you; they're just trying to get you to straighten out."

"I'm trying, Evelyn," I reply, half meaning it. I stand and place Sterling on the floor by his cat bed. "I'll text you when I'm up there."

There's a yellow Post-it next to my laptop that catches my eye as I hang up. It's screaming for my attention so badly that I wouldn't be surprised if it grew legs and chased me around the house. I start a debate with myself. Lie on the couch, drink, take some painkillers, and watch horror movies all day in a daze with Sterling slumbering on my chest, or pick up that Post-it and follow what's scribbled on it. I cross the room and pick up the small yellow note, staring at it for a few seconds before shoving it in my pocket and grabbing my car keys.

I've had many addictions throughout my life. They all have a voice, demanding to be heard, seducing me to give in to them. Once that starts, I am powerless to ignore it. I *have* to have it—I have to quiet the voices and quench the desire for whatever the evil of the day is.

Today it's an address across town, and the voices lead me right out of the house to my midnight-blue Camaro. I listen to some of my favorite rock music while I drive, windows down, hair blowing. I haven't felt this undead in a long time.

This part of town is not overly familiar to me, but with the help of the GPS, after about thirty minutes I am soon turning down the quiet residential street scribbled on the sticky note, and slowly creeping past each house until I reach number 1999. That number excites me, and it's got nothing to do with the Prince song about a fucking party. It's the year I grew a pair, left the shit-storm of a mess that was my home, and went out to live on my own.

The house I'm hawking is a small cape-style, and is very cookie-cutter with its blue shutters and matching front door. The grass needs to be cut and mail is spilling out of the mailbox, and I'm sure it's because she hasn't bothered with it, and not because she's on a vacation in the Hamptons. A small silver SUV is parked in the driveway. I wish I could see the backyard, but I can't risk someone seeing me if I go creeping around back there. My veins thrum as I examine the house and everything around it. *Everything that is her.*

No, this isn't stalking. Not really. I'd call this interested observation. Bright colored flowers line the brick walkway to the front door, and wind chimes dangle from a low-hanging oak tree branch, creating a soft melody floating in the breeze. A small gnome and three bunny statues surround a stone birdbath with no water in it. She likes whimsical. I bet she likes angels and fairies, and she smiles at butterflies and marvels at hummingbirds.

The only way to make someone happy is to *know* what makes him or her happy. Alternatively, the way to instill fear in someone is to know what scares him or her. Knowing how to use those feelings to spin a web of seduction and trust takes patience and control.

I've got both.

On my way home, I grab a monstrous steak and cheese sandwich and a six-pack of beer. I eat it in the living room and give small pieces to Sterling, who likes to supervise all things food-related. When I'm done, I wander into Katie's room and sit on the edge of her small bed. The kitten has followed me in and walks around slowly, sniffing everything, his little ears twisting around. Sometimes my mind goes screwy and I think I can somehow undo this and bring Katie back, as if it were all a big mistake or a bad dream.

After staring at Katie's things for a while, I take a few sleeping pills and check Tabitha's page before I prepare to pass out on the couch. She hasn't posted anything in quite a while, but I still check every night, just to see if she's shared any new thoughts, and today she has.

*"Whoever said life is too short obviously never endured heartache or loss,*

*because life is too long. It's one long, miserable day that just drags out forever... I hate this life."*

How fucking true. Life is really for the happy people.

I miss Katie more than I can put into words, but she's my daughter, my flesh and blood. Remembering how I heard Tabitha crying in despair at Nick's grave, I know damn well if I had died in that crash, no one would be crying over my grave or still missing me months later. I'm oddly jealous over Tabitha's intense love for her husband.

There's another picture I found in one of her many online photo albums where she's sitting on an old staircase, looking up into the camera, her huge eyes half hidden under her bangs, her small cleavage pushing out of the black dress she's wearing. I've saved it to my computer so I can look at it whenever I want to and fantasize about her on her knees, gazing up at me in that same way with those big enchanting eyes.

She's stirred me.

VANDAL

I throw some clothes into my saddlebags and hop on my bike, looking forward to going to the lake for a few weeks. The past three months have been torturous for me, living in my house without Katie and I need to get away from all that. On my way, I stop at the cemetery to visit Katie once more before I go, and also to check one of my foot pegs that I heard rattling. Once in the parking lot, I take out my tool bag and tighten it up.

Off to my right, I hear a sound coming from the direction of my tree. I put my tools away and push my hair out of my face, looking toward the noise. Wiping my dirty hands on my jeans, I take another teddy bear from my bag and head for Katie's grave.

I can hear her crying, but can barely see her this time because she's sitting on the ground on the other side of the headstone. Seeing her again is unexpected, but I can't resist going to her because I've thought about this too fucking much to just walk away. It's like she's been handed to me.

She startles at first when she sees me, staring up at all six-foot-four of me with a small amount of fear in her teary eyes. *Those eyes.* Holding my breath, I wait for some glimmer of recognition, but there's none. I slowly exhale.

"You've got black stuff on your face," she says, sniffling. Her voice is softer than I expected it to be.

I kneel down in front of her and rub my thumb across her

cheek, smudging the stain of tears and make-up under her eye. She flinches a tiny bit and sucks in a breath.

"So do you," I say.

My heart is thundering in my chest just from touching her warm, soft flesh. It's the same feeling I get when I cut myself—only this is far better. This is its own heartbeat, its own breath, its own blood and fear.

*I fucking want it.*

She wipes at her face with the back of her hand and rips her gaze away from mine, landing on the bear I'm holding.

She nods her quivering chin towards it. "You're holding a teddy bear."

I turn the soft toy in my dirty hands. "I am."

"Why?"

I glance over at my daughter's grave. The sun is shining through the leaves of my tree and casting a ray of light onto her stone, making it glow. I take this as a sign.

Looking back at Tabitha, I hold the bear out to her. "I was going to give it to someone, but I think maybe you need it more."

Her hand shakes as she takes it from me and she cradles it against her. "Thank you." Her voice is slightly above a whisper. She swallows hard and squeezes her eyes shut. Katie would want her to have it. The bears were always meant to cheer someone up. Why not a grieving widow?

I can't take my eyes off of her. She absolutely takes my breath away. She's so beautifully damaged. She's wrecked. I can see it in her lifeless eyes. And now I want to fix her in the only way I know how.

Standing, I offer her my hand. "Wanna go for a ride?"

Her eyes widen and her fingers tighten around the bear before she slowly puts her other hand in mine. I pull her up to her feet and her head barely reaches the middle of my chest. She looks down at the grave and takes a deep shuddering breath.

"Yes," she finally says, nodding a little. "I'd like to get away from here."

That's all I need to hear.

She follows me to the bike and surprises me when she just gets on the back without any reaction or question. I can see the defiance in her as she plants herself on the seat and stuffs the bear into her purse. She doesn't look at me at all—she just stares off into the distance, completely expressionless. I start the bike and the engine roars loudly, but she doesn't even jump at the sound. I tie my hair back, put my sunglasses on and turn to the side to peek at her. I don't wear a helmet, as this is a no-helmet-law state, and I don't have an extra one on my bike for her. She doesn't seem concerned about not having it, like most chicks are. Maybe she's like me and is also daring fate. *That's right -- we're the ones that got away. Wanna try again?*

"You gotta hold on, darlin', or you're gonna fly right the fuck off."

"Not sure I'd care," she replies, but wraps her arms tightly around my waist.

She's going to be mine, I have zero doubt. *Yes, baby. Embrace the darkness with me.*

I pull out of the parking lot, leaving her car and our lost loved ones behind. As the wind whips our long hair behind us, I think we both feel that this is the start of letting go.

The lake house is about an hour away, tucked deep in the

mountains. I have no fucking idea what I'm doing, but her hands clasped around me as we ride along the tree-lined curvy roads ignite all sorts of dark thoughts inside me. The feel of her warm thighs spread and pressed against my legs makes my cock ache.

Riding my bike has always been an escape for me—just me and the road and the wind, and nothing else. Having a chick wrapped around me, giving me a hard-on, is an invasion of the Zen I usually feel when riding, but I ain't gonna complain.

A few times, she rests her cheek against my shoulder, her arms squeezing me tighter, hiding in me.

*Melting into me.*

The driveway is dusty and gravelly, and I take it slow when I turn in so we don't wipe out. I park just in front of the garage and kill the engine. She takes the cue and hops off, walking around a bit to stretch her legs as I unlock the garage and push the bike in next to my hot rod. She walks even further away as I pull my stuff out of my saddlebags and I find her standing by the lake at the edge of my back yard a few minutes later.

"Where are we?" she asks when she hears me walk up behind her.

"My place." I follow her blinkless stare over the water. "Wanna come inside?"

She nods absently and crosses her arms, hugging herself. I've never seen a person look so incredibly lost before.

I cock my head towards the house. "Come on." I step away, and she follows a few feet behind me.

Sterling is sitting in the hallway when we walk in as if he's been waiting for me, and he meows softly when I lean down to pat his head.

"Oh no!" She's on the floor instantly, scooping him up in her arms. "What happened to him?"

I throw my keys on the credenza by the door. "Yeah, a friend gave him to me. His name is Sterling. He was tortured by some sick fucking kids and lost his eyes. He's okay though -- not in pain or anything. It's amazing how he gets around actually."

Her mouth drops open in horror, and she starts to stroke his head, and of course he's loving it. "Poor little guy," she coos. She looks up at me. "It's so nice you're taking care of him. He's just precious."

So, Sterling is a chick magnet. I'll have to thank Evie for that little bonus. I shrug. "It's no big deal. I just feed him and let him hang out."

"I want to kill those fuckers that hurt him." Her voice is laced with hatred, and I like it. She's a spunky little thing beneath all that sadness.

I head for the kitchen and take out two bottles of water that Evie has left in the refrigerator, along with a shit-ton of other food for me. Tabitha follows me, still holding the cat.

Grinning, I offer the water to her. "He can walk, ya know," I tease. Her face reddens, and she gently puts the cat back down on the floor and watches him prance across the room. Straightening, she wipes at her eyes and looks around.

"Can I use your bathroom and wash my face? I'm kind of a mess."

I step closer to her, and she doesn't back away from me. "I like messes," I say, my gaze traveling from her pouty lips up to her eyes. I push a strand of hair out of her face and tuck it behind her ear, my fingers lightly touching her flushed cheek. She holds her breath but doesn't break eye contact. "The bathroom's down the hall."

When I take a step backward she practically runs down the hall, away from me.

I should take her home. What I'm doing is wrong, but this part of me always seems to win because there's just more bad in me than there is good. Besides, being bad is way more fun.

She comes out after a few minutes, her hair brushed and the

dark stains of mascara cleaned off her face. "Sorry I looked so bad . . ." Her voice trails off.

"Grief isn't pretty."

She shakes her head. "No . . . it's not."

I put my water bottle down and move closer to her, leaning my hip against the kitchen counter. "So I gotta ask. Why did you come here with me?"

She tilts her head a little and bites her lip. "To forget."

"Forget what?"

"Just . . ." She looks off out the window at the lake. "Everything." Tears start to fall down her cheeks. "Him . . . me . . . the pain of losing him. All of it." She chokes and wipes at her eyes. "It's killing me. I feel like I want to die, and I don't know how to make it stop. I've never been this way, ever."

I think back to her social media statuses, how happy and whimsical she was before the accident, and what a shame it is that her light has been snuffed.

*By me.*

"I'm scared of the thoughts I have. I feel alone, like no one is really listening to me. They just want me back how I was . . ." She coughs and takes a sip of water, and I'm mesmerized by her pink lips around the rim of the bottle. "I'm not that person anymore, and I'm tired of trying to be. I'm just . . . exhausted. I don't want to think, or do, or *anything* anymore. I want it all to stop. I want a reset button. And I have no idea why I'm telling you all this. You're just a stranger on a bike."

*Oh, I'm so much more.*

I did this. This cute, pixie-like girl doesn't smile anymore because of my mistakes. I can't change the accident or bring back Katie, Renee, or Nick, but I can fix Tabitha. I can flip her all-the-fuck back around again. I know this without a doubt because I know myself, and I know pain, and I know pleasure, and I know how to unfuck and refuck and fix fuck, and it starts with breaking her down, gaining her trust, and renewing her.

I don't know shit about love and romance, but I know that true submission goes far deeper than love. It gives more; it takes more. Love is fragile and can be destroyed. Submission is strong and only strengthens with time. Love leaves people weak and devastated, as she is now. Submission heals and awakens. Submission is love on fucking steroids. Men like me have a radar for women that need to submit, and she's silently screaming for it just as much as I've been silently begging to give it. Maybe I'm wrong, but my gut tells me I'm right. Or maybe I'm just twisted.

I lift her chin and force her to look up at me. "You probably won't believe me, but I understand more than you know. I know exactly how you feel." I take a deep breath and search her eyes. "I can help you, if you want me to. I could help you forget. I can help you out of this bad head space you're in. But you'd have to trust me." I sound like a psycho, but I can't pick the right words for what I'm trying to say. I curse myself for being verbally challenged.

"I don't even know you." Her voice shakes.

"Sometimes, we can't trust what we *do* know, and we have to trust what we *don't*."

She lets out a little sarcastic laugh. "You really think *you* could possibly help me? I've already talked to a therapist and she's useless as shit. I feel like she's . . . like she's analyzing me. Judging me. I stopped going."

"I'm not a fucking therapist. But I'm pretty sure I can make you feel things you've never felt before, and it'll be way better than what you're feeling now. How does that sound?"

She licks her lips, absorbing my words, the glimpse of her tongue making my cock twitch. "All right, then. I'm all yours," she says with a daring lilt. "Make me forget, if you think you can. Make me want to live again. I've tried everything else."

I waste no time accepting that challenge and bring both my

hands up to the sides of her face to hold her still as I take her lips with mine. I kiss her, feather soft, barely touching her lips, tasting her breath, lingering close to her and lightly running my tongue along her bottom lip, and she quivers and shivers beneath my touch. She gasps but opens her mouth for my tongue to explore hers. Her hands clutch at the sides of my shirt, hanging on to me.

After a few moments I pull away, and she sways on her feet. I put my hands on her waist to steady her, enjoying the effect I have on her immensely. It's exactly what I wanted.

"You okay?" I ask, studying her face.

"Yeah . . ." She brings her hand up slowly and touches my hair, as if she's petting a wild zoo animal. "Your hair is so shiny and pretty." She says it so softly, mostly to herself, then tugs my hair, trying to bring my head back down to her for another kiss. Oh, this little girl has some spark in her. I grab her hand and flash her an evil grin.

"Tell me what you want, darlin'."

She shakes her head and tries to pull her hand out of mine, but I hold onto her. "Say it." It's a gentle command for me to gauge her willingness to give.

"More of that," she whispers, and another tear slowly slides down her cheek. She brushes it away with her finger, her cheeks reddening. "I'm sorry . . . I cry a lot lately . . ."

I lean my head down and rest my forehead against hers. "Don't apologize. Even the sky cries."

I close my eyes and inhale the coconut scent of her shampoo for a few moments and then lift her up, wrapping her legs around my waist and kissing her long and deep, my hands on her ass, holding her body tight against mine. She circles her arms around my neck as I carry her down the hallway to my bedroom, kicking the door shut behind me. Sterling hasn't been around any sex activities yet, and I don't want to find out if he's going to try to get in on the action or start a purr-fest.

I drop her on the bed and fall on top of her, trying not to crush her. She's the smallest chick I've ever fucked and my mind is racing with ideas of what I can do with someone this short and light. That can wait though. Today will be for her.

I expect her to lie there, frozen, but she's in a frenzy, pulling at my shirt, trying to get it off me. I'm pretty sure this is more about an inner rebellion for her and not exactly wanting *me*, but I'm okay with that. At least for now. I sit on top of her and let her tug my shirt up over my head. Her hands still and her eyes widen as she takes me in, her focus wandering over the colorful tattoos that span my arms and chest. I know that my looks are most likely a shock to her, and she's probably not used to a huge muscular guy with long blue-black hair, covered in tattoos, crawling all over her. By the time I'm done with her, she'll have little memory of any men before me. She'll be Vandal-ized for life.

Capturing her hands in mine, I pin them over her head on the mattress, slowly sliding my body down hers until my lips meet hers again. I kiss her hungrily, demanding her breath, then move my mouth down her neck, sucking and biting her delicate flesh, marking each inch I touch with lust. I want to see the evidence of fucking her when we're done, and I want her to see it, too. The fabric of her thin blouse rips down the middle with a quick, well-practiced tear, exposing a purple bra stretched over her breasts. I glide my tongue between her soft mounds, my hands squeezing her through the satin material. I flick my tongue over her nipple, wetting the thin fabric that covers her.

Leaning up off of her a bit, I reach down and pull the small knife from my ankle strap and flick the blade out of its case with a quick snap of my wrist. Her eyes flash with fear and her breath quickens as she watches me bring the blade closer to her. I slide it between her breasts, under the small piece of material, and yank it up quickly, slicing the bra in half. The two pieces of fabric fall to each side, exposing her breasts. I close the blade and toss the knife to the floor and give her all my attention. Her tits are small in my hands, but firm and round, her nipples pressing against my palms as I gently squeeze and caress them.

My lips meet hers for a rough kiss. "You. are. exquisite," I whisper slowly before I drag my tongue from her lips, down to suck one of those taut little buds into my mouth while I tease the other in my hand, twisting the nipple between my thumb and forefinger. Her body writhes beneath me, pressing against mine. Her hands finally realize they're free and she tangles them in my hair as I feast on her breasts until she starts to moan.

Standing slowly, I move to the end of the bed, watching her intently as she watches me. I grab one of her feet and pull off one shoe, then the other. She's chewing on her lower lip as she watches me, fighting an inner battle. Part of her wants to stop me, and part of her wants to go over the edge to escape the pain and grief, but we both know she's not turning back now.

Reaching for her waist, I yank her jeans and panties down in one quick pull and throw them to the floor, pausing to drink her in for a moment: naked, and pale on my dark comforter, and just so breathtaking. A long, jagged scar runs down her side, and a few more are on her legs. Of course, these are from the accident. My sins engraved in her perfect body, forever.

Locking my eyes onto hers, I kick my boots off, unbuckle my belt, unbutton my jeans, tug the zipper down, and step out of them. She stares at the ceiling as I go to the nightstand to get a condom and quickly slip it on. My cock is hard as a rock, jutting out from my body, aching to get into her sweet pussy.

Crawling between her legs, I run my hand slowly down the inside of her thigh, my fingers welcomed by her wet, satiny lips. She doesn't know it, but this is just as hard, just as out of bounds for me as it is for her. I think this girl may ruin me even more than I'm going to ruin her.

Her muscles clench around my fingers, dragging me out of my

thoughts. She spreads her legs for me in silent invitation, and I thrust my cock into her, hard and deep, causing her to cry out, her back arching up.

"Holy fuck," she gasps. *Yes.*

Lowering myself onto her, I kiss her savagely as I pump in and out of her tight pussy, fisting her hair in my hand so she can't move her head away from me. Our eyes lock on to each other, prying into each other's souls. She wraps her legs around my waist and digs her nails into my back, hard, dragging them down and digging deeper with each thrust of my hips. I can feel the warmth of my blood under her nails, and it feels like heaven.

She whimpers, and I kiss her lips more softly. "Don't stop," I whisper hoarsely against her mouth. "Scratch me. Hurt me. Let all your pain out on me."

And she does. The harder I fuck her, the more she sinks her nails into me and bites my shoulder and neck. The pain does nothing but turn me on even more, my head reeling with such euphoria that I feel dizzy and utterly lost in her. I want the world to stop right now in this moment, with my cock buried in this broken girl who is tied to me in our united, twisted devastation.

She climaxes wildly, thrashing beneath me, nails grating into my ass, screaming everything except for my name, because she doesn't know it yet. I hold out until she's panting for breath, and then I move in and out of her slowly, deliberately, deeply, inch by inch, savoring every tight, wet part of her until I explode.

She starts to tremble and cry as her orgasm fades, and I ease out of her, quickly pulling the condom off and throwing it in the small trash bin next to the bed. Rolling onto my side, I gently put an arm around her.

"It's okay," I soothe, pulling the comforter up to cover her.

"I'm sorry . . . I'm just so tired, and I haven't slept in so long . . ." She covers her face with her hands. "I don't know what I'm doing. I'm so fucking scared."

"Stay right here."

I pull my jeans on and go into the bathroom, rummaging in the medicine cabinet until I find what I'm looking for, then grab her some water from the kitchen and head back to the bedroom, sitting on the bed next to her and holding the pill and water out to her.

"What is it?" she asks, warily.

"It's just a Valium. It will help you sleep."

"Here?"

"Do you need to go home?"

She shakes her head while twisting her wedding band around her finger. "No. There's nothing there. I hate being there. He's everywhere."

"Then take it and let yourself sleep as long as you want. Okay?"

She looks at me with narrowed eyes. "Are you sure?"

"Yes. Trust me, I've had a lot of sleepless nights. You'll feel better if you get some rest. I'll be right out in the living room with the cat. I won't bother you at all."

She shrugs, pops the pill in her mouth, and swallows it with some water while eyeing me over the bottle, then falls back onto the pillow and looks at me with a dazed expression on her face.

"I have no idea who you are or what the hell just happened. I don't do things like that. Ever. I don't know what's happening to me."

Grinning, I pull the comforter up around her, much like I used to do with Katie. "Neither do I, for what it's worth. Now sleep."

# chapter nine

TABITHA

The sun shining on my face wakes me. I sit up groggily and look out the window at the lake. It's pretty here, and quiet. Almost serene. I quickly glance around the room that I slept in. Vaulted ceilings with raw wooden beams, hardwood floors with thick area rugs, cherry-wood furniture . . . a huge stone electric fireplace takes up one corner of the room. Everything looks rustic and expensive, and out of place for the guy who claims to live here. Heat rushes between my legs as memories of him flip through my mind like a slow-motion movie. He's like no one I've ever met before. His voice, so deep. Sexy, but soothing. That amazing long black hair. The smudged dirt on his face and hands. Muscles like a wrestler, and all those tattoos. I swear his eyes were black as the ace of spades.

I think back on how those dark eyes bored straight into the very depths of me as he moved in and out of me. He knew exactly how to touch me, where to touch me, as if we'd been making love forever. He knew how to take control and just let me *be*.

*I let him touch me.* The guilt of it makes me shiver. Nick would be so disgusted by me if he could see me now, and that's how I want it. The man I love is gone, so it only seems fair that the woman he loves should be gone, too.

Faint voices coming from somewhere out in the house break my thoughts. There's a female voice mixed with his deep one.

*Holy shit, I don't even know who he is.*

*You are a pig, Tabitha. A whore.*

I look for my clothes and find my jeans at the foot of the bed, and my shirt and bra on the other side of the room, torn in pieces. The knife is lying on the floor, and I shiver as I remember how the blade felt against my skin, cold and sharp.

*You liked it.*

I pilfer his dresser and find a white T-shirt. It's huge, so I tie a knot in the back and creep out into the hallway, wondering if I should go to him or just hide in the bedroom. The voices are coming from the kitchen, so I slowly make my way down the hall, hoping I'm not interrupting something I shouldn't be. For all I know, he could be married, and I could have just slept in his wife's bed.

She sees me first and stops talking, her face literally freezing in mid-sentence. She turns to him. "Um, who's that? I didn't know you had company. Why the hell didn't you say something?"

"She was sleeping." He's making coffee, wearing nothing but jeans. Even from where I'm standing, I can see the long scratch marks I raked into his back last night. Can't she see that? Why isn't she questioning it?

She keeps staring at me in such a way that makes me think this must be some sort of girlfriend. She doesn't look mad though, just shocked.

"I . . . I'm sorry. I just—" I mumble not knowing what to say. "I should go."

*How, you idiot? You came here with him.*

"No," he says, running his hand through his hair. "You stay. Evie's just a friend. My cousin's girlfriend, actually."

"*Fiancée,* actually," she corrects.

He makes a face at her. "Whatever." He turns to me. "She was just checking in on me and the cat."

She nods in agreement with him. "I got worried when I didn't hear from him last night, so I just drove up to check on him. I didn't mean to interrupt." She grabs her purse and keys. "I'll be going then." She glares at him on her way out. "Call me later." She turns to me. "Nice meeting you."

"You, too." I debate whether I should ask her for a ride, but she's out the door too fast. I'm not sure I buy this story of her being a cousin's girlfriend or fiancée or whatever she is.

I stand in the hallway awkwardly, feeling as if something weird just happened, like he didn't want her to see me here.

"Um, I'm sorry. I woke up and heard voices . . ."

"It's fine; forget it. I was trying to let you rest. Feeling better?"

I step farther into the kitchen and look around. "Groggy. Is it tomorrow? Did I sleep all night?"

He nods and goes to the fridge, taking out a glass carafe of orange juice. "You did. OJ?"

"Yes . . . thank you."

He pours the juice into a small glass and hands it to me, our fingers touching. I catch his eyes traveling down to my chest.

"You look good in my shirt." He raises his eyebrows at me.

I'm sure I blush a thousand shades of red. I can't believe I stood here with my nipples visible in front of his friend.

"You ripped my shirt. And my bra. I took this out of your dresser. I hope that's okay."

He hooks his fingers in the waistband of my jeans and pulls me closer to him. "I'll buy you a new shirt."

Being so close to him again quickens my pulse. I've never had a one-night stand before, I have no idea if that's what this is, or how I'm supposed to act now. On television, the girl usually goes home the next day and they never speak again.

*Slut. You fucked someone you met at your husband's grave.*

I squeeze my eyes shut and try to ignore the voices. They never seem to stop.

When I open my eyes again, I see that he's watching me intently, as if he's trying to read my mind.

"No, I don't need a new shirt. Thank you though. I should go. Can you take me back to my car?" *That's still at the cemetery.*

He lets out a deep breath. "I was thinking . . . I'm staying here for a month. Kinda like a mental vacation or something." He slowly brushes his hand down my arm and grabs onto my hand. "Why don't you stay with me? You kinda look like you could use a vacation, too."

I must have heard him incorrectly. There is no way this total stranger just asked me to spend a month with him.

"Excuse me?"

"I think you need it. I've seen you in the cemetery before. I watched you."

I pull away from him quickly, as if he's on fire. "What? Why? Are you sick? You don't watch people in a cemetery. It's a sacred place. What the hell is wrong with you?"

He doesn't even flinch or defend himself. He just answers me calmly. "Because watching you made me feel."

"What the hell could watching a woman cry at her husband's grave possibly make you feel?"

He stares me right in the eye. "A lot of things, actually. But envy, mostly."

"Envy?" I repeat incredulously. "Of *what*?"

"Meaning that much to someone."

The raw honesty of his answer is so unexpected. I cross my arms over my chest and stare at him. "I really don't know what to say to that. I'm sorry."

"I lost someone, too," he says, looking down at the floor. "I meant what I said yesterday." He looks back up and meets my eyes. His eyes are dark and full of so much pain, and I wonder if mine look the same way. Is that what people see when they look at me? "I can help you forget," he continues. "To help the pain go away. And you can help me, too."

"How?"

"Stay here with me. Give yourself to me—to us—for a month. Let go of everything. Trust me, it will set you free of all this crap you're feeling. It will help both of us. It'll just be you and me. No one and nothing else. Let me take care of everything."

I back away from him, trying to understand what exactly he's saying. "I don't understand . . . give myself to you? What does that even mean?"

He closes the space between us, taking my hands in his again, which is oddly comforting to me. "Sometimes it's better if you don't understand it, and just let yourself feel it as it's happening. Just let go; don't think about it. I won't hurt you. I promise I'll take care of you, and I'll take it all the fuck away."

I shake under the intensity of his stare, and his words that could mean a myriad of things. Scary things that happen in the dark. I've read about this sort of thing in romance books, and remember thinking it was sorta scary but also sensually exciting. "Will it be . . . sexual?" My voice trembles and I lick my lips, my mouth suddenly dry.

"Yes, some of it. Sometimes I may gently tie you up, so you can't touch me, and you're at my mercy to touch, to make you feel, and all you can do is just lie there and enjoy it." His eyes take on a spark as he describes what he wants. "Or I may command you to touch me because sometimes it feels good to be told what to do, and it feels good for me to have someone listen to what I want and do it. But it's much more than that. It's not just about sex. It's much deeper than that. Much, much deeper."

"And at the end of the month? Then what?"

"You'll be stronger, and I will be, too. We'll have a bond. Other than that, we'll have to see. Neither one of us is in any frame of mind to think that far ahead."

*This isn't what I was expecting.*

I can go back home to the empty house, the loneliness, the overwhelming responsibility of everything, or I can stay here with this mysterious, fascinating stranger and let him do whatever it is he wants to do that he thinks will help me. Nothing can get worse. I've already reached rock bottom with losing my husband, quitting my job, bills piling up, and contemplating suicide daily. Nothing matters to me anymore. This guy could murder me right now and I don't think I would even care. Or he could fuck me again and make my mind sear into a hot frenzy, as he did last night, and make me forget everything for a little while with his insane body, electrifying touch, and soothing voice. Plus he has a stash of Valium somewhere in this house, which I can use to implement my Plan B of going to sleep forever if this doesn't go well. It's a win win.

"All right. I'll stay."

Heat flashes in his eyes and he kisses my lips possessively, squeezing my hands tight in his, not letting go.

I return his kisses with equal fervor. Something about him has rattled me. Denying him anything seems like it would be impossible, and I'm just too exhausted mentally and physically to question it or him. If he wants to take care of me and take me on some erotic emotional ride, why the hell not? If it changes my life, great. *If I get what I want, even better.* If it doesn't go well, then at least I experienced something different and daring, and didn't take the safe way out.

# chapter ten

VANDAL

The sight of her wearing my old, white T-shirt, her nipples straining against the thin fabric and the visible bite marks going down the side of her neck, is enough to make me want to throw her on the kitchen table and fuck her brains out. Damn Evelyn for showing up here and disrupting our morning. All that matters now is she agreed to stay. Being with her has ignited a fire in me that I thought was snuffed out a long time ago.

I lead her wordlessly down to the bathroom and undress her, then myself. She shivers as I trace my finger down the scar that runs down her side. The skin is pink, jagged, and new. She shoves my hand away and attempts to cover herself, and I immediately place my hand back along her ribs.

"Don't ever push me away." I keep my voice low and even. "Tell me how this happened."

"No." Tears instantly flow down her cheeks, her pain always so close to the surface, just pouring out.

"You have to let me in if this is going to work."

She leans back against the sink. "It's from the accident my husband was killed in. We crashed into another car. I guess a piece of the car cut into me." She looks down at the scar. "It's ugly."

Kneeling in front of her, I drag my tongue along the length of the scar that goes from her hip to the side of her breast, goose bumps rising on her flesh. *I did this.* This could have killed her. She can't be more than a hundred pounds; I have no idea how she lived through the accident. *I wish my baby had been as lucky.*

"You're beautiful," I tell her, and it's true. She's got classic, almost old-fashioned beauty. Porcelain skin, big sky-blue eyes, natural blond hair. She's actually very cute. Too cute to ever be with a guy like me under any normal circumstances.

"I'm not. Not at all."

It's always the most beautiful people who have no idea that they are.

"You are. Every inch of you. Whether you see it or not, I see it," I stand and take her face in my hands, forcing her to look up into my eyes. "I see *you*."

We shower together, but she's despondent as I caress her body with cream lavender soap. The hot water stings the deep scratches she made in my back last night, but I don't care. I'll take any pain I can from her because I deserve it as much as I want it.

"Does your little plan include me having any clothes? And what about my car?" She finally speaks when we step out of the shower.

I take one of the towels we just dried off with and fold it into a nice, neat square, placing it on the floor in front of me.

"I'll get you some clothes and take care of your car. Kneel."

"How are you going to take care of my car, exactly?"

"I'll have it towed to your house. Or here, if you prefer. Is there anything else that needs to be taken care of, like, at your house? You have any pets, or any shit like that?"

"No, I don't have any *shit like that*. But I'll call my neighbor and tell her I'm going to be gone; she can keep an eye on my place."

I nod and point to the towel. "Kneel."

She looks at me quizzically. "Why do you keep saying that?"

She reaches for her clothes, but I take them away from her. "No. Kneel down on the towel for me."

"You're serious?"

"Very."

She kneels down, naked, and looks up at me. My cock

immediately stiffens, and she's trying to look at anything except my dick.

"Why am I down here?" she asks.

I can't help but smile at her because her innocence is very different from what I'm used to. It's turning me on way more than the experienced subs and overly outgoing women I've been with.

"To suck me." The way her lips wrapped around the water bottle earlier was too much for me to ignore. I brush her wet hair away from her face and watch her reaction, which is priceless. Her eyes literally bug out. She shakes her head and her mouth falls open, which only furthers my desire for her.

"I don't do that." She bends her leg and pushes up to stand, but I gently put my hand on the top of her head and hold her down.

"You will."

She looks at me defiantly, knocks my hand away and stands up. "And if I don't?"

Ah. She wants to play. I expected this though, and I know exactly how to handle her.

Shrugging nonchalantly, I wrap a towel around my waist. "I won't force you. I want you to want it."

I walk out of the bathroom and leave her there, knowing she'll react as I think she will. Call me a douche, but women always want me. I have some kind of sexual magnetism about me that makes them crazy, like dick catnip. She's going to need some time, but I can't push her too hard since she's mentally fragile right now. I go to the living room, sit on the couch, and flick on the television. Sterling jumps next to me, and I pet him absently as I wait for her to come out, which takes about five minutes. She stands in the archway of the room and watches me for a few moments, a towel wrapped around her.

"You're going to ignore me now?" she finally says.

*Yes.*

I say nothing and continue to scroll through the channels.

"Hello?"

I don't even look at her. I'm very good at being an asshole, and I own it. A few more minutes pass until she comes and stands in front of me.

Finally, she kneels and puts her hands on my thighs and I turn the TV off, throw the remote to the side and give her my full attention, unwrapping the towel from my waist. The defiance I saw in her eyes earlier has been replaced with something between desire and anger, but that's normal. Learning to read her body language, eyes, tone of voice, and mannerisms is going to be my focus for the next few days.

I take my cock in my hand and pump it slowly as she watches in fascination. Her lips part slightly as she stares and her hands grip my thighs. I'm torn between jerking off while she watches me and wanting her to suck me. *Decisions, decisions.*

She surprises me by putting her small hand over mine, both of our hands fisting my rock-hard cock. She watches us move together and then lowers her head onto me, her lips coming down over the slick head, her tongue swirling around my fingers. A long sigh escapes me and I pull my hand away as her mouth moves further down, taking me deeper. *Fuck.*

I lean my head back against the couch and close my eyes, loving the feel of her mouth on me. Her pussy and her mouth are both exquisite, and just from the little bit I've had of her so far, I'm not sure how I'm going to be able to let her go in a month.

I've always gravitated to trashy girls with loud voices, sketchy pasts, and zero morals. They're willing to do anything I tell them to, not caring if it's going to hurt or humiliate them. Deep down, they just want attention, so they let me use them. Tabi isn't like that. She's sweet, classy, and thoughtful. Getting her to do erotic things just for me is a turn on. I like corrupting her innocence, and then seeing it renew itself so I can do it all over again.

She grips the base of my cock with one hand while she sucks me, her other hand moving up my leg, over my hip, and stopping at my abs, splaying her fingers out over my muscles.

Suddenly her mouth and hands are gone. My eyes fly open, and I turn to see her walking away, out of the room.

*What the fuck?*

I jump up and follow her. "Hey, where the hell are you going?"

No one has ever walked away from me during sex before.

She looks over her shoulder at me as I stalk her down the hallway to the bedroom. "How does it feel to be walked away from?" she quips.

This is a first, and not something I'm about to let go. She just pushed a button she shouldn't have pushed.

I catch her easily and wrap my arms around her from behind, pinning her against me.

"You want to play?" I whisper in her ear. "Then let's play." I reach into the nightstand and pull out the long black nylon rope that I hid in there a long time ago, holding her to me with my other arm. In seconds, I've got her hands tied expertly behind her back before she even realizes what's going on. Once tied, I turn her around to face me.

"What the hell do you think you're doing?" she demands. "Untie me."

"Not a chance," I say, nipping at her neck. "I was trying to go slow with you, but you've made that impossible." I kiss her mouth, licking her lips. I can taste myself on her. "I live for this, sweetheart. You don't know it yet, but you're going to love it."

She tries to protest again, but I quiet her by kissing her, my hand going up to her breast to gently pinch her nipple. She lets out a little cry.

"Now kneel," I say.

She glares at me and doesn't move.

"Don't make me repeat myself. That will be the last time you ever tease me."

"I'm sorry." Her voice is shaky, and I think she's probably afraid of me now, which is both good and bad.

"Show me." I gently push her down until she's kneeling in front of me, wobbling a little while she tries to balance herself.

With her hands tied at the base of her spine, she can only use her mouth to grab my throbbing cock. I refuse to help her. This would be easier on her if I sat on the bed, but now I want to teach her a lesson. Nobody fucks with me -- not even her.

Now that she's got me pissed off, her mouth feels even better. On the couch she licked and sucked me slowly and that felt fucking amazing, but now she's sucking me hard and furious, and that's waking up the animal in me. I wind my hand in her hair and hold the back of her neck as I thrust into her mouth, not enough to choke her but enough to let her know that I'm in charge. Her moans vibrate around my cock, telling me she's not exactly not liking this.

She makes me come in her mouth way faster than I want to, but I can't hold it back. I pull out slowly and watch her swallow, gulping and glaring at me while a drop of my cum drips down her chin. I reach down and wipe it with my thumb, then glide my thumb over her bottom lip, smearing myself on her like lip-gloss.

"We need to have a little talk," I tell her, lowering myself down to the floor to sit with her.

"Untie me."

"Not yet." She glares at me but I ignore her. "Look, you know what's going on here. The power play between a Dom and sub is a delicate balance, but it *can* work and it *can* be a really deep experience for both of us."

"Dom and sub? You mean like *Fif—*"

I put my finger on her lips. "Don't even say it. I need you to respect me, not provoke me. I *will* take care of you. I'll make you feel things you've never felt before. I can help get you out of this depression you're in, and all the other overwhelming feelings you have, but you have to trust me." I reach behind her, untie her hands, and gently rub her wrists. "You have my word I won't hurt you. Think of this as a total mental and physical vacation. You don't have to worry about anything. *Everything* is my responsibility now. All you have to do is what I ask you to do." I raise her wrist to my lips, kissing the flesh that is red from the rope, eliciting a short gasp from her. "A big part of this is giving up power, putting total trust in someone else, allowing them to take control, and respecting them in return." Her eyes don't leave mine as I kiss her other wrist. "Ya know how when you go for a long drive with someone, and you don't have to pay attention to the road at all? You can just watch the scenery, daydream, take a nap, listen to some good tunes, and trust that they'll get you to where you're going safely? It's like that." She raises her eyebrows at me doubtfully, but there's a glimmer of hope there, too. "Just let me drive. Can you do that?"

"Yes. I think so."

"Do you *want* that?"

She thinks for a moment, and I hold my breath nervously. She might say no, ask me to take her home, and I'll never see her again.

Now that I've spent some time with her, I don't want her to go.

"Actually, I do."

I breathe again. "Good. I want you to. I can see you're going to provoke me because I think you like the cat and mouse. That's fucking great, but I'm going to need to know when 'stop' or 'no' is what you really mean."

"Like a safe word? I've read about that."

"Yes, exactly. Pick one."

She thinks for a moment. "Red. It means stop."

"'Red' it is."

"Can I ask you something?"

"Of course."

She looks at the rope on the floor. "You've done this before?"

I pick up the rope and coil it neatly. "Yes. I've always had this . . . need. Craving. Fetish. Whatever you want to call it. I tie up all the women I fuck; I always have. But a lot of that was just for fun and didn't touch on the serious aspects of the lifestyle. I've never actually been in a true D/s relationship full-time though. I've always wanted to, but I never found the right person that I thought I could try it with. It's complicated."

"But you do with me? Some random girl you met in a cemetery?"

"Yes," I reply. "Without a doubt."

"I really don't know much about any of this sort of thing. I'm definitely intrigued, but I'm not going to be a slave."

"Fuck no, I don't want that either. For example, I'm friends with this couple . . . the woman is president of a corporation and she has a ton of responsibility and stress—it's fucking crazy. But when she's home with her partner, she's submissive and he's the Dom. She needs that with him because she gets to let go and relinquish control to someone she trusts and loves." I study her face for a reaction or some hint of understanding, but she's just tilting her head at me, listening intently, much like a child does when hearing a bedtime story. *Like Katie did.* "I know it's hard to understand. Every relationship is different. It's a total give and take. For a lot of people, it gives them balance."

She nods. "That makes sense. I can understand that."

"Some people, they're into the pain and degradation. Like you mentioned, they want a slave, or want to be a slave. For me, it's a mix of things." Taking her hand, I stand and guide her onto the bed with me where we can be more comfortable. "I think what started this is my childhood. I was beat up by my adoptive father a lot. He liked to belittle me and put me down, and not let me have anything or be able to do anything. He was a control freak. He liked to lock me in my room alone. So I think I have a need for control now, to get what I want."

She interrupts me. "You really like that? The ropes, too?"

"It's an incredible rush to fuck someone who can't touch you, and on the flip side, to have sex with someone that you're restrained from touching. Tell me, how did it feel to suck me with your hands tied behind your back?"

Her cheeks redden, and she looks down at her pink-tipped fingers clutching the blanket.

"Tell me," I coax. "I want to know everything you're feeling."

She takes a deep breath before answering. "It was scary . . . but also exciting, in a really weird way. You're gonna laugh at me for this, but I've always hated giving oral because I thought I was doing it wrong, or not good enough, and I had a fear of swallowing and choking." She peeks at me from under her long, dark eyelashes. "But with you kinda demanding it, and having my hands tied, I didn't have the chance to back out. It made it easier, as backwards as that sounds."

"See?" I smile at her. "Giving up control and fears can be good. And it made me happy as fucking hell."

"Did it? I really made you feel good?"

"You made me feel way better than good. I never get off that fast. You just looked so fucking beautiful, and provoking me to chase you down pushed me right over the edge."

I'm treading on delicate ground here. Getting involved like this hadn't been part of my plan. Not that I really had a plan. I just knew I couldn't stop thinking about her after seeing her, and I just had to get closer to her. *Feel* her. *Hear* her. Be part of her. I wasn't expecting to actually like her. Or to want her so fucking much. Or the possibility of her liking me.

*I'm fucked.*

I stand and cross the room to my walk-in closet to get some

clothes. When I return she's staring at the wall, not blinking. A lot like Sterling does.

"I'm gonna run out for a little while."

Her head snaps up. "You're leaving me here?"

"Yes." I don't want her with me in case I run into someone who recognizes me, and I'm not ready yet to tell her I'm in Ashes & Embers, or that I'm the guy who crashed into her.

Her eyes fly to me wildly. "When are you coming back?"

"Relax. I'm just running to the store. I'm going to grab some things I need, and some clothes for you. What size are you? Little?"

"Small. Why can't I go with you?"

I shake my head and pull a black T-shirt over my head. "No. Listen to me. I'm going to trust you to not touch my shit while I'm gone. If I find out that you touched any of my stuff, I will fucking spank your ass raw. Come with me." I head out into the living room and she follows me. "I want you to sit on this couch with the cat and not move, all right?"

She scowls at me like a child. "What is your problem? I'm not going to steal your stuff."

I'm not worried about her stealing anything; I'm worried about her finding something with my name on it, and I don't have time to go through the entire house to see what's lying around. I keep this place really clean and don't have mail sent here, but I'm sure there must be something with my name on it somewhere.

"I know you're not. I just don't like people going through my personal things."

She flops on the couch, pulls the cat onto her lap, and picks up the television remote. "I have zero interest."

"Do you need anything? Any kind of food you want?"

"No, thank you. I barely eat anymore."

"That's changing tonight. I'm making us dinner."

"You can't make me eat. I'll use the safe word."

"You can't use the safe word for dinner. That's ridiculous, and not even funny."

She shoots me a dirty look, and I suddenly feel as if I'm living with a teenager.

"I won't be gone long," I tell her, picking up my car keys.

"Should I expect any random women to show up while you're gone?" she asks, a touch of sarcasm in her voice.

I smirk and cross the room to stand over her. "Were you jealous of Evelyn?"

"Who's Evelyn?"

I want to spank this girl so bad I can taste it. She's such a little instigator. She flip-flops from being quiet and depressed to sarcastic in about two seconds.

"You're begging for a spanking, ya know."

"Just go already." She's not even looking at me.

"Stand up."

"Why?"

"Don't question me. Just do it."

She puts the cat gently next to her and stands up, twisting her hair around her finger and chewing her lip.

"Kiss me goodbye." I soften my voice to ease her nerves.

"I don't like goodbyes," she says, her voice thick with sadness.

"I can understand that. Then just kiss me because you like me."

She peeks up at me beneath her messy bangs. "Maybe I don't like you." I know she's only half teasing, but her words cut me and kill my mood. Which is really different for me, because I don't like many people and couldn't give two shits if they like me or not. But I want *her* to like me, and even more than that, I want her to want me.

"Hey, I'm used to people not liking me. Join the fucking club." And with that I leave, slamming the door behind me.

I take the car I keep up here instead of the bike because I can't cram too much stuff into the saddlebags. On the way to the store, I blast some music to try and raise my mood, but it's not working. Maybe I should just take her home and stop playing with fire with this situation I've created. I shouldn't be fucking around with the widow of someone I accidentally killed. It's pretty much the most fucked up thing I've ever done. Lukas would kill me if he knew, and Storm would have a goddamn coronary. Ash would try to ban me from the fucking planet. *Self-righteous assholes.*

But this girl . . . this little broken doll of a girl that used to smile and write silly status updates like *"omg! This cookie is amazing!!"* has entranced me. She's woken my desires and eased some of my pain already. I crave both her dark silence and her sensual innocence. I want to catch her smile with my lips, feel what she feels, see what she sees. I need her to be happy, because I believe it's contagious, and I want her to infect me with it. Giving her up is not something I'm ready to do.

I pick up a few grocery items, some sweatpants, T-shirts, and panties for her, and then wander into the craft store that is conveniently located next door. She's way too delicate for my usual industrial ropes and chains. Instead, I want to bind her with silk ribbon and long strings of pearls, to tie her beauty within beauty, and then defile her with my ugly darkness just so I can undo it again.

As I drive back to the house, I play last night over in my mind. I'm surprised at how willingly she came with me and let me touch her. I don't think I misjudged her in thinking she's a good girl that doesn't sleep around. She turned me on like mad and I want to believe that she wanted me just as badly, but I know that's far from the truth. It must be that she has reached a level of destruction where she wants me to ruin her and is using me to facilitate her own mental demise.

*Shit.*

# chapter eleven

TABITHA

The blind kitten purring on my lap has a therapeutic effect on me, his internal motor like a lullaby. I gently rub my fingers on his forehead. One would think that a kitten that was tortured and who'd completely lost his eyes would be scared, timid, hiding from people. But he's not. He's totally loving and trusting, willing to give life and humans another chance.

I haven't had a pet since I was a little girl, but this adorable furball is making me want one. It would be nice to have a sweet cat like this to cuddle with at night, rather than being all alone in the house. I wonder if the guy would let me have him. He really doesn't seem like the type who would want to have a disabled pet.

"You want to come live with me, little guy?" I say in a baby voice. He purrs louder and rolls on his back so I can rub his tummy, making me laugh.

I think I accidentally upset the dominant dude. I didn't mean to, really—I just can't seem to control my emotions at all anymore. I'm a total mess since Nick died, and I feel as if I'm flailing off the edge of a cliff most of the time. Just a few months ago, life was so different. We were trying to have a baby. We both had good jobs. We had great friends. We were happy, at least most of the time, and more than most couples I know. A lump forms in my throat as the memories envelope me.

And now . . .

Now I'm lying on some guy's couch, a guy I let tie me up for a blow job and fuck me, a guy who threatened to spank me and wants me to submit to him. There is something incredibly alluring and sexually magnetic about him, something taboo. I *want* to give in to him, and I don't even know why. Maybe I'm just trying to punish myself.

He was right about the release of control and it making me feel better. It really did, so very much, but not in any way that I have ever felt before. It was exhilarating, like falling without a net, yet knowing I would be caught. It felt dirty, too, and as much as I tried to fight it, it turned me on.

*You're disgusting.*

There is sadness deep in him, a darkness living there that pulls him under. He's hiding so much from me, not letting me see all of him, and I know there is more to him than he's letting on, more than I assumed he would be. He's a Pandora's box that I should probably not play with, but even after just one day, I feel hooked. I honestly think his need for control stems from a fear of abandonment and loss. If he controls the relationship, then he can't be blindsided or hurt.

While he's at the store, I consider calling a cab and getting the hell out of here before I get in deeper, but I can't bring myself to do it because I'm too intrigued by him and what he's offering. I like how he's melting the ice around me, helping me feel again, awakening feelings I've never felt before, helping me find a new me.

Yesterday I wanted to die, but today I just want to kill the girl I used to be and meet the girl I could be.

It's a start.

A door shutting and the kitten jumping wake me up. I look around, disoriented, and he's standing over me, holding some bags.

"I'm sorry. I must have dozed off."

"Don't apologize, I want you to rest. You're exhausted. And too thin."

Still drowsy, I follow him to the kitchen and help him take the stuff out of the bags, which feels strangely domestic and familiar. "I thought men liked thin women."

He winks at me and my insides melt for days. "Not me. I like some curves so I can hold on to you. You're way too skinny. My dick weighs more than you."

I make a disgusted face at him. "Ew. That is so . . . ugh. I don't even know." I shake my head and busy myself with the groceries while he laughs.

I check him out as he's putting things in the refrigerator, his long, black hair cascading over his muscled back and shoulders. Yesterday my head was too messed up and foggy to notice how gorgeous and sexy he is. He's got the kind of carnal looks that stop a woman in her tracks and make her wet instantly just by looking at him. His dark skin, facial features, and long, black hair definitely hint at him being Native American. And those muscles and tattoos . . . *wow.*

"I'm sorry I upset you earlier . . . before you left."

He shrugs it off. "I don't get upset." *He's lying.*

"I thought this worked both ways?"

"What do you mean?"

"This morning, you said you needed to know what I was feeling. I need to know what you're feeling, too."

"I really don't talk about my feelings. Sorry." He pulls bottled water, assorted fruits, and toiletries out of the bag. "I need to know your feelings so I can understand your needs better and help you."

I take the milk carton he's holding out of his hands and put it into the refrigerator. "And who helps you?" I ask him pointedly.

"I bought you some clothes," he replies, completely ignoring my question and gesturing towards a bag on the table.

After dumping out the contents of the bag, all I see are black sweatpants, basic T-shirts, and plain bikini panties.

"Geez. This is fashionable," I joke.

"No need for fashion. I'll have you naked most of the time and on your knees," he says, and then pauses. "Or on all fours."

My traitorous pussy quivers in response.

I try to change the subject. "What about my car?"

"Write down your address and I'll call a tow truck to have it taken there. I'll pay for it." He opens a drawer and hands me a pen and torn piece of paper with a hotel emblem on it.

"Don't you have a job?" I ask him, writing down my address. "And a name?"

He takes the paper from me and gives me that long stare of his, as if he's looking right through my eyes and straight into my thoughts, making me feel vulnerable and exposed.

"We'll talk about that later on," he finally answers.

"Seriously? We're going to talk about your name *later*?"

He doesn't waver. "That's what I said."

"Don't you want to know mine?"

"No. I'll call you what I want to call you."

"Fine," I mutter, and take off out the sliding glass doors in the kitchen that lead to the backyard, sure to close the doors behind me so Sterling can't wander out. There's a chilly breeze coming off the lake. All I've got on is his thin T-shirt, but I don't care. There are no other houses around that I can see from here, so no one's going to see my pointy nipples and naked legs.

Walking over to the short wooden dock that extends from the yard, I find a dingy tied to it. It's hard for me to picture him in this tiny boat; he's just too big and I think he would sink it. I climb into it and untie the rope from the wooden post. There are two oars but I don't use them; I just let the wind blow me slowly across the water. From the middle of the lake, I can see a few other houses, each with their own docks and boats. I didn't explore his house while he was gone, but now I wished I had. There were definitely other rooms—I just lacked the interest in seeing them. Maybe there's a guest room that he will let me stay in while I'm here. Unless he expects me to sleep in his bed every night. *With him?* I'm not sure I can do that.

I wiggle my left hand, staring at my engagement ring and wedding band. All my memories feel so far away, and I don't understand how that can happen in just a few months. Everything feels as if it happened a lifetime ago. I can't remember the happiness I felt every day before the accident. Now it feels like a movie I watched, and not like it happened to me at all.

Sometimes I'm not sure if I'm grieving the loss of Nick or the loss of myself.

I peer over the edge of the boat and see a face looking back at me in the water. I don't even recognize myself anymore. The girl in the water looks like a sad wreck.

The boat bobbing in the water is making me sleepy, and I wish I had a blanket and pillow with me so I could just curl up on the cramped floor of the boat and sleep. Better yet, I wish I could fall over the side, float to the bottom of the lake, and just stay there.

Dom dude is just as much of a mess as I am. Possibly even more so. He seems sad, but also devious and a bit of an asshole, and yet I see fleeting glimpses of care and compassion in him, too. The fact that I got on a motorcycle with him so easily without a second thought and let him bring me here to his house in the woods scares me terribly.

Turning to look back at the house, I see he's standing on the dock with a bottle in his hand. I've drifted out further than I thought and doubt the wind will be nice enough to lead me back, so I pick up the oars and row back. His eyebrows furrow together when I near, and he grabs the rope from my hand and ties it to the post. I watch his fingers expertly tie the knot, and wetness pools between my legs, thinking of how he tied my hands almost the same way.

He takes my arm and helps me onto the dock. "What the hell are you doing? I thought something happened to you." He picks up his bottle of vodka and takes a swig. This cannot be good.

"What could happen? I was just floating around."

"Next time, tell me. You can't just disappear on me like that."

"I wish I could just disappear. And why are you drinking?"

"Because that's what I do." He puts his arm around me and leads me towards the house. "It's too cold for you to be out here like this."

As soon as we walk through the doors, I can smell food cooking, so he must have started dinner while I was out on the boat *disappearing*. He doesn't strike me as the cooking type, but I guess he's just full of surprises.

"It smells delicious. What are you making?"

"Chicken cordon bleu and rice pilaf."

I can't hide the impressed and surprised look that must be on my face. "Really? You made that?"

He takes another sip of vodka before answering me, and I'm starting to worry about why he's drinking and how much of that he's going to be doing. I really don't want to be stuck out here with an angry—or psycho—drunk.

"Yes, I made it. My grandmother loves to cook, and sometimes I just go to her house and spend the day cooking with her."

Picturing that scene brings a smile to my face. I don't know many men who would hang out with their grandmother cooking, especially ones that look like he does.

Sterling waltzes into the room and starts to wind himself around my ankles, meowing up at me.

"Aww . . . he's talking. He's such a cutie."

He takes yet another drink, and opens a small pantry door, pulling out a bag of cat food. "He's hungry. This little fucker eats nonstop."

I take the bag out of his hand and fill the cat's dish, laughing at how quickly he runs over to start devouring his food. "Don't call him a fucker. He's just a kitten. Maybe he was starved as well as tortured."

"Shit, I never thought of that."

I put the food back in the pantry and spy more alcohol in there, way in the back.

I turn around and eye him. "Why are you drinking so much?"

"This is nothing. Trust me." Thin red veins are spreading in his eyes, and his words are starting to slur just a little bit. The fuck is he doing to himself?

"Do you have a drinking problem?" I demand, folding my arms across my chest.

He laughs. "I have a lot of problems."

Irritated, I take the bottle away from him. "I won't stay here if you're going to drink." I pour what's left in the bottle into the sink, hoping it doesn't put him in a rage.

"What the fuck?" he yells. "Why did you do that?"

I back away from him a little. "I refuse to stay here if you're going to be drinking. Forget it. No way in hell am I going to let you put a finger on me or be wielding knives and tying me up or whatever crazy shit you plan to do if you're drunk or high. You said I had to trust you and there is no way I can do that if you're drinking. I can't go there."

We engage in a stare-off for a few minutes. His eyes are dark with anger and his fists are clenched at his sides. The fact that I don't know anything about him or what he could do to me quickly comes to the forefront of my mind.

"You keep fucking walking away from me," he finally says.

"And?" I prod, raising my eyebrows at him.

"And what? I don't like it. Don't do it again."

"Fine. No more drinking or I'll walk home."

He sighs and blows out a breath, running his hand through his hair. "All right. If it bothers you that much, I won't."

"It does, and thank you."

"Come here."

I don't budge.

"Come. Here," he repeats.

I relent and step forward, stopping a few inches in front of him to crane my neck to look up into his face. His hand brushes across my cheek. "Why do you run off?" he asks, his voice low and soft, his eyes fighting to close.

Shrugging, I lean against the warmth of his hand. "I don't know, really. I'm constantly feeling like I have to run away . . . like being someplace else will somehow make me feel better. It never does though, and I usually end up just crying or getting mad at myself. I don't know how else to explain it other than my brain and my heart feel lost."

He stares into my eyes for a few moments and I know that he understands. Finally, someone understands. "We'll even you out and you'll feel better." He leans down and kisses me. "Come into the bedroom with me. I need to measure you."

Confused, I let him lead me to the bedroom. "Measure me?" I question. "For what?"

He pulls the T-shirt over my head, as if it's just the most natural thing to be doing, then guides me to step out of my panties while I hang on to him for balance.

"I'm going to buy you something," he finally says.

Well, that piques my interest. What could he buy me that I would need to be measured naked for? I recall reading about a psycho that kidnapped a woman and kept her in a box under his bed for weeks, taking her out only to abuse her. A flash of fear rips through me at the thought of that happening to me.

He goes to his dresser and comes back with a cloth tape measure, and begins to measure my height, my chest, my waist, my hips—almost every part of my body. He types it all into a note program on his phone.

"Okay, you've really got my mind going. What are you going to get me?"

He slides his hand between my thighs. "It's a secret." His finger presses up between my already moist lips. "It will take about a week to get here once I order it." He slowly slides his finger in and out of me and bends down to kiss my neck, sucking the base of my throat. I lean back, stretching my neck to feel more of his mouth on me. His teeth graze my skin, sending shivers down my spine.

"Spread your legs for me," he whispers, and I obey, spreading my feet farther apart. I run my hands up his arms and grip his shoulders as he pushes two fingers inside me. He pulls my hair, stretching my neck back even more, and ravishes my flesh with his lips and tongue. "Take your hands off me and put them behind your back."

My heart sinks a little. I like touching him and feeling his muscles. I love how strong and solid he feels.

"I'll fall over," I protest.

He bites my lip. "I won't let you fall. Ever."

My hands drop and clasp together behind me at my lower back.

"Good girl." He puts his arm around me and holds me against him while he finger-fucks me with his other hand, pistoning in and out while his thumb rubs circles over my clit. My legs quake and weaken as he brings me close to orgasm. His fingers are like magic, knowing exactly where and how to touch me, making it hard for me to stop my body from grinding against him. I have to focus on keeping my hands behind me, and not grabbing on to him.

"You want to come, don't you?" His voice is a sexy, raspy whisper in my ear. He slows his hand down, barely moving inside me. I press my sex against him, needing him to keep going, but he doesn't move, and holds me back from riding on his hand.

"Yes . . ." I try to kiss him, but he moves his lips away from mine, teasing me, taking everything away. I struggle not to whimper with want.

"Beg."

All pride goes out the window. "Please . . ."

"Again."

God, he's a cruel bastard. "Please, let me come."

He groans and thrusts his fingers inside me, swirling them around my core, his thumb working my clit as if his life depends on it. His lips find mine again, and he kisses me so deeply, so passionately and so demandingly, it's as if we have to kiss just to breathe and survive. I've never felt such intensity in a man's kiss before, and it drives me further to the brink and then pushes me over the edge. I'm tumbling into orgasm, my muscles clenching around his fingers buried deep inside me. He holds me tight as my body quivers against him, my legs threatening to give out. His kisses slow until they are soft and lingering, his lips just barely touching mine, our breathing slowing together.

Gently lowering me down onto the bed, he holds me while I come down from the orgasm high.

"I think dinner is ready," he says, breaking the silence. "Let's go eat and then I can play with you some more."

Damn, is he serious? I don't think I can take any more.

"Be right back," he says, and disappears down the hall. He returns with the clothes he bought for me and lays them on the bed.

"Get dressed and come join me for dinner." He kisses me once more. "That was perfect, by the way. I love making you beg and come."

My limbs are wobbly, like wet noodles, as I get dressed. I really feel like I need a nap to recover after that escapade, but the smell of the food is making my stomach grumble so much that for the first time in months, I actually want to eat.

I find him in the kitchen, and he looks so out of place with his long hair and tattooed muscles standing over the island stove. Sterling is at his feet, literally howling at the top of his tiny lungs.

"Oh my, what's up with him?" I ask.

He shakes his head. "It seems he's yelling at the smells. I think it woke up his tapeworm or something." He looks down at the kitten, who's rubbing at his ankles. "I don't know what the fuck Evelyn was thinking, giving me this cat. I don't know what to do with him."

"That girl who was here gave him to you?"

"Yeah. She volunteers at some pet rescue or something. I don't really pay attention."

"Why would she give you a blind kitten?" I wonder again if maybe something is going on between them. Giving someone a pet is kind of an intimate gift.

He fills two plates with rice and chicken and carries them over to the table. "She thought he would help me. At least, that's what she said."

"Help you with what?"

"Grief, I think. Go sit down." I know he's dismissing the

conversation to avoid talking about it, but I want him to tell me who he's grieving and how long it's been for him. I want to dig deep into him, as he plans to do to me. Does he feel the endless agony of loss that I do? Does it tear his heart out every time he thinks of her?

Is his future an empty pit of darkness like mine is now?

# chapter twelve

VANDAL

She's staring off into space and doesn't even look at me when I sit down at the table. From the expression in her eyes, I can tell she's thinking about him. *Not me*. She's slipped away from me again, even without walking off.

I cut the chicken on her plate into small pieces. "Your eyes should always be on me when I enter the room," I say evenly. "And I should be the only man you think about."

She turns her head suddenly, as if she just realized I was there. "Huh?"

"I'm telling you what I expect and need."

She nods absently and looks down at her plate. "Thank you for making dinner."

"Don't thank me until you try it."

She smiles a little and takes a bite, chewing slowly. I like watching her mouth as she chews and swallows. There are so many things I want to do with her mouth.

"This is delicious." She takes another bite. "I haven't eaten real food in so long."

"What have you been eating?"

She shrugs her shoulders. "Coffee and crackers. Sometimes a milkshake."

I laugh at her answer. "Coffee, crackers, and milkshakes?" I repeat. "That's the most bizarre combo of food I've ever heard."

"I lost my lust for food when Nick died."

Christ. The accident I caused forced this girl into starving herself. Just great.

"What do you usually like to eat?" I ask.

"Hmmm . . . vanilla lattes, chocolate mousse, salad, homemade chicken noodle soup, cookies, pumpkin ice cream—"

"Whoa, what? Did you say pumpkin ice cream?" I almost choke on my food.

She nods and takes a sip of water. "Yup. It's amazing."

"It sounds disgusting."

"Dude, you have to try it. I could eat it forever."

"Don't call me dude. Maybe we'll get some if you're good."

She almost squeals with happiness over that. Who knew ice cream would be the thing to finally get some real happiness out of her?

"What do *you* like?" She tilts her head at me as she waits for my answer, and I love how she's looking at me as if she really wants to hear what I'm going to say.

"To eat?"

"Yeah . . . or anything else you want to tell me."

"As far as food goes, I like meat and vegetables. I'm not into all that sweet stuff you mentioned. I like rough sex, fast cars, loud bikes, pain, music, ink, and little blondes on their knees."

She almost spits her food out. "Well, that's an interesting list," she says.

"Your turn."

"My list is much more boring than yours. I like soft music, reading, art, angels, nature, photography . . . and big, long-haired guys with control issues." She says the last part with a shy smile that fuckin' makes my heart leap. I put my fork down and push my plate away.

"Come over here," I command.

She blinks at me. "What?"

I grab her hand, tug her until she stands, then pull her onto my lap.

"I thought we were eating." The slight nervousness in her voice fuels the fire growing in me.

My hand is already down her pants, seeking the heat between her legs. "You're going to be dessert." Lifting her up effortlessly, I sit her on the table in front of me, yanking the sweatpants and panties off her, spreading her legs wide.

"Are you crazy? We can't do this on the dining room table—"

Ignoring her, I lift her legs onto my shoulders and lap at her open pussy, immediately shutting her up. Her head falls back, knocking her water over. She tries to sit up and I push her down, keeping my hand in the middle of her chest to keep her still. I caress her soft folds with my tongue and suck her clit into my mouth, gently biting. She squirms and pushes her hips up against my face. She gets turned on so quickly, I'm going to have to teach her to slow down and savor every moment. Grabbing her hand in mine, I guide hers down between her legs, coaxing her to touch herself. She pulls away but I hold her wrist there until she catches on and starts to rub her clit as I plunge my tongue deep into her. Her legs tighten around my neck and I stop moving, letting her fuck herself on my tongue while she fingers herself. When I feel her start to come, I grab her hips, pulling her half off the table and pushing my tongue deeper into her. She yanks at my hair. "Stop! Please . . . I can't take anymore," she begs.

I move my lips up to her stomach, kissing her and tracing slow circles around her belly button while her body finally relaxes beneath me, then pull her onto my lap, her legs spreading around my waist.

"You're delicious. Much better than pumpkin ice cream," I tease. Her face is flushed, her hair sticking to her damp forehead.

"You're exhausting. I've had more orgasms in the past twenty-four hours than I've had in a year." She quickly covers her mouth and closes her eyes, shaking her head back and forth as the words leave her lips and she tries to move off me. I put my hands on her waist and hold her.

"Don't do that," I say, noticing the tears brimming in her eyes. She looks away from me. "You don't have to feel guilt for enjoying what we do."

"I shouldn't have said that . . . it's disrespectful to him."

Once again I lift her chin to look at me. "One, don't break eye contact with me. And two, I want you to say whatever you're thinking. You're allowed to feel. I *need* you to feel."

She's quiet for a few moments and plays with my necklace, turning it over in her fingers.

"I've never been fucked on a table before."

"You still haven't been. I licked you, but I didn't fuck you."

She gives me a crooked smile. "Same thing."

"Not at all. I can demonstrate the differences if you want."

"No! Jesus." She chews her lip and peeks up at me. "I've . . . *you know* . . . more than you have though."

Fuck, she's adorable. "Gotten off?" I say.

Her cheeks redden and she nods. "Yes."

"I'm not keeping a scorecard, babe. If I want to make you come, I'm going to. If I want to get off, trust me, you'll know it. If you want it, just ask. Is that what you're hinting at? Do you want to get me off?"

"No . . . I just didn't want you to be mad at me that you haven't."

I slide my hands under her shirt to cup her breasts. "I'm not one of those guys who thinks just because he gets a chick off that she owes him one back. The fun for me is making you come, watching you squirm, hearing you moan, tasting you, making you obey me, and pushing your boundaries." I roll her nipples between my fingers as I talk and watch her eyes flutter closed.

My cell phone vibrates in my pocket. What the fuck? Why can't people leave me alone for one fucking day? I let out a frustrated sigh and pull it out to check the screen. It's Lukas.

"Hey," I answer, knowing if I don't talk to him he'll psycho call me for hours until I prove I'm alive.

"Hey, man, how's it going?" he asks casually.

"Just relaxing."

"Good. Evie called me—"

I blow out a breath. "What the fuck. She has such a big mouth."

"She said you had a girl up there?"

"Is there a problem with that?"

"Not at all. I'm glad you're getting some. I was just surprised to hear."

"She's staying with me for a few weeks."

"Shit. That's not like you."

"Call it therapy."

"Anyone I know?"

"Nope."

"Are you doing okay otherwise? Sobering up?"

"Actually, the deal was she would stay if I don't drink, so there's your answer."

"I like her already. Maybe me and Ivy can come up next week and hang out?"

I knew this shit was coming. "I'm not sure if I'm ready for a double-date, Lukas. Not sure she is either." I watch her face as I talk, her eyes fluttering closed as my free hand slowly roams over her body.

Lukas continues, "Call me in a few days and let me know. I'll bring some steaks, we can hang out and jam a little, build a bonfire . . ."

*Ugh.* "I'll think about it." Seeing Lukas will drag me back to reality and bring me out of my Tabitha bubble. He'll remind me of Katie and how she's not here anymore.

"Have you talked to Ash?" he inquires.

"Fuck him."

"He's gonna let you come back, Van. Just get your shit together."

"I'm working on it." I grab the back of Tabi's neck and pull her down for a quick kiss. "All right, man. I gotta run. I'll call you." I end the call before he can say anything else.

"Who was that?"

"My brother. He wants to bring his chick up here and do couples shit."

"Oh."

"Look . . . I don't do things like that. I don't date."

"I understand. I don't want that either. What's he like?"

"Like me, only younger and nicer."

I stand and lower her to her feet, giving her a playful slap on the ass. "Clean up the table and meet me in the bedroom in half an hour."

"Okay . . ."

I wasn't expecting Tabi to affect me, but she is and it's freaking me out. For a few minutes, I actually forgot who she was, and what I did. It all felt . . . normal. Like I'm just a normal guy and she's just a normal chick, and we met randomly and hit it off. I wish my life could be that normal, and not the dysfunctional mess it's always been. I've never gotten attached, but damn, this girl is somehow getting under my skin. In a different time, under different circumstances, she would have been perfect for me. *I* could have been perfect for her.

She comes into the room forty minutes after I left her to clean up dinner. I'm actually glad she's late, because now I can do what I've been itching to do.

Punish her.

"You're late." I'm sitting on the bed with black shorts on and nothing else, the pearls and ribbon waiting next to me.

"I know. I played with the cat for a few minutes and took a quick shower. I had rice in my hair."

I cross the room and go to the closet, take out a thin foam pillow, and throw it on the floor a few feet away from the bed.

"Undress and kneel on this."

She opens her mouth to protest, and I put my finger to her lips. "No debates," I say. "Undress slowly so I can enjoy it."

She's trembling as she takes her clothes off in front of me, awkward and unsure of herself, showing zero confidence in how beautiful she is and the feelings she's stirring in me. Naked, she walks to the small pillow and drops to her knees.

I bend down next to her and put my hands on her back. "Lower your head 'til your forehead touches the floor."

She pops her head back up and looks over her shoulder at me. "Seriously?"

"Stop. Do it." I raise my voice a little, getting annoyed. I hate having to repeat myself. Hopefully she'll learn that soon.

I gently guide her into position, legs tucked beneath her, forehead on the floor, arms outstretched, palms down. Her small, thin body looks so graceful this way, like a statue. I run my hand down her spine.

"Are you comfortable?" I ask.

"What do you think?"

"Just yes or no. No bratty remarks, or this will be way worse for you and a lot of fun for me."

She sighs into the carpet. "Yes."

"We're going to start doing this the right way, now. Any time you want me to stop, and I mean really stop, you use your safe word and everything stops. If you're restrained, you have to be still and calm after saying the word so I can release you without you getting hurt. Do you understand?"

"Yes."

"Do you trust me to take care of you?"

"Yes." She fidgets on the floor. I gently caress her back.

"Just relax your body and your mind. Don't stiffen up."

"I'm trying to." Her shoulders relax and she unclenches her fingers.

"I know, and you're doing great. You look fucking stunning. You have no idea what seeing you like this does to me." I plant a kiss on the middle of her spine and watch goose bumps sprinkle over her flesh.

I'm like a kid in a toy store. There are so many things I want to do with her and say to her, and have her do to me. It's almost overwhelming. I've fantasized about someone like her for more than ten years, and thought it would always be just an unattainable fantasy. And now here she is, on my floor, open to me. If only this could last, but I know better. It will end . . . and it will end badly.

"From now on, I don't want you to shower unless you ask me first. I want to bathe you myself sometimes." Bathing is part of the bonding and after-care process, and one of the parts that I'm most looking forward to with her. I have a desire to care for her that I've never felt with another woman.

She turns her head on the floor and blows her hair out of her face to look at me. "Oh my God. Seriously?"

Her sarcasm completely severs my mood, like having ice thrown on me, and pulls me out of the scene.

"Ya know what? Fuck it. Get up."

Standing, I grab the pearls and ribbon and throw them into the nightstand drawer.

"Just go to bed," I say, angrily. "I'll take you home tomorrow."

I leave her sitting there and go out to the living room, seething mad and disappointed. The universe is obviously punishing me for my sins, constantly getting in the way of any happiness. It just doesn't happen, no matter what I fucking do. I should have never gone near her; every part of it is wrong on so many fucking levels. My desire for her has clouded over all of my judgement.

*Fuck.* I want to cut myself wicked bad, and I have no razors here. I lean my head into my hands. Ever since the accident, my brain feels as if it's trying to claw its way out of my skull when I get mad or stressed out. I want to rip my own fucking head off right now.

"Are you okay?" Her voice is soft but still startles me. I didn't even hear her come into the room. She touches my head carefully. "Are you sick?"

"Just go away. We're not doing this."

I lean back on the couch and try to focus on her in the dark room. She's still completely naked and is standing way too close to me.

"I'm sorry," she whispers, and then kneels on the floor in front of me and clasps her hands behind her back. "I know I'm a sarcastic brat. It's how I deal with things when I'm upset or scared. I didn't mean to disrespect you."

"Please, just go to bed." I can't stand having her like this in front of me. She makes me feel as if I'm going to lose my fucked up mind.

"I don't want to go, I want to stay here with you. I promise I'll be better. I want to see where this can go with us."

My heart speeds up, and anticipation kicks in upon hearing those words. "Do you mean that? Do you know what you're saying?"

"Yes."

"You can't play with me. This is serious for me . . . for both of us. It's not a fucking game."

"I know, and I don't want it to be. I did some web research on my cell phone while you were at the store. I've read a little about this sort of thing before. I understand what it is. I'm just nervous."

"I know you are. I am, too." I let one brick out of my wall and pray she doesn't destroy me with it.

"Can I kiss you?"

*Fuck me.* She's asking for permission.

"No," I answer, even though I want her kiss more than I want to breathe. "Turn around and bend over the coffee table."

Disappointment crosses her face, but she silently turns and does exactly as I ask, bending over the low table and resting her forehead against it, her hands still clasped behind her, her beautiful ass offered to me. I run my hands slowly down her ribs, over her hips, and further down to squeeze her tight, round ass. I want to ram my cock into her and make her scream my name so badly that it's making my entire body ache just holding back from ravishing her.

I slide my finger between her cheeks all the way down to her lips, parting them and feeling her wetness. She wants this. Maybe just as much as I do.

I lift my hand and bring it down on her ass cheek with a smack. Not as hard as I've done to others in the past, but enough to make her jump and gasp.

"Will you listen to me from now on and not be a brat?"

"Yes." We both know she's lying, but that's okay.

I smack her other cheek and she jumps again.

"You sure?"

She turns her face to the side, her cheek resting against the table.

"I'm positive. I want you to help me. I don't want to be numb anymore."

I rub my hands over her ass cheeks, soothing the sting for her. "Me either, baby."

I really wanted to tie her up with the six feet of fake pearl strings I bought, but seeing her like this, I decide to put that off and stay in this moment.

I quickly take my clothes off and get on my knees behind her, pushing her and the coffee table forward to give me more room. I rub the head of my cock against her lips, teasing her and letting her wetness mix with my precum, lubing us both. Sliding into her slowly, I let her adjust to me so she's not in pain. I close my eyes and savor the feeling of being inside her, the sounds of her mewling and sighing the only noises in the dark room. Grabbing her hips, I pull out and then plunge full force back into her, my balls slapping against her thighs. She lets out a whimper and puts her hands on the table to steady herself as I thrust in and out of her tight sex.

"Hands back," I growl. She puts her hands back and I clasp her wrists with my hand, holding them tight, my other hand gripping her hip, pulling her towards me to meet every thrust. "You feel so fucking good," I praise, tilting the angle of her a bit so I can go deeper and press against her more sensitive spots.

She tightens around me as she simultaneously starts to moan and shudder, her breathing quick and shallow as she comes on my shaft. The delicious tightening and spurt of wetness almost makes me come on the spot when I realize I'm bareback inside her. No wonder it feels so good. *Fuck me.*

I pull out and shoot all over her back and hands, jetting across her spine. Leaning back against the couch, I catch my breath for a minute and then pull her up to her feet. "Come with me, baby."

She follows me to the bathroom and watches me quietly as I run a bubble bath for her. My throat and heart clench when I realize I just poured Katie's bubble soap into the tub to bathe a girl I just spanked, fucked, and came on.

"Um, did you just . . . without a . . ." she says while we wait for the tub to fill.

I test the water temp and turn to face her. Her blue eyes are wide and her skin has paled two shades.

"I did. But I pulled out. I'm sorry . . . I got so caught up I just forgot. I never do that, I swear." I feel like a freakin' amateur.

"I got the birth control shot after Nick died, to help reduce the bad cramps I get," she says, looking at her toes. "But I'm kinda worried about where you've been."

Well, shit. She doesn't beat around the bush, now does she?

"I'm clean." My voice is defensive.

She looks at me with narrow eyes, and I really don't blame her. I picked her up in a cemetery and fucked her seven ways 'til Sunday. Several times. I'm sure I don't exactly give off an impression of clean and crabless.

"You think I would do something to hurt you?" I ask, turning off the water. I can feel the familiar anger building up inside me and I try to quench it.

"Well, you *did* forget."

"Yeah, I did, but if I had some kind of fucking disease, I wouldn't be touching you in the first place. I'm not that much of a douche."

She eyes me some more, and I run my hands through my hair in frustration. "I swear to you, I'm clean."

"Okay," she finally says. "I believe you."

"Good, now get in the tub before the water gets cold." I help her in, and she settles down under the bubbles. I'm assaulted by a flashback of Katie bathing here not too long ago. My heart clenches and the familiar pain in my chest makes itself known. *Not now. Please.* I grab a clean washcloth from the linen closet and sit on the floor, wishing this bathroom had a big Jacuzzi tub so I could fit in there comfortably with her.

"Can I ask you something?" she says, idly playing with the bubbles.

"The answer to that will always be yes."

She gives me a cute sideways smile and blows the bubbles towards my face. "This is part of it? Bathing?"

I nod and slowly glide the washcloth over her body under the water. "Yes, it's referred to as after-care sometimes. It's to soothe you, relax muscles that may be sore after using restraints, to clean you, of course, and to show you that I care about you and want you to feel safe and taken care of. And it helps to bring us closer, because it's intimate."

"Have you had other girls like me here?"

"Actually, no. I've never had any girls here. I don't live here full-time; I only stay here sometimes."

I follow her eyes to the pink bottle of bubble bath with the smiling kitten on it. *Shit.*

"Then why do you have that? You really don't look like the type who would be taking pink bubble baths. No offense."

I take a deep breath and rub her back with the cloth in slow circles. "It was my daughter's."

I did not want to go down this road. Not now. Maybe not ever. I can't lie to her about this though. Not when I'm trying to gain her trust and submission. I can't have her doubting me about diseases and bubble baths and thinking I'm either a pervert or feeding her lies.

"You have a daughter?"

"She's gone." That's all I can manage to say. I can't verbalize anything else about it. I haven't had to say the words before now because everyone I know knew Katie died. To actually say it, to say she is dead with my own mouth, is sickening to me. I never want to hear my voice say those words again.

Tabi looks upset, her eyes softening and watery. She grabs at my hand under the water. "I'm so sorry. I had no idea. Is that why you were there? When we met?"

I nod and slip my fingers between hers. I always want to be

touching her in some way, maybe because I'm afraid she's going to just disappear.

"How old was she?"

*No. I can't say it.* I shake my head.

"Recently?" she coaxes. "A few months ago?"

"This year."

She stares at the bottle of bubble bath, unblinking, and shivers.

"Around the same time Nick died, then."

"Yeah, I guess around then."

"Help me out?" she asks, rising from the tub.

I wrap her up in a big towel, but the mood has completely changed. "Are you all right?" she asks. "Maybe you should put on some pants and we can talk?"

I have no idea what one thing has to do with the other, but I go to the living room to put my shorts back on and flop on the couch on my back, staring up at the ceiling. *Fuck.* One good day. That's all I want. One day without pain eating through my heart. That's what I want for her too. Why is that so fucking hard?

She sits on the couch next to me, trying to read my face, with the towel still wrapped around her thin frame.

"Can I get you anything?" she asks. "You don't look too good right now. You've gone pale."

I bark out a short, sarcastic laugh. "A lot of alcohol would be great. Can you lift the ban?"

"Absolutely not." She lays her hand on my chest, over my heart, and traces my ink. "Do you want to talk about her?"

I throw my arm over my face to cover my eyes. "No. Never."

# chapter thirteen

## Tabitha

After he told me about his daughter last night, he succumbed to what appeared to be an emotional stress migraine and shut down. At least, that's what I call them when I get them, and I get them a lot. It's kinda like a brain overload. His grief has dragged him into a very dark place, and for some reason I just didn't expect that in him, or for it to affect him so deeply. I felt such an intense need to console him, but I was at a loss as to how. I know from experience that you really can't console a person in grief. Words are useless space fillers. He is so incredibly closed up, and I have no clue how to get in other than to give him what he seems to want so badly -- my submission.

I sat with him on the couch for hours with Sterling in my lap, unable to sleep myself but comforted by both of them sleeping near. I quietly left not long after midnight and slept alone in his bed.

He's not on the couch this morning though, or anywhere in the house from what I can see, and for a moment I panic, thinking he left me here. But then I see him outside, sitting on the dock, playing a guitar. I slide the glass doors open and walk across the woodsy yard. The music he's playing is beautiful and haunting, the kind of sound that goes straight through you and awakens your emotions and gives you chills. It's the kind of music that I would play on repeat over and over and over again until it was impossible to unhear it.

My heart skips a beat as my eyes rove over him from behind.

He's shirtless, his wide, muscled shoulders flexing as he plays the strings, his long black hair hanging down to the middle of his spine, covering the tattoos that adorn his entire back. His head is tilted down slightly as he plays. I sit next to him and just watch him, his fingers gliding effortlessly over the strings, the song drifting over the lake. He is such an enigma, this rock-hard man with the bad-ass attitude creating this ethereal, soul-touching sound.

When he finishes the song, his eyes open very slowly and meet mine.

"That was incredible," I say in awe. "I didn't know you played the guitar."

He puts the instrument off to the side. "That's an acoustic bass." He gives me a crooked cocky grin.

"Well, I know nothing about musical instruments, but whatever it is, I seriously have no words for how beautiful that was. It was just . . . wow. Seriously."

"Thanks. Music is a big part of my life. If you want to hear beautiful, you should hear Lukas play the violin."

"The violin? Really? I don't think I've ever heard anyone play the violin in person."

"He fuckin' rocks it. He can play metal songs on ,it too. It's pretty wild."

"I hope I get to hear him play someday. Maybe you could play some more for me?"

He cracks his neck to the side with an audible pop. "Yeah. Maybe later."

"Do you feel better? Your headache, I mean."

"I do. How do *you* feel? Are you sore?"

"Sore?" I'm not sure what he's asking me.

He bends his knee up and leans his arm on it. "Yeah. I rammed you pretty hard last night."

My pussy immediately quivers at his words. *Sweet Jesus.* Who asks questions like that?

"Um, a little bit, but it's all right."

He stares at me intently and chews on a toothpick he's got hanging out of his mouth. "I'm not good at slow and easy."

"Maybe you just need to practice." The words come out before I consider that he'll take that as a challenge.

An evil but sexy smile spreads across his lips and I know that's exactly what he's thinking.

"Soon, your gifts will be here, and I'll have a lot in store for you."

"More ramming, I assume?"

He throws his head back and laughs. "You're such a little smart-ass, ya know that? I'm starting to like it. And yeah, there will be some ramming, but a lot more than that."

I'm not sure if I should be worried about this or not. I'm definitely intrigued.

"I'll have some rules," he says.

"I'm not surprised. Such as?"

"For starters, you should kiss me good morning every day and thank me."

"Thank you for what?"

"Ramming you the night before," he half teases, quirking one eyebrow up.

I can't not giggle at him. I'm starting to like our little sarcastic talks and the way he makes me laugh even when it's the last thing I want to do. Especially with him.

"I see," I say. "Should I start now?"

He leans into my neck. "You want to kiss me, don't you?" he whispers in my ear, his breath hot against me.

I turn my face towards his. "I do," I whisper back, my heart beating faster. The way he makes me feel when he's near is indescribable and beyond the usual butterflies I have felt in the past when I met someone new and exciting. I feel as if I've known him so much longer than just two days, as if there is some kind of timeless connection between us. Maybe death and guilt do that to people.

He touches my cheek and runs his thumb across my bottom lip. "Kiss me then. Make me feel like you mean it."

Swallowing nervously, I tilt my head and kiss his lips. I don't want it to mean anything, but it's starting to. I just don't know exactly what that meaning is yet.

"What are you doing to me?" I ask him softly, looking into his dark eyes, our noses touching.

His hand tightens at the back of my neck. "*Everything.*"

I'm tumbling fast and hard into the web he's weaving, clinging to the hope that he really is bringing me out of my depression, making me want to feel and live again. What's scaring me is he's making me want *him* so much. My lips meet his again and I kiss him the only way I can right now—soft, questioning, searching. His breathing grows heavier and he wraps an arm around me, holding me against him. I move my lips down to kiss and gently suck his neck and he groans, his hand sliding down to squeeze my ass. Kissing my way back up to his lips, I pause and peek up into his hooded eyes.

"Fuck, darlin'. You're killing me." He sighs.

I touch his stubbled cheek and kiss him again. "How so?"

"Your touch is so soft. No one's ever kissed me like that."

"Oh." My voice drops with disappointment. I guess he's used to something better, something sexier.

"Hey," he says. "That's a compliment. Don't get down."

I shake my head a little. "I'm just not good at this."

"Cut it out. You don't want to start the day with a spanking, do you?"

I giggle. "No."

"Then don't stop kissing me."

We spend the entire morning on the dock, kissing and stopping for him to play some songs for me, then kissing more. Once I started kissing him, I felt as if I couldn't stop, as if he were my anchor to keep me from drifting back to Nick's memories, the depression, the guilt, and the suicidal thoughts. Maybe if I hang on to him long enough, I really will be okay. Maybe he will be, too.

"I'm gonna go for a ride," he says abruptly, grabbing his bass and standing up. "I won't be gone too long."

"Okay . . ." I'm taken aback that he wants to leave and wonder if I did something wrong. I follow him into the house. "I could go with you?" I suggest, standing in the doorway of the second bedroom, watching him put his bass in its carrying case and then into the closet.

"I kinda want to be alone."

*Ouch.*

"Oh."

"Can you cook?"

"Cook?" I repeat.

He winds a hair-tie around his hair that he's pulled into a ponytail. "Yeah, as in dinner?"

"Yes. I think I can manage that."

He ruffles my hair like I'm a little dog or a small child. "Good. I'll be back in about two hours. I'd like it if you have dinner ready when I get back. That's something I'd like to happen a lot, actually, as part of our arrangement, so if you need any cookbooks or groceries, let me know and I'll get what you need."

"Okay. Can you get me a charger for my cell phone?"

"Sure. Anything you need, just let me know." He takes a few more steps towards the door that leads to the garage and then turns back. "Part of this is me giving you things to do so you don't fall into a rut. You understand that, right? I'm not just trying to be a dick."

"Yes. I understand that."

"And I'm glad you're interested enough to do some research on a D/s relationship. That means a lot to me. I know we haven't really talked much about all of it, and that's my fault. I just want you to be careful about what you read online. Like I said, people have their own reasons for getting involved in this kind of relationship, and I don't judge what they do if it's something I'm not into, but a lot of what you see and read could be . . ." He looks up, as if he's searching for the right words ". . . scary for you, for lack of a better word. I don't want you to get freaked out thinking I'm going to hang you from the rafters for days, or share you with other men."

My stomach lurches. "Wait, what?"

"No, I'm not into that. Relax. I'm more into the submission, restraints, emotional boundaries, power, trust . . . that stuff." He closes the distance between us and puts his hand on the side of my neck, under my hair. The warmth of his fingers feels comforting to me, and eases my fears. "I want us to explore it all together and find what works for us. If you read about something that you want to try, tell me. Or, if you read about something that is a definite no *fucking* way for you, make a list of those, too. How's that?"

Nodding, I try to dredge up my voice. "Yes . . . that would be good I think."

He gives my neck a gentle squeeze. "I guess I wanted to make sure you were going to stick around for a while before we really talked about everything, which is ass-backwards, right?"

Letting out a little laugh, I agree. "Yes, but I understand. This whole situation has been a little unconventional."

"Do you regret coming here?" A shadow of worry shrouds his face, and it's becoming increasingly obvious that whatever this is between us is important to him. But why do this with me? Surely he has no shortage of women, with his looks and sexual talents. What the hell is he after?

I don't answer right away because I want him to sweat it out a little. "No, not yet," I finally say.

"Well, here's a warning, baby. My goal is to make sure you never regret it. So if you're gonna run, you better run now." He pulls me to him, forcing me to stand on my tiptoes to kiss him, then he lets me go and walks away.

"Don't forget dinner and don't go through my things," he reminds me. "And feed the furry, sightless one."

I'm still standing in the hallway when his motorcycle starts and then roars off out of the driveway, the sound fading as he drives further down the mountain road.

My first impulse is to go to sleep until he comes back. That's what I've been doing for months: sleeping my life away. Waiting for Nick to come back when he never will. Waiting for my own life to just end. But first I wander around the house. I've been in such a fog that I haven't noticed how gorgeous and unique this place is. It's small, but modern, with an open-concept layout, vaulted ceilings with exposed raw wooden beams like I saw in the bedroom, skylights, and floor-to-ceiling windows in the living room, dining room, and master bedroom. Everything is clean and in its place, hinting at his control-freak nature. Native American decor fills almost every room with wolf statues, Indian pottery, dream catchers, wall paintings, and the focal point of the living room—a huge colorful headdress mounted above the fireplace. I'm sure it's authentic, and I wonder where he got it and if it's a family heirloom. A huge tapestry hangs from the wall in the foyer with an image of an Native American family on it, real feathers hanging from the corners of the frame. The wraparound couch and accent chair are deep chocolate brown suede with cream throw pillows. A white, thick, faux-fur blanket is folded along the back of the couch. I wish I had noticed that when I was napping the other day because it looks extremely cozy.

Hanging on the wall above his bed is a huge charcoal sketch of a wolf in the snow that is absolutely breathtaking. A sense of peace and comfort envelopes me in this house, and I wish I could stay here forever and never go back to my real life.

I slide open the cabinet in the credenza by the front door, curious to see what may be in there. Inside is an envelope of photos of him holding a baby. As I flip through the photos the baby is getting older, growing into a little girl. She had his eyes, and was incredibly adorable, always smiling. The love that is evident in his eyes around her surprises me and tears my heart to shreds. For some reason, I assumed him to be an uncaring, cold father. My heart hurts for him, now, even more than it did before. I carefully put the pictures back where they were, almost wishing I had never seen them.

"Come on, Sterling," I say, heading for the kitchen with him at my feet. "Let's see what kind of dinner I can make."

VANDAL

The road is long and void of many cars, with sprawling views over the various lakes that scatter the mountain. This has always been my favorite road to ride. The turns are perfect, like the curves of a woman, and spaced out just right. The air is clean and crisp and feels good in my lungs. When Gram suggested I buy a "mental vacation house," I knew this was where I wanted that house to be. As luck would have it, the house I now own had just gone on the market when I started house hunting. Built ten years ago and barely lived in, it had everything I wanted.

Hanging out and playing my acoustic this morning with Tabi fucked me up. Bad. The way she half-closed her eyes and swayed to my music, becoming one with the song and feeling it course through her veins as I do spoke volumes to me. She would be an amazing muse. Hell, she *is* an amazing muse. That melody I played this morning was everything she's made me feel pouring out of my soul. Music has always been how I best express myself and she totally felt it. This chick might really get me.

Her willingness to give in scares the shit out of me because the more she lets me do, the more I will want to do, and I want to do a lot. She brats out and resists a little, but I can see in her eyes and feel in her body that she wants everything I'm unleashing upon her. She melts beneath me like butter.

I ride into one of the nearby towns and buy a charger for her cell phone, feeling like an asshole that I basically kidnapped her and took her without any regard to anything she might need. Like clothes, which worked in my favor, but it was still an epic douche maneuver. On my way to the register, I see a display of little angel statues and one is holding a cat, so on a whim I buy it for her. I grab a box of cookies, too.

Pulling out my phone, I log into the portal of my indoor surveillance cameras and find Tabi in the kitchen, holding Sterling, staring into the open refrigerator. Her mouth is moving so I turn up the volume on my cell phone.

"Let's just order some take-out and tell him we cooked it. Do you think he'll know?" she's saying.

I laugh, watching and listening to her. She's having an entire conversation with the kitten and pretending he's answering her. A big smile spreads across my face, and I shake my head in amusement as I watch her moving around the room, opening and closing cabinets while having a conversation with my cat. She's fuckin' adorable.

I ignore all the emails in the inbox of my phone and log out. I'll deal with all that shit later.

As I'm putting the stuff I bought into my saddlebag, a pretty girl walks by and tries to get my attention. When I ignore her, she comes over to me.

"Oh my fucking God, aren't you Vandal Valentine? From Ashes and Embers?"

"Yup." I try not to make eye contact with her because female fans can be like psychotic vultures sometimes.

"Holy shit! I love you guys!"

"Thanks."

"Is this your bike?"

*No, I'm stealing it.*

"It is."

"Motorcycles are so fucking sexy. Will you take me for a ride? I would *so* love that!"

I lower my sunglasses over my eyes before standing to look at her. "Sorry, I'm heading home."

"Do you live up here? I live right down the road."

"No, I'm just visiting a friend."

She forms her big red-lipsticked mouth into a fake pout. "Well, that sucks!"

I mount the bike and nod at her. "I'll see ya around."

I ride away quickly before she tries to jump on the back or some other crazy-ass shit. That scene was a harsh reminder that I can't take Tabi for a ride with me because the same thing could happen if we stopped to get a cold drink or to use the restroom, and I'm not ready for her to know who I am or to subject her to women like the one in the parking lot.

*Will I ever be?*

I've fucked myself into a corner, good. Once our month is up, I have to take her home and I have to get back to my life. Since Asher's got me on fucking band probation, I'm definitely going to work at the tat shop with Lukas because sitting around doing nothing is just going to invite me to start drinking and partying all over again. There will be no way for me to continue with Tabi in my day-to-day life and not have her find out who I am, and eventually find out that I'm the one who caused the accident, and then she'll leave.

*Unless . . .*

Unless I take this to a higher level, and let her live with me and keep her entirely secluded from everyone. Never let her meet my friends or family. Or maybe just let her meet Lukas and Ivy but make them keep their mouths shut about the band and the accident. I would hide her from my public persona and not subject her to the fans, the prying eyes, the photographers, and the rumors. She might actually like that since she acts as if she wants nothing to do with the outside world. She hasn't mentioned any friends or family that she wants to talk to. I don't think she has any interest in going back to work or living in that house she shared with her husband.

*That could work.* She would have to stay willingly, of course. I could sell my house and buy a new one for us, something she likes and that has a lot of theme rooms for us to play in.

The thought of selling my house has crossed my mind several times to escape the memories of living there with Katie. The constant pain of that will continue to eat me alive. In a new house, I could keep Tabi and give her everything she wants and needs, and have her safe and content. I would cherish her like the little doll that she is and she would never want to leave. I could see those big eyes staring up at me every single day, hear her orgasmic screams of pleasure, let her dig her nails into me. We could explore so much of each other. She could be totally mine and I wouldn't mind being totally hers. At all. My heart pounds against my ribs and my cock grows harder the more I think of how amazing life could be with her. She could make my fantasy a reality.

I've basically just devised a plan to keep this woman as a pet.

*I'm a sick fuck.*

As I walk through the garage door into the kitchen, I'm greeted by her bouncing over to me, a big smile on her face, clapping her hands.

"You're just in time. Dinner is ready. And I didn't ruin it!"

Her giddy excitement over non-ruined dinner is cute but also serves as a warning for meals to come. Too bad I can't get her into a cooking boot camp with Gram.

I kick off my boots and throw them onto the shoe mat by the door. "Is this a new accomplishment for you?" I ask, grinning.

"It is. Nick worked a lot and always came home at odd hours so we kinda lived on frozen dinners most of the time because they were quick and easy to make without any planning."

"Trust me, I've eaten my fair share of frozen pizzas and fast food drive-thrus, but I'd much prefer a real meal whenever possible."

"You better order some cookbooks then, or else I'll be making you grilled cheese and soup every day."

"Is that what I'm eating tonight?"

"No! There was a big package of ground beef in the fridge, some eggs, and bread. And I found all your spices, so I made a meatloaf. I cut up some potatoes and made mash with a little bit of sour cream."

Smiling at her but with a look of suspicion, I peer into the oven expecting to see a misshapen mass of meat, but it looks perfect.

"I'm impressed, baby. It even smells good. I'm gonna go wash the road off me—why don't you set the table? I'll be back in ten." Realizing I'm still holding the bag of things I bought for her, I hand it over. "These are for you."

"Oh, my charger? Thank you! My phone finally died last night. I'm going to have to call my mother and best friend to let them know where I am." She goes to the oven and checks on the meatloaf. "I'll do that after dinner . . . I don't want to hear all the lecturing right now."

I'm a little worried about how those conversations will go and how she's going to react to them. Is she the type to cave if someone else gets on her shit about something she's doing? What the hell would she tell them about me? Or, maybe she won't mention me at all and will lie about her whereabouts.

After a quick shower, I find her at the table, holding the little angel statue with a faraway, almost sad, reflective look on her face.

"What's wrong? You don't like it?"

She has tears in her eyes when she looks up at me. *Shit.* What the fuck did I do wrong now?

"I love it. I kinda collect little things like this . . . but you wouldn't know that."

*Yes, I do.*

"I love the little cat with her. This will always remind me of being here with you and Sterling. Thank you." She wipes her eyes with her napkin. "And you got me cookies! Are you one of those rare men that actually *listen*?"

Taking my seat at the table, I grin over at her and slice the meatloaf, place the first slice on my own plate and the second on hers. "I never used to be. I guess I didn't want you to go into cookie withdrawal."

Her meatloaf turned out excellent and her mood is considerably better than it's been before. Her eyes are brighter and she looks more alive. She's much more animated when she talks to me, too. My own mood is better as well now that I have her to look forward to.

"Can we watch a movie tonight?" she blurts out as she's clearing the table after dinner.

"A movie?"

"Yeah. I thought we could just sit on the couch together and watch a movie. Don't you do that?"

"Not usually with a chick. I fuck them and then they go."

She stops and stares at me as if I've grown five heads. "You're kidding, right?"

"No, I'm dead serious."

I watch her load the dishwasher, clanking the dishes together, glaring daggers at me. "How did you manage to have a child with someone? Were you married? Living together? You must have had some kind of relationship, right?"

Rage boils inside me. Is she seriously judging me? And bringing up my dead daughter?

"That shit is off-limits." I stand up quickly in anger, banging into the table.

"Why? It's a normal thing to be talking about." She slams the door of the dishwasher and crosses her arms, waiting for me to say something.

"Not for me. It was a big clusterfuck, if you have to know. She was just some stripper I met and partied with. I was wasted and sloppy. I never wanted anything else to do with her, and I sure as shit didn't want to have a kid." I take a deep breath, hating what I just said. I don't regret Katie. She was the best thing that ever happened to me. "After the baby was born, I wasn't allowed to see her, but that bitch dragged me to court to get child support and made sure I didn't have any visitation because I was too fucked up on drugs and alcohol. It took me three years to get straight and pass enough tests to see my own kid. I had zero relationship with her mother. I hate that bitch."

Tabi cringes away from me. "I'm sorry I asked," she says. "I'm just trying to get to know a little about you."

"Trust me, baby, it ain't pretty. The more you know, the less you're gonna like. Be glad you're in the dark."

I leave her in the kitchen and sink into the couch, wondering how shit can go so bad so fast. What the fuck?

"Are you going to do that to me, too? Fuck and go? Spank and go?" she asks, stalking into the living room.

That is not a question I can easily answer right now, but I have to or she'll keep digging at me. She wants to know where she stands, which is only natural. Women like labels, titles, and definition. Unfortunately, I'm so messed up in the head that I really don't know what I'm doing anymore. I've acted on crazy impulses, one after the other after the other, and now I've got this girl in my life that I know I shouldn't have, but all I can think about is keeping her. And she's fucking clueless, getting mind-fucked left and right, giving into dark desires, giving me permission to dominate her in the hope that she'll get out of the hole of grief she's in, and find what? What is she hoping for? I don't know. But let's be fucking honest here: I'm digging her out of one hole and putting her into another one.

"You can't even answer me. Fuck you." She stomps down the hallway and slams the bedroom door. I let her. Going after her is just going to fuel the fire that's burning in both of us right now.

I pinch the bridge of my nose and focus on calming my breathing. I need to regain control of our relationship, and stay in control at all times. She keeps skewing me off, distracting me from my role, and that's my fault. I took responsibility of her when I brought her here and invited her into this with me. It's my responsibility to teach her and guide her, protect her. I lean back against the couch and meditate, calmly making a mental list of everything I have learned and need to adhere to. *Cherish her. Respect her. Be patient. Stay in control.*

I want this woman. I refuse to screw this up anymore than I already have. Somehow, in some way, I have to make this work and build us a foundation that will protect us when the truth finally hits. I can lie and hide and be a fucking bastard, but eventually the truth will surface. I will *not* lose her.

She didn't come to me last night and I didn't go to her. Instead I stayed on the couch with Sterling. I dreamt of Katie—she was smiling and laughing, as she always did. Nothing significant happened in the dream—she was just there with me, happy. I tell myself this is a sign from her, maybe even a visit, to let me know that she's okay.

FedEx comes while I'm making coffee, delivering six boxes of various shapes. I carry them all to the guest room, put my coffee on the dresser, and start cutting the boxes open. I'm glad she's still sleeping so I can prepare everything for her and hide what I'm not ready to use yet in the closet.

I have everything spread out on the bed when my cell phone beeps with a text message. I pull it out of my pocket.

***Sydni: I'm back home. Can you come see me? We should talk.***

Shit. Fucking bad timing.

***Me: Kinda busy. Maybe next week?***

***Sydni: It's important. Please come today?***

***Me: You're a pain in my ass. I'll need about two hours to get there. At the lake now.***

***Sydni: K. I'll be here. Just come in. Door's unlocked.***

Pocketing my phone, I step out into the hall, closing the door behind me, and run right into her. Her hair is rumpled and her eyes are rimmed red.

"Hey," I say.

"Hey," she replies, not meeting my eyes. "Is there coffee?"

"Yeah. Come on, let's talk for a few minutes." She follows me to the kitchen and stares out the window as I make her a cup of coffee.

"Can we get some vanilla coffee?" she asks when I hand it to her. "That's my favorite."

"Yeah, make a list and I'll go shopping tomorrow. I have to go out for a few hours, so I can't go today. I'll be back around dinner time."

"Again?"

I nod. "Yeah."

"You were gone almost all day yesterday."

"So?"

Her bottom lip starts to quiver but I refuse to play into this and allow the drama to continue.

"Are you seeing someone else? Do you have a girlfriend?" Her voice cracks and she grips the coffee mug tighter.

"We aren't dating. That's not what this is." I stick a toothpick in my mouth and roll it around between my teeth. "But there aren't any other women, either. Only you."

She sniffles and pushes her hair behind her ear. "Why can't I come, too?"

*Jesus.* So this must be what it's like having a girlfriend—all these emotions and questions . . .

"No," I say sternly. "I want you to stay here. Eat something light around two o'clock. I'll be home at four. Your gifts came today and I have exciting plans for us tonight. After I leave, go into the guest room. I have presents waiting there for you."

She immediately perks up, her eyes growing wide, and a small smile creeping across her face. "Presents?"

"Yes. And by the way, you forgot the first rule."

She tilts her head and looks at me quizzically. "Oh! The good morning kiss?"

"Yes. That."

"We had a fight last night."

"No, we didn't. You had a tantrum. Let's not start it up again, all right?" Grabbing her hip, I pull her against my body and bend down to kiss her neck. "I can't wait 'til tonight," I whisper into her ear.

She shivers and holds on to my arms, resting her head against my chest. "Me, too," she whispers back. "Don't forget me while you're gone."

"Not a chance." I lift her head up to face me. "No bad moods while I'm gone, okay? Today's going to be a good day and tonight will be amazing. Trust me."

Picking her up, I sit her on the kitchen counter and kiss her hungrily, thoughts of what tonight will bring deepening my desire for her even more. Her legs wrap around my waist and her hands entwine around my neck. Knowing she misses me when I'm gone is a good sign.

Reluctantly, I pull away. "I better go. I have to meet with a friend, that's all. Be good. Try to groom the cat if you can. There's a brush in that drawer over there."

She smiles at me. "Okay . . . I think I can do that."

My thoughts are consumed with Tabi, Tabi, and more Tabi while I ride over to Sydni's. I wish I could have just stayed at the house with her and not wait until tonight to see her with her gifts, but I can't blow Sydni off. Her timing completely sucks though.

When I get to her apartment I let myself in, as I've done hundreds of times.

"I'll be right out!" she screams from the bathroom. I help myself to a drink from the refrigerator and wait for her out on the back balcony.

"Sorry, hon. I slept way too late today and I'm still suffering from that awful jet lag." She's wearing her usual denim shorts and a tank top and is rubbing her damp hair with a towel. Her eyes are red with puffy bags underneath.

"You look tired as fuck," I tell her. "You need to slow down."

She sits, and crosses her lean, tan legs. She lights up a cigarette, her long, fire-engine red hair hanging over her face and almost catching a spark. Last time I saw her, her hair was blue.

"Tell me how you're doing. I'm so sorry I wasn't here, Van . . ."

I wave my hand at her. "Not your fault, Syd. You were touring in England—that takes precedence over everything else. I get that." I shrug my shoulder and shake my hair out of my face. "I'm doing better. I haven't had a drink in like, two days." Oddly enough, I don't even miss it.

"Well, that's a start, pal. One day at a time."

"So they say."

She yawns and stretches her fully tattooed arms out and above her head, her white tank top straining over her large breasts that normally I stare at, but today I look away.

"I ran into Talon and Ash at the studio yesterday, and they told me you're out for a while." She takes a drag on her cigarette and watches me for a reaction.

I roll my eyes in disgust. "Yeah, I guess they had a vote and don't want me wrecking their sacred image with my drunken outbursts. I don't know who the fuck they think they can replace me with on such short notice. Even wasted I play better than most of the hacks out there."

She smashes her cigarette into a marble ashtray on the table. "Me," she states simply.

"You, what?"

"They asked me to play the tour with them."

I almost fall over. Sydni can totally fucking rock. Her all-female rock band, Sugar Kiss, is one of the best out there. I've known her for years and they've opened for us more times than I can count. I gotta hand it to Asher: it's a genius marketing move to stick a hot girl in the band for a few months.

Running my hand through my hair, I look over at her, speechless. "I really didn't see this coming, Syd."

"I know. Neither did I. Vandal, listen. This isn't permanent. I only agreed to do it if it's just for a few months for this tour, until you come back on board. I'm not going to leave Sugar to be a permanent member of A&E. I couldn't really say no; the ties run deep here, you know that . . ."

I nod. "I know, I know."

"I won't do it if you're not okay with it. That's why I wanted to see you. I'm not going to risk our friendship for this; I respect you way too much, man. And just so you know, Ash kept saying that you were coming back." She gives my hand a quick squeeze.

I swallow and flick my gaze away.

"I appreciate that. I do. I'd much rather it was you than some other asshole. You'll do fucking great, and I like not having to worry about the replacement trying to oust me for good. I'm fucking back next year. I've got some new material I've been working on—it's fuckin' sweet."

She lets out a sigh of relief. "I can't wait to hear it . . ." She pauses and stares out over the balcony for a few moments. "Vandal, don't hate Ash so much. He's got a lot on his plate, and the band is his baby. It's all he's got right now."

"Yeah, yeah, yeah." I don't want to think about Asher and his problems. I have my own, and his could be much worse. "You gonna be okay jumping into another tour so soon? With new material?"

"Fuck yeah. I got this."

I push myself away from the wooden railing. "I better get going, I have to ride back up to the lake."

She stands and walks with me into the house, putting her hand on my back before we reach the front door.

"You could stay," she hints, her voice sultry. "It's been a while."

Measuring my control, I sigh and turn to face her. "We shouldn't, Syd. Let's not complicate shit." I pause and decide to tell her the truth. "Plus, I kinda got someone waiting at home for me."

Surprise and disappointment dance across her face. "You? Really?"

"It's still new. We're trying to figure it out."

"I think that's great, Vandal. I really do. You deserve some happiness."

"No, I really fucking don't, Syd. I'm a douche."

She looks me in the eye and shakes her head defiantly. "I've known you for a long time. You're difficult, and you're fucked up, but you deserve to be happy. Maybe I'll get to meet her someday?"

Fear courses through me like acid in my veins. "I don't know. I got a lot of shit to figure out."

She leans against the doorframe and opens the door for me. "Be good, buddy. Stay in touch, and don't worry. I'll make you proud standing in for you."

"I know you will."

TABITHA

As soon as he's gone I run to the guest room like a little kid and open the door, my insides jittery with anticipation of what could be waiting for me. On the middle of the bed are two boxes, one medium and one large, each wrapped in purple matte paper with a big black bow, and a brown suede journal. I'm not sure what to go to first, but curiosity makes me pick up the journal. I sit on the bed and open it to find handwriting on the first page in calligraphy-style writing.

*Tabitha,*

*This will be our journal, and I hope to fill all the pages as our story grows. I'll write in this book each morning to tell you what I want you to do for me that day, or maybe just tell you something I'm thinking about. I want you to do the same. Tell me how you feel and what you want, and write it in here so I can read it the next day. Sometimes writing thoughts is easier than saying them. This is meant to be a safe communication tool for us, and hopefully, a memoir for us to read back on someday.*

*On the bed is your first present. I want you to take a shower and use the body soap and shampoo I bought for you. Then put on the items in the box. Take your time and let yourself enjoy everything. I know you will look beautiful.*

*Then, go to the bedroom and lie on the bed in the waiting position I taught you, and wait for me to come for you.*

*V*

*V?* What the hell? How long has he known my name? And why have we gone days without using our names? I want to hear him say mine just as much as I want to say his and feel it on my lips. Tonight I'm going to insist he tell me what his name is.

I tear the wrapping off the large box and lift the lid. Pushing the white tissue paper to the side, my breath catches when I see what's inside. I lift the corset out of the box and hold it up. The man has taste, I'll give him that. Now it all makes sense and I know why he measured me—he wanted to make sure this would fit my body perfectly. The thought of that causes my sex to flutter and dampen. The idea of a man ordering expensive lingerie for me is crazy erotic, even romantic. The corset is a deep, cherry color, with small roses embroidered into the fabric and black satin side strips. Next I pull black stockings and a garter belt out of the box, and matching panties, the same fabric as the corset. Laying everything on the bed, I open a smaller box that's nestled inside the larger one. Inside is a necklace made out of black material that looks like webbing with tiny sparkling crystals, and black gem earrings. Holy wow. None of this looks cheap. I lay the necklace down carefully, hoping I don't get it in a tangled mess. Lastly, I find matching fingerless gloves, and a calligraphy style pen.

I unwrap the medium-sized box to find a myriad of toiletries: shampoo, conditioner, body wash, body oil crème, toothbrush, perfume, and makeup. Once again, all expensive-looking and labeled with brand names that I don't recognize at all. I take the caps off the bottles and inhale the scent of each one, reveling in the sweet fragrances.

Staring at all these items on the bed, the bigger picture starts to form for me, not only about what he wants and needs, but what I can have. With someone else, I would think this was creepy and scary. But I don't feel that way with him. This seeps of sensuality and desire, of a lifestyle that could transcend any fantasy I've ever had. Just touching the fabric excites me. I've never had expensive lingerie like this before. It's exquisite.

I leave everything in the guest room and close the door behind me to make sure Sterling doesn't sneak in there and rip anything or get fur on it. For a blind cat, he still manages to get into everything.

Glancing at the clock, I'm disappointed to see it's not even noon yet. I have a feeling this day will drag just because I am attempting to look forward to something. Not knowing where he went bothers me. Nick would never just leave and not tell me what his plans were.

*Oh God.* How can I be comparing Nick to him? I choke back the tears that threaten to instantly fall. *No.* Today is supposed to be a good day. I will *not* fall apart.

After I give Sterling a quick brushing, I take a long shower using the bath products he picked out especially for me. They each smell like lavender and vanilla, which I once read is supposed to have a calming affect. I leave the conditioner in extra long so my hair will be soft and silky, my mind wandering to how my body trembles when he pulls my hair.

I dry my body off and spread the body oil over my damp skin. It absorbs slowly and sends a warm tingle through me, much like his touch feels. Using my finger, I rub a tiny bit between my legs, between my folds.

Next, I blow my hair out straight and apply a little bit of makeup. I never wear lipstick, but in the makeup bag is a deep red lipstick that matches the corset, so I put it on, assuming he must want me to be wearing it or else it wouldn't be with the rest of the items.

He said to eat light but I'm so nervous I can't even think about food without my nerves churning my stomach. To be obedient as promised, I force a few crackers down and sip some apple juice while I stare out the window at the shimmering water. I'd love to go float around in the boat again, but he gave me strict instructions the other day not to go on the lake when he's not home. I think he's afraid I'm going to fall out of the boat and drown.

When I can't stall anymore, I go to the guest bedroom and try to figure out what I'm supposed to put on first. Chewing my lip as I finger all the items, I pick the corset, pulling it up and buttoning the front. It's tight, but not so much that I can't breathe. The front barely covers my breasts but pushes them up and together, giving even my small cleavage the appearance of voluptuousness. Next I step into the panties.

The garter belt and stockings are completely foreign to me. Sitting on the bed, very carefully I pull up the black stockings, wiggling them to my thighs and attaching them to the garter belt. I feel incredibly dressed up to still be so naked. Once I have the necklace, earrings, and gloves on, I look at myself in the full-length mirror that's mounted to the back of the door.

*Wow.*

I look so . . . different. I don't think I've ever looked sexy before, but with this on, I do. I even *feel* sexy. Twisting and turning, I look at myself from every angle, loving how curvy I look. How did he know what to pick to make me look this way?

*3:45*

Waiting in the position he taught me, my head down, arms stretched with hands laying flat above my head, I focus on slowing my breathing until the jitters subside, the fidgeting stops, and I feel peaceful while waiting for him. Quiet confidence washes over me.

The roar of his motorcycle soon fills the silence, then the grinding sound of the opening and closing of the garage door. Next, a soft-spoken greeting to Sterling, followed by heavy footsteps in the hall. The bathroom door opens and closes, and the hiss of the shower fills my ears. The sun sets and darkness comes, leaving me in the bedroom with no light.

I continue my breathing exercises, taking slow, deep breaths to calm my suddenly racing heart. The anticipation is like a drug, bringing me higher, taking away all other worries and problems. Nothing exists in this moment except us.

His presence in the room is all I can feel. I don't move or turn as a match strikes and an amber glow casts seductive dancing shadows on the walls.

I can feel his eyes on me, prowling over every inch of me. *Does he like what he sees? Is he disappointed?*

"Stand for me."

A million butterflies take flight in my stomach and soar between my legs as I slowly stand, giving my limbs a moment to wake up.

I stand before him, eyes on the floor, hands clasped, and wait as he circles me slowly like a panther stalking his prey, stopping behind me.

"You look absolutely breathtaking." His voice is deep and sexy, drenched with raw truth. I never doubt his words because his voice religiously holds so much emotion. Circling again, he stops in front of me.

"How do you feel?"

"I feel beautiful. Thank you."

"You were made to be dressed this way, to be spoiled with beautiful things."

He's completely naked, his cock already hard and glistening in the candlelight. I swallow as he goes to the nightstand and takes out the pearls and ribbon he had the other day.

*How long ago was that? It feels like years.*

"All I could think about today was seeing you like this. I hated leaving you."

Kneeling in front of me, he runs his fingertips lightly from my ankles over my calves, up to my thighs, then around the backs of my legs, and up to cup my ass, pressing his face between my legs. His fingers hook beneath the fabric of the panties and pull them down slowly, letting me step out of them.

Pressing his face between my legs again, he flicks his tongue out and lavishes me with a few slow, long licks before standing up. He guides me to the bed and lays me on my back, then climbs on top of me, straddling my body, his cock pressed between us.

"And I did see another woman today." He takes one of my wrists and wraps it with a length of ribbon intertwined with the pearls, then ties it to the headboard. Anger and heartache broil in me. How dare he leave me here alone while he went to another woman? I squirm against the binds, wondering if he tied her, too, and feeling sick at the thought.

"A woman I used to fuck. A lot," he continues, giving the ribbon a hard yank, tightening the bond.

My heart and stomach lurch at his words. *Please no.* Jealousy spreads through me like wildfire.

He grabs my other hand. "I didn't fuck her this time though." The ribbon tightens around my wrist as he secures this one like the first.

With my hands tied above my head, he leans down just inches away from my face, his silky hair falling down over my breasts, tickling me. "Ask me why, Tabitha," he whispers, the sound of my name on his lips in the dark sending jolts through me.

"Why?"

"Because you've ruined me already." His lips touch mine briefly. "You've taken all the fun out of fucking other women. There's no way they can compare to what you're giving me." This revelation makes me happy. I want him all to myself.

He slowly runs his finger up the front of the corset and stops to caress the tops of my breasts that are spilling over the top, begging to be freed of the tight material. "How can I eat fast food when I've got this five-course meal waiting for me?"

Relief mixed with fear replaces the jealousy I felt earlier. What dark road am I going down with this sexual deviant only wanting *me*? Do I want to be the sole object of his desires?

*Yes. I don't want anyone else to feel the magic he can create. He's mine.*

He lowers again, his lips at the base of my throat near the necklace, then rains kisses across my chest, his tongue finding my small cleavage, licking the sides of my breasts as his hand comes up along my ribs and rests openly over my neck. His other hand methodically starts to unfasten each tiny button of the bodice, exposing me inch by inch. His hand tightens slightly around my neck. *Oh shit.*

Once unbuttoned, he lifts the corset out from under me and tosses it to the side.

"Do you like what I picked out for you?"

"Yes." My voice is strained from the pressure of his grip around my throat, and I wonder if he's going to strangle me.

"There's a lot more I'm going to give you." His hand cups my breast, his lips sucking my nipple into his mouth, flicking his tongue over the tip, igniting an ache deep between my thighs. His mouth descends between my breasts, down my stomach, and over my mound. His hot mouth devours my pussy, his tongue probing and lapping. My pulse quickens, and my body presses up against him, my thighs parting with want. His grip on my throat tightens sporadically as he licks and sucks my delicate flesh. He's so big, that his body completely covers mine, and he can reach every part of me easily. My legs tremble as I grind against him, so close to orgasmic bliss, and then he abruptly pulls away. I suck in a few ragged breaths, and my eyes fly open to see him moving out from between my legs to kneel on the bed beside my head, his hand still clasped on my neck. He takes his massive cock into his free hand and presses it against my mouth.

"Open." His deep voice pierces the silence. I obey and he slides the thick head past my lips. My hungry gaze travels up the length of his body. He looks like a god, looming above me, the flickering candles throwing an orange glow over his broad muscled chest and dancing along his blue-black hair. He pushes his thick shaft further into my mouth, causing me to gag. Pulling out slightly, he allows me to catch my breath before sliding back in, his cock hitting the back of my throat. Relaxing my muscles as much as I can, I suck him farther into my mouth, my head bobbing up and down off the mattress slightly, swirling my tongue over his girth. His grip on my throat heightens the intense sexual and emotional bond I feel growing between us. Everything I thought I knew about sex and making love is derailed as my trust grows for this man who's got a chokehold on me while I suck him, with my hands bound to his bed by satin ribbons.

His eyes burn with lust as he watches me suck him, his hand moving from his cock to gently caress my cheek, his thumb gliding over my top lip that's stretched around him. Releasing my throat, he runs that hand down the length of my body and thrusts it between my legs, inserting one, then two fingers inside me. I moan against his cock and suck harder as he fingers me, his thumb rubbing fast circles against my clit. I'm almost there again, squeezing my thighs against his hand, when he pulls his hand away. I pull my mouth from him in wild frustration.

"Oh my God, stop stopping," I beg, breathlessly. Laughing sadistically, he crawls between my legs and lies on top of me, leaning up on his elbows to stare down into my face.

"What's wrong, baby?" he teases, rubbing his dick against my thigh.

I thrash my head to the side and yank my wrists, wishing I could put my hands on him and pull him into me.

"You're torturing me!"

"I love to." His lips come down on mine and he kisses me savagely, winding one hand beneath me to grab my ass and pull me against him. I coil my leg around his and rub against him like a cat.

"It's mean," I whine when he lifts his lips from mine.

"You'll come when I let you," he murmurs, burying his face into my neck and pressing his shaft against my swollen, waiting folds. He goes up on his knees between my legs and lifts me up, shoving a pillow under my ass. Slowly sliding his long cock into me, his eyes fixate on mine, watching my every reaction. I can't break away from his hypnotizing gaze. He lifts my black stocking-clad legs up above his head, brings them together, and leans them against his left shoulder, his hand clasping my ankles together. Turning my body slightly, he plunges into me deeper, making me gasp. My fingers clench around the ribbon restraints in fervor as he bucks into me. His hand still wrapped around my ankles, he turns his head and slowly runs his tongue along the arch of my foot. The sensation sends ripples of tiny electric shocks through my body and I start to climax, praying to every God in the universe that he doesn't stop. As my body trembles and clenches around him, he leans down on top of me, my legs still over his shoulder and now pressing against my chest, almost bending me in half, and drives fast, deep and hard, into me.

He comes so hard that I actually feel him explode inside me. I lie beneath him as he rocks inside of me slowly for a few minutes, allowing us each to catch our breath, then he rises and gently lays my legs down, pulling off the stockings and rubbing my calves and thighs as I stretch them out. *Shit,* I thought he was going to snap me at the waist. He unties my hands and rubs my fingers, wrists and arms silently for a few minutes, soothing the sore muscles from being tied in place. I watch him put the ribbons in the nightstand and take out a soft black cloth, which he uses to gently wipe me between my legs.

My head is fuzzy and I feel a bit delirious from the onslaught of everything that is him. Everything about this man is so consuming and powerful that surrendering to it all seems the easiest way to deal with being overwhelmed.

His lips catch mine and we kiss in the candlelit room, slowly, sweetly. *Tenderly.* Holding me in his arms, our naked bodies wrapped around each other, he continues to kiss me softly while his hand caresses my back. This gentle side of him is not something I was expecting and it assaults my heart. I can no longer tell if this is lust or something more happening between us. *I'm falling for him.*

"You have to tell me your name," I say softly. I simply can't go one more day not being able to say his name. He rolls over on top of me, pinning me beneath him.

"I don't have to tell you anything." His voice is low and sexy.

Staring up into his eyes, I plead with him silently. I need to hear him say it. I need the honesty of who he is. His dark gaze locks onto mine and I can see the struggle behind it like a tormented storm. I tentatively touch his cheek. *Please. Say it.*

He takes a deep breath, his chest pressing against mine. "Vandal," he finally says.

My eyes flutter closed as his name seeps into every pore of my being, the sound of it resonating through me, possessing me. *Vandal.* Some people are truly cursed by their names, their destiny sealed the moment it's stamped into the world as who they are. Who they will become. What they will *do*.

"Wow," I exclaim. "That's an interesting name. I've never heard it before."

"Good." He exhales and holds me tighter. "I want you to sleep with me tonight."

Swallowing the lump in my throat, I can only nod in the dark.

# chapter sixteen

VANDAL

My heart stopped when I told her my name, waiting for the recognition, the hatred, and the accusations to follow. Waiting for her to somehow know who I am. I mentally prepared myself for it. I even bought a pack of brand new shiny razor blades on the way home, knowing tonight she would ask my name. I could slice and dice all night after she spewed well-deserved verbal daggers at me and left me here to bleed and hopefully die. It didn't happen though. She stayed right here in my arms, sweet and soft.

My heart beats in rhythm with hers against my chest. Maybe this is meant to be. Maybe for once the universe has decided to give me a pass. Maybe the powers that be are finally bored with fucking me.

She lays her head on my chest and stares up at me with those wide, innocent eyes.

"What secrets are you hiding?" she whispers.

I hold her gaze, and I do what I do best. I capture her lips with mine and drag her into that place where desire shadows denial.

"If I tell you, you'll hate me forever."

Her breath hitches and she traces her finger down my cheek and presses it softly against my lips.

"Then don't ever tell me."

She falls asleep in my arms and I let her stay there. I don't know how she manages to do it, but I want to break all my rules for her. It's easy because all I want is to see her smile and be the one that makes her happy. I want her to love me like she loved Nick.

*No.*

I want her to love me *more* than she loved Nick.

When I wake up, she's still in my bed, but she's curled up on her side facing away from me. I can't take my eyes off of her sexy back, the delicate curve of her spine. As I run my palm over her pale skin, ideas flow through my mind like a kaleidoscope. She moans softly while I caress her.

I know what I'm going to do today.

She's eyeing me suspiciously with a grin on her face as she sips her coffee at the table.

"You look strangely happy this morning," she says. "Should I be worried?"

I grin back at her. "Maybe a little."

"Will you be leaving again today to not fuck another woman?"

"No, smart-ass. I'm going to spend the day with you."

Visible pleasure spreads across her face. I finish off my omelet and push the plate away.

"Last night was perfect. *You* were perfect, Tabi. I could tell you learned some things from your reading."

Her cheeks redden. "I like when you call me that. And last night . . . all I can say is wow." She fingers the rim of her coffee cup and peeks up at me. "The way you make me feel . . . and the things you bought for me . . ."

"Today I have another surprise. I have to go down in the basement for a few minutes to get what I need. While I'm down there, I want you to make the bed and put your gifts back in the guest room. I'll put them away. I don't want you in that closet because I have more things in there for you and I want them to be a surprise."

"Okay . . ."

"I wrote in the journal this morning while you were still sleeping. Please read it while I'm downstairs so you can be ready."

She frowns. "I didn't have time to write in it yet though."

"That's all right. You can whenever you want."

"I really like the journal idea. It's kinda sweet."

"Sometimes it might be, sometimes not."

Downstairs, I find everything I need. I'm glad I store some of my extra supplies here. Once again I'm venturing into taboo territory, but as usual, I just can't stop myself. I like doing what I'm not supposed to be doing, and I especially like doing things I'm not supposed to do to Tabi. Mostly because she likes it, and I like that she likes what we're not supposed to be doing.

Being bad can be very, very good.

She's exactly where she should be when I go back upstairs, sitting at the dining room table. I know she sprayed bleach cleaner on the table and all the chairs, as I asked in the journal, because I can smell it.

I open the window to let some air in. "I don't want you to get a headache from the bleach smell," I say, then grab Sterling. "I'm going to put him in the bedroom while we do this. I can't risk him jumping on my stuff or knocking shit over."

While I'm putting the cat in the guest room, I see the journal has been moved, so I grab it to see if she's written in it, and she has, right under my entry. I skim through my words and then study hers.

*Tabi,*

*In just a few days, you have become a very bright light in my very dark life. Last night was everything I hoped it would be. I love how you trust me. I don't think I will ever get enough of you. I can see the change in you already and I hope you see it in yourself. You've changed me, too. I never had a plan with you, and I still don't. I like where we're heading though.*

*There's something I need to do with you and I think you will love it. I hope you will.*

*Clean the dining room table and the chairs with the spray bleach under the sink. I'll meet you there.*

*Vandal,*

*I don't know what's happening between us. I didn't have a plan either —I just wanted to feel again, and not be so numb and lifeless. You're giving me that. Yes, it's a lot different than what I was thinking, but I have no regrets. At least not yet.*

*The bleach sounds scary but I'll do what you say. I wouldn't want another spanking.*

*Tabi*

Grinning, I close the journal. Her snarky comments always make me laugh.

I methodically lay my equipment out on the table as she watches with a slightly horrified look on her face.

"Um, what are we doing, exactly?" she asks.

"I'm going to tattoo you."

Her eyes go wide and she looks from me, to the gun, to the inkwells and back to me again.

"What? You can't just tattoo a person. I could get an infection or something. And you need to know how to draw, don't you? You can't just start jabbing with that . . . thing." She gestures at the gun and looks up at me as if I've completely lost my mind.

"Tabi, I'm a tattoo artist. I have been for about ten years. My brother and I own a shop. I can show you the website if you want, and you can see my portfolio. And all this stuff is brand new, totally clean and sterile. I know what I'm doing."

"Are you serious? You're a tattoo artist?"

"Yes. A fucking good one, too. People wait months to have me do their ink. You should feel very privileged."

She's still staring at all the equipment. "I don't know. Is it safe to do here?"

"Yes."

"Will it hurt?"

"No," I lie. She narrows her eyes at me. "Okay, a little," I add. "It feels kinda like a bunch of fuckin' bee stings. Me? I like it. I think it's therapeutic. Like acupuncture. I like pain."

"Bee stings?" she repeats. "That sounds painful. And you're weird."

"I think you'll be okay. I'll be nice and gentle."

Doubt is clear on her face. "You really want to do this to me?"

"Yes. But only if you want me to. If you're really against it, I won't do it. It's going to be on you forever, so I want you to want it."

She studies the tattoos on my arms for a few moments.

"Did you do these?" she asks.

"I did some on my left arm. I did the dragon. Lukas did my right arm."

She lightly touches my skin, tracing the designs. "Well . . . what did you have in mind for me?"

"Angel wings on your back. I was staring at your back this morning while you were sleeping and I just thought how fucking gorgeous you would look with angel wings. Your skin is so pale and perfect. It'll be beautiful on you."

She contemplates this, chewing her lip. "I kinda always wanted a tattoo but Nick wouldn't let me." Her gaze shifts to the floor.

I scoff. "Let you? What the fuck? You needed permission?"

"You are really in no position to be making judgments about what other men do or what kind of control they try to inflict on their wives. He thought tattoos were for strippers and girls like that. He didn't want me to look trashy."

"Is that how you feel, too?"

"No, I always thought body art was beautiful. I used to photograph a friend of mine who's a model, and she had a lot of them. They were really sexy on her. They were tasteful though. Not stupid things that meant nothing."

"Is there some kind of design you'd prefer? I'll do whatever you want. You don't have to go with what I want."

She graces me with an adorably wicked grin and touches my hand, suddenly leaning over to kiss my lips. "I forgot to kiss you this morning. And thank you for the ramming," she says.

"You're not doing so great with that rule."

"I know."

I lean back in the chair and wait for her. "So, what's it gonna be, darlin'?"

Nodding slowly, her smile comes back. "Yes. I think I'm gonna go for it. But only if you go slow. Will you stop when I ask you to?"

"Of course. I'll give you a lot of breaks, but once we start the design, we have to finish it. Even if we work on it every day for two weeks. I'm not going to let you walk around with a half a design on you."

"Ew. Deal."

"Have you decided what you want?"

"I want you to do what you picked. That will mean the most to me."

Nodding, I try not to let her see how happy that makes me. "Do you think you can straddle the chair backwards so I can get to your back? You can get up and stretch whenever you need to."

"Sure."

I get the rest of my gear ready while she turns the chair and moves it closer to me. "Should I take my shirt off?" she asks.

"Yeah, and your bra, too, if you're okay with that."

She peers back at me. "Isn't that unprofessional?"

"Immensely."

It's hard to concentrate once she's sitting there topless, even with her back to me. I try to compose myself.

I gather her hair and lay it over her shoulder. "Keep your hair in front," I say, opening a sterile rubbing alcohol pack and wiping her back with it.

"How big is this going to be?"

I sit back and stare at her blank skin, trying to envision it in my mind. She's so tiny. I picture it taking up almost her entire back, if she has the patience for it.

"I was thinking two huge angel wings, taking up pretty much your whole back. It would look incredible, but it would take some time to do, depending on how much you can handle at once. Or if you just want small wings, I can do that, too. It's your body, so you tell me."

She grabs her cell phone and starts fiddling with it, then turns and thrusts it at me. It's a web image of a tattoo similar to what I described. The art isn't as good as mine, but it's not bad. "Like this?" she asks.

"Yeah, but my detail and shading will be much more realistic than that. But yeah, that size."

"Yes! That's what I want. I'd love that."

"Let's get started then. Try to keep still, and let me know if you need me to stop."

I snap my black gloves on and get to work. She yowls two seconds after I start. I pull back.

"Ouch! That *does* hurt. Shit!"

I stifle a laugh. I've seen girls react this way at least a hundred times. "You kinda get numb to it after a while. Do you want me to stop? There's just a tiny black line."

"No!" she wails. "I'm doing this. I will *not* wuss out."

"Good girl."

"Just talk a lot to distract me."

We talk casually as I work on her. She tells me some funny stories about when she was a little girl, and I tell her a few of my tamer childhood stories. I want to tell her about the band, and more about my music, but I'm afraid that could lead to too many possible links for her to connect the dots and figure out who I am. *Shit*. For the first time in my life, all my lies are making me sick.

"You're doing great, babe," I say after about an hour and only two short breaks. "Are you feeling okay? I've had a few chicks pass out on me before. Two guys, too."

"Are you kidding? Sucks for the guys. How embarrassing is that?"

"Very."

"I feel okay. A little sore."

I stop and take a few moments to really look at the design. It's coming out totally sick. "You're going to be tender for a few days. You might not want to sleep on your back."

"Okay . . . what about other stuff?"

"What other stuff?"

"You know . . . with you."

Leaning forward, I kiss her shoulder, being careful not to touch her back or let my hair brush over her raw skin. "You mean sex?"

"Yes, that, and the other stuff."

I stand up and walk around her chair to kneel in front of her. "I'll go easy on you. There's lots of positions I can put you in. Or we just won't do any of that."

She nods but doesn't say anything else, just chews on her lower lip.

"What's wrong?" I ask her.

"Is that all there is . . . for us? Just sex?"

*Fuck. I'm not ready for this.*

I stand and head for the refrigerator. "You want a cold drink?" I pull out a soda and she's right behind me when I turn around.

"Hey, get back over there where it's clean. I don't want you walking around getting cat fur or what-the-fuck-ever on you." Grabbing her elbow, I lead her back to the dining room.

"You're avoiding the question," she accuses me.

"Tabi . . ."

"Vandal. It's okay if that's all this is. Just be honest about it."

I relent and fall into my chair. *Be honest*. Do I even know how to do that?

"No. That's not all this is," I finally say, but I have no idea what else to add because I honestly just don't know what I'm feeling right now, but I *do* know that this is more than just sex, and that scares the shit out of me.

She stares at me with her big eyes. "Really?"

"Really."

She accepts that. For now.

We decide to do the left-side wing today and the right side tomorrow. I take a picture of it with her cell phone and she jumps up and down with excitement and gingerly places her arms around me when she sees it. I cover it with bandage and plastic and help her put her T-shirt back on.

"I have an idea," I throw at her as I clean up my gear.

"Do tell."

"Why don't we watch some television tonight? Like you wanted to the other night?"

Her excitement grows even more. "I would love that!"

Later that night I'm doing something I never thought I'd be doing. Sitting on the couch with a chick lying against me, eating pretzels and chocolate, watching a stupid comedy. I don't know how I got here or what the fuck this is anymore. Something is *happening*.

By the end of the movie, she's asleep, so I pick her up effortlessly and carry her to the bedroom. The past few days and then the tattoo must have exhausted her because she doesn't even wake up when I remove her sweatpants and pull the comforter over her. Maybe this is what love feels like. Just taking care of someone and trying to make them happy.

I crawl into the bed next to her and pull her against me, being careful not to hurt her back. Sterling jumps up and curls at the foot of the bed. I wish Katie were here. If she was, she would love Tabitha, and she would be head over heels for Sterling.

*But neither of them would even be here if Katie were alive.*

Screaming cries wake me from a dead sleep and I bolt upright, thinking Katie is having a nightmare. My feet just about hit the floor when I realize it's not Katie; it's Tabitha. She's thrashing in bed next to me, whimpering and crying.

I gently shake her. "Tabi . . ."

She smacks at me and kicks me, still screaming. I grab her hands to avoid another hit to the face. "Tabi, wake up."

Waking with wild eyes, she stares at me as if she doesn't recognize me and yanks herself away from my grasp.

"Hey . . . it's okay. You had a bad dream."

Her eyes slowly focus on me and she settles down a little. "I had a dream about the accident again," she says, her entire body trembling with the aftermath of the dream. "I can see the lights coming at us and I scream, but I can't make them stop. I can't get the car to stop."

*Shit, she remembers. I don't remember any of it.*

"Come here," I say softly, and after a few moments, she moves into my embrace, but doesn't put her arms around me. I wrap my arms tightly around her and lean my cheek against the top of her head, wishing my touch could suck all the fear and pain from her.

"I hate it, Vandal. It's awful. All I can see is the lights and then I'm lying in the road . . . and everything hurts so much, and there's blood on me, and I don't know where Nick is . . . and there's a baby crying, and I can't make it stop." She sobs against my chest, oblivious to the fact that her words just turned my veins to ice.

*A baby crying . . .*

How could I be so stupid to think that just because I remember nothing from the accident that she wouldn't either? A baby crying means that Katie didn't die right away, as I convinced myself she did. *As everyone led me to believe.* She was alive and she was alone in that twisted fucking mess. Crying. Where the fuck was I?

I swallow hard. "There was a baby in the accident? Where was the baby?" I try to keep my voice even.

"I don't know...still in the other car I think. I couldn't see her. It was just awful. I don't want to think about it." Her entire body shudders.

"Shit . . ." I hold on to Tabi as my own tears choke out. Knowing that Katie was alive and hurt, scared and alone before she died, is ripping my heart to shreds.

"I miss him so much . . ." Tabitha utters against my chest.

Vile jealousy coils inside me, snaking around my grief. Fisting her hair, I yank her head up, finding her lips in the dark, my tongue seeking out hers. Her hands cling to my shoulders, her nails digging into my flesh. Pushing her down hard, I fall on top of her, kissing her savagely, using my leg to push hers apart.

"Ow!" she shrills. "Vandal, stop!"

I pull away from her instantly, snapping out of the fucked up frenzy I'm in. *What is wrong with me?*

"Fuck! I'm sorry, I forgot about your tattoo. I'm sorry," I repeat, apologizing for so much more than just hurting her back. *I'll say it a thousand times.*

She turns on her side, away from me, crying into the pillow. Her fingers that just moments ago were clinging to me are now clenched to the blanket. I stroke her hair, hoping to soothe her. "I'm sorry, Tabi. I didn't mean to hurt you."

"I know . . . please . . . I want to be alone."

The words slice through me like a burning blade. She wants to be alone to think about *him*.

I reluctantly leave her in my bed, alone with her grief and nightmare. Grabbing the blanket from the couch, I go out to the back deck and settle myself in one of the lounge chairs under the pitch-black sky that is riddled with gem-like stars and a bright crescent moon. All is quiet except for the chirping of crickets and an owl in the distance. Sometimes being out in the night calms me, and I sure as shit need that now.

*Katie*. Tabitha heard her crying, and I want to know where my baby was. Was she trapped in the car? I want to force Tabitha to tell me everything she remembers, where she was, and where the sound of the crying was coming from. I want to grab her and demand that she tell me what she saw, what else she heard. She must remember more.

I can't do any of those things though. No normal bystander would ask those questions, and she'll know I either have something to do with it or she'll think I'm some kind of fucking lunatic for asking crazy questions.

If I dwell on this I'm going to lose my mind over it. I want a drink so bad right now I can practically feel the burn of the alcohol just thinking about it. Or I could take a pill and let it pull me to sleep—anything to make this pain go away again.

*Don't do it.*

*Think about Tabitha instead. Focus on her.*

Breathing deeply, I close my eyes to divert my thoughts. My head is twisted like a pretzel over this girl. I have no right to feel jealousy over her deceased husband. I may have distracted her for a few days, but she's still grieving and missing him. Reliving the accident in her dreams is not helping. I know too well what that feels like.

I brought her here to make her forget, give her something new, and now I don't want to *be* the distraction, because distractions are temporary and unfulfilling. For the first time in my life, I want more than a quick fix. I want to *be* more than a quick fix for someone, more than a novelty.

I hate that Tabi's in bed alone, haunted by her own awful memories of the accident. She's crying for the man she loved and lost, a good man that deserved her love. A man who isn't the monster of her nightmares.

That's me.

# chapter seventeen

VANDAL

When I wake up the next morning, she's lying on top of me, snuggled under the blanket. She must have come out here in the middle of the night after I fell asleep. *She came to me.*

I stretch my cramped legs, and her eyes flutter open and focus on me.

"Hey, you." I tuck her hair behind her ear and wrap my arm around her. "What are you doing out here?"

She snuggles into my shoulder. "I missed you."

"I'm sorry," we both say at the same time.

"You have nothing to be sorry for, Tabitha. I was being an asshole."

"And I was being overly emotional, as usual."

"You're allowed to be. You've been through a lot and I'm probably not helping."

She props herself up on her arm to look me in the eye as she talks. "That's not true. I know I've only known you for a few days, but you've woken me up a lot. Here's the thing . . ." She fingers my necklace, lost in her own thoughts for a moment. "I want to say this the right way, but I don't know if there *is* a right way."

A burn spreads from my stomach straight up to my heart as I come to the realization that she's going to leave and she's trying to say goodbye.

"I'm just gonna say it the best way I can right now, okay? Nick and I had a really special relationship." Ugh, I don't want to hear about Nick. *I don't want to hear how much you loved him.* "He was a good guy, he treated me great, he was polite, and he was always in a good mood. That's just who he was, and he was easy to love. Everything with him was just easy. There were no fights and no guessing. I know I'll never find someone like him again, or be able to love someone like that again." She swallows and peers up at me. I want her to stop talking before the bad part comes. I don't want to hear the *we can be friends* spiel.

"I don't think I could ever be in a relationship like that again without always comparing it to what I had and missing him. It would never be fair to put someone else through that." She shakes her head a little. "But you . . . you are *so* different. You're moody and mysterious, and you've got this . . . this *thing* about you that just makes me want to get closer and closer to you. You bring me out of myself. You're unpredictable and a little bit scary, but you're also protective and make me feel safe. The kind of relationship you want is so deep and dark and sensual. It's all so *raw* and challenging. It's not comfortable and easy. Loving you won't be easy, I can see that. That's what I need. Something totally different than what I had. That's what I want." She pauses and plays with a lock of my hair, twirling it between her fingers.

"Vandal, I don't know where this is going or if it's gonna last, and I know it's too soon for either of us to be thinking about it right now, but someday, if it happens, I could see that with you," she says.

"Shit. I thought you wanted to leave." Letting out a big sigh, I grab her hand and link her fingers with mine. "So, yeah. I could see that too. With you. Maybe someday." I wonder if she can feel my heart pounding in my chest at the thought of a someday with her. A someday I want really fuckin' bad.

A shy but happy smile dances across her lips. "Is it weird we've only known each other a few days? Does it feel a lot longer to you? Tell me it does, or I'm going to feel stupid."

"No . . . it feels longer to me, too," I agree, reminding myself that I stalked her for a few weeks before actually meeting her.

She crawls on top of me and straddles me. Cupping her hands on my face, she slowly leans into me and kisses my lips.

"I want you," she whispers.

"Then take me."

She wiggles out of her panties and then reaches down between us to push my pants down. My cock is already rock-hard just from the words she spoke. She wraps her hand around me and slowly glides it up and down before lowering her sweet, tight pussy onto me. Sucking in a breath, I grab her hips, remembering not to grab her sore back. She lets out a faint moan as she takes me into her, her hands splayed on my chest for balance.

I never let a chick ride me. I always have to be in control. But having her on top of me, watching her slowly move above me with her eyes closed, pouty lips parted, and her head thrown back, I can't think of anything else I'd rather have done to me.

Leaning back, I let her take control and do all the work, giving her the freedom to enjoy herself at her own pace, even though the urge to grab her by the hips and bounce her up and down hard on my cock like a pogo stick is very tempting. There is something amazing about seeing a shy woman come out of her shell, gain confidence, and harness her own sexuality. I ain't gonna lie: I haven't met many shy women, but this one here—she fucking dazzles me.

"I don't know if I can go through this again. I'm still sore," she whines as I set up my tattoo gear on the table.

"We can wait a day or two if you want. I'm not going to force you." I gently lift her shirt to check out the ink I did yesterday, and it looks fuckin' hot as hell on her. The feathery wings are some of my best work.

"It's gorgeous," I tell her. "Once this all heals up, it's going to be sick. You have to let me add it to my portfolio." I run my finger slowly down her spine and dip my head down to whisper in her ear. "Then I'm going to bend you over and fuck you so I can watch these wings flutter on your back when you come."

She turns her head to me. "Oh, so that's why you wanted wings on my back?" she teases as I pull her shirt up over her head.

"Maybe . . ." I reply, grinning.

"I thought it was because you're setting me free."

"That, too. So, are we gonna do this or do you want to wait 'til tomorrow?"

She flops down in her chair and turns away from me. "No, let's get some done. I'll suffer through."

I grab Sterling and shut him in the bedroom with a bunch of his catnip toys, and then put my mp3 player into the speaker dock so we can listen to some tunes while I work on her.

Pulling on my black latex gloves, I study the ink from yesterday. There are a few areas I'll go back to later to add in some additional shading for depth. I like my art to have a lot of dimension and realism.

"Damn! I forgot how much it hurts!" she yells when I start on her. "I feel like you should put a leather belt in my mouth for me to bite on."

My cock strains against my jeans from that visual. "I think I might do that, darlin'. Only, not for this."

"I'm not going to think about that right now," she replies. "So your brother is a tattoo artist?"

"Yes."

"And he plays the violin?"

"Yup."

"Wow. That's a lot of talent for one family."

I let out a little chuckle. "If you only knew." I wipe her back with a white cloth. "Do you have any brothers or sisters?"

"I have an older sister."

"What's she like? Are you close?"

"She's the opposite of me. She's tall and gorgeous—she always looks absolutely perfect. She married this mega-rich guy and lives in a mansion and drives a Porsche. They have twins, a boy and a girl, who are equally perfect. I don't see them often; she's way too busy being a socialite to be bothered with her awkward little sister."

"Do you want to live in a mansion, too?" I ask her, although I think I already know the answer. That's just not her style.

She shakes her head. "Gawd no. I swear I get lost in her house. I stayed there once, and I couldn't even find my way from the guest room to the kitchen. My dream house is like this place here."

"Here? My house?"

"Yes. I love it here; it's so peaceful and cozy. I bet it's gorgeous in the fall and winter, too. I'd love to take photos up here; I could totally go crazy with ideas."

"If you like it that much, you can stay here. You could live here if you wanted to." Yeah, I'm jumping the gun, but I don't give a shit. I want her to live in a place she loves, that inspires her. I owe her that much.

"What? Are you crazy? You can't just let someone live in your house."

"Not someone . . . just you."

"Why? You barely know me. I mean a few weeks is okay but not like . . . indefinitely."

I apply some slight pressure on her back. "Lean forward a little, babe, and don't wiggle around," I say, starting the lower feathers at the small of her back. "I'm not sure we ever really know anyone, Tabi." I wipe the blood away and resume working. "I know a shitload of people who have known each other for years, and one turns out to be a douche or a bitch, and then they're like, 'What the fuck just happened?' So, I don't put a lot of value on time known; I put value in my gut feeling about people, living in the moment, and dealing with the shit later."

"That's really kinda romantic, Vandal, in a very *you* way."

"Ya think? I'm serious though. You can stay here as long as you want; I don't mind. Even after I go back home in a few weeks. If you want to stay here and chill, take some photos, and just figure life out, I'm fine with that."

She's quiet for a moment, and I'm glad she can't move away. "I don't think I'd like it as much without you here," she finally says, her voice lilting with sadness.

I wipe ink and blood off her back again before answering her. "I could come back on the weekends. It's not too far. Maybe not every weekend, depending on what I've got going on. Think about it for a while."

What I really want is to take her home with me, but I have no idea how I'd keep her from finding out about the accident and the band and every-fucking-thing else in my life that I'm not ready for her to know. If she stayed here, and I just came on weekends, I could keep her isolated from the rest of my life and not drag her into all that shit.

That is, if she even wants to see me after our time here. I can't stop myself from just assuming that this is going to continue. I've never thought of a woman as a long-term fixture before. They all had an expiration date. But with Tabitha, the more I'm with her, the more I don't want it to end.

"Do you have a job?" I ask her casually, even though I already know the answer.

She blows out an exasperated breath. "I quit my job after Nick passed away. I just couldn't deal with it anymore. I couldn't get out of bed most days, and when I did actually go in, I couldn't interact with the people there at all. I was a mess. I spent most of the day in the bathroom crying. They would have fired me eventually." She sighs. "I had a long talk with my boss, and she agreed to say the company laid me off so I could collect unemployment for a few months while I tried to get out of the depression I was in."

"That sucks. I'm sorry about all that. What did you do for work?"

"I was just a receptionist. Nothing exciting."

I frown at the back of her head. "Don't say it like that. At least you had a job, and I'm sure you were great at it. You have a really sweet voice and a fuckin' gorgeous smile. That's what people want to hear and see."

"Well, thanks. It's not really what I wanted to do with my life."

I pull off my gloves and put my hands on her bare shoulders. "Let's take a break. Turn around."

Turning towards me, she stretches her arms out and above her head, her naked breasts lifting up perfectly. Impulsively, I lean forward and plant a kiss between them.

"You look so fuckin' sexy sitting like that; I forgot what I was going to say."

She smiles sheepishly. "Was ramming involved?"

"Surprisingly, no. I wanted to ask you what you *want* to do for work."

"Hmm. My passion is photography." Just saying the words makes her smile, and her eyes light up. "So, I guess in a perfect world, I would love to be able to take photos, do theme shoots, sell my photos, and maybe have a photo book published. I really love artistic shoots."

"Then that's what you should do."

"I wish, but it takes a while to get to a point to actually make any money. If ever! Nick and I talked about it, but I guess I have to agree with what he said; it's a nice hobby but not something I could really ever make money doing."

I really want to say that Nick is a douche dream-killer, but I hold back so I don't upset her. Maybe he was just trying to be realistic.

I line up more ink cups on the table. "I think we all need to chase our dreams if we can. I was a struggling artist for a long time, playing my bass for shit money and tattooing, living in the friggin' ghetto. Then one day, my life changed."

She tilts her head, her blond hair falling down over her breasts. "What happened?"

"I got a letter from someone claiming to be my grandmother. I had no idea who this woman was. My father bailed when I was about four years old, and my mother was a junkie. I was adopted by another couple when I was five, but they weren't good parents. I had no one. Then I get this letter from someone claiming to be my father's mother, and she wants to meet me. She insisted she had no idea I even existed until a few weeks before she wrote the letter."

"Wow . . . what did you do? When was this?"

I shake my hair out of my face and start to fill the tiny cups with ink. "I ignored it. This was six years ago. I basically said fuck it. Like, where the hell was she when I was getting the shit beat out of me by my adoptive father? So, about two months later, this tiny old lady shows up at my door. I was hungover, and I had some nameless chick in my bed, so I told this old lady to get the fuck off my doorstep." The memory is still so vivid in my mind that it makes me laugh remembering the face Gram made and what she did next. "I tried to shut the door and she stopped it with her foot and barged right into my shitty apartment. She yanked the girl out of my bed and pretty much threw her out, ordered me to take a shower, and trashed all my weed and booze while I was in there."

"Holy shit!"

"No kidding. I was mad as hell. But like, she's maybe five feet tall and pushing ninety. What could I do?"

She giggles, covering her mouth with her hand. "Oh my God. What did you do?"

"I sat there and was like, what the hell do you want? And she told me that she was my grandmother, and the whole fucking deal. Apparently, my father was a pretty famous musician when he was younger, which I obviously had no clue about, and he was an asshole. I guess he was screwing women left and right and then disappearing if they got pregnant. Same shit happened to my brother, Lukas. No one knew about him either. Gram found out about us at the same time and hired a private detective to find both of us. I guess she hadn't talked to my father in years due to some shit that had gone down."

"Yikes!"

"So, she tells me that my filthy rich grandfather passed away and she wanted to make sure all her grandchildren got their inheritance. Including the ones that her son threw away."

Her eyes go big, and she hangs her mouth open. "What? Seriously?"

"No lie, baby. Five mil later and suddenly I've got a brother, a grandmother, a bunch of cousins, and an aunt and uncle. And the wild part is, they actually wanted us to be part of the family. I didn't even want the money. I said no. But Gram kept insisting, and she kept showing up at my place, and finally dragged me to her lawyer's office, and then to her house. It was some fucking crazy shit. It changed my life. Me and Lukas hung out and got to talking, found out we both were kick-ass tattoo artists. We put some of our money together and opened a shop. Then I got in the band, and I bought these two houses, blah, blah, blah. The rest is history, I guess."

Shit. I shouldn't have mentioned the band. Too late now. Hopefully she won't question me about it, and if she does, fuck it.

She's sitting there with wide eyes, mouth dropped open, just staring at me in awe. "Vandal, wow. That's all so . . . unbelievable."

"Yeah. It is. Still kinda surreal to me. Gram is awesome though. She makes the best fucking cookies; they're like crack and can fix any bad mood or drama."

"She sounds amazing. Maybe I can meet her someday?" she asks cautiously, and I know what she's asking is more than just wanting to meet my grandmother. She's trying to see if I'm going to keep her around and if I like her enough to bring her around my family. I've never done that though. I've never brought any chick around my friends or family. Yeah, sometimes if I had something going with a girl they would come to concerts to hear me play, or be hanging around my place sometimes, but I never actually wanted any of them to meet my family. I had no interest in any of that. What scares me is that I can see Tabitha talking to Gram—drinking tea and eating cookies in the kitchen with her like I've seen Evie do.

Do I want to be like Storm? Having a girl with me all the time? Being part of my family? Holding my hand and being all smiley and cutesy and disappearing in dark corners together?

*No.*

I want the evil twin version of that. I want what I've been fantasizing about for years. I want a live-in sub who gives herself to me whenever I want or need her. I want her to only want me, only need me, and be bound to me forever. I want her to trust me without question or hesitation, and accept me no matter what. I want her to be open to all the dark and deviant things I want to do with her and want them as much as I do. I want her to be on her knees, bent over, begging, gagging, and ravished by me and still want more. And after all that, yeah . . . I want her to adore me, be by my side, and maybe even love me. I want to never feel alone and abandoned again. And if she can give me all that? I'd love the fucking hell out of her and let her sit and eat cookies with Gram as much as she wants.

"Can we keep going?" she asks, her voice subdued. "I can't wait to see it." She turns her back to me so I can continue her tattoo.

She never got an answer to her question, but I let it stay that way, hanging between us. *Fuck.* I hate this black cloud that's looming over us, waiting to explode into a tornado of lies, deceit, and grief.

We are a ticking time bomb. Not even Gram and her cookies can fix this shit.

# chapter eighteen

Tabitha

Two weeks. Fourteen days. No matter how I think of it, I can't grasp that in such a short amount of time, my life has changed in ways I never could have imagined. I'm so immersed in Vandal that I can barely remember him not being part of me. He's a drug that I cannot get enough of. A little is never enough; I always need and want more.

When he's not touching me, all I can think about is when he will touch me again. Making him smile has become a daily goal for me. While once all I wanted was to sleep, now I don't want to sleep unless I'm in his arms.

Like now. I've just woken up, my back against his chest, his arm tight around me, our hands linked and curled at my breast, our naked bodies spooned tightly against each other perfectly. I move slightly and he moves with me, his cock already hard and pressing against my ass. He slips his hand out of mine and slides across my stomach and up over my hip, then down to my thigh, lifting my leg up and back over his. He raises his head off the pillow and sinks into my neck, his lips warm and moist, as he slides his cock into me slowly from behind. My body instinctively arches back to curve to his, opening up to him. He lifts my leg further, and I roll forward just a little, angling my ass up to meet his thrusts. We are one perfect fluid movement, completely in sync with each other's bodies. I have never felt such an intense physical and emotional closeness to someone as this.

"I love fucking you when you're barely awake," he groans in my ear. "You're so soft and warm."

"Mmmm . . ." I murmur, turning my head to meet his lips.

"You want me to fuck you awake every morning, don't you?" His hand delves between my thighs, his fingers stroking my clit expertly.

"Yes," I pant, rocking my body back against him.

"Beg me and I might."

"Please . . ."

His teeth graze the flesh behind my ear as he pumps deeper into me, forcing a moan out of me. "Please what?" he demands. "Don't make me pull words out of you, Tabi. Beg for what you want, or you won't get it."

His raw, commanding voice turns me on like a vibrator on warp speed. I squeeze my thighs together around his hand and reach back to wind my fingers around his neck, grabbing a handful of his hair in the process. "Please fuck me every morning forever," I breathe, as my body starts to tremor.

In one swift movement he pushes me down on my stomach and lifts my hips up, driving his cock back into me. "Forever's a long fucking time, baby. You're gonna have to beg better than that."

"Please . . . fill my pussy with your cock every morning."

"For . . .?" He pounds into me so hard I swear he's slamming into my cervix. My muscles contract wildly around his girth as the ripples of orgasm course through my body. My hands clench his cotton sheets.

"Forever," I gasp as my body shudders around him, and his hot cum spurts deep inside me. His hands slide up my hips and gently caress my back.

"Your wings look so perfect," he says softly, still breathing heavy. "I love watching your back when I fuck you; you have no idea how gorgeous you look."

At the end of my first week with him, he gave me an e-reader after he learned that I love to read. Along with my usual romance novels, I purchased a bunch of books about light BDSM lifestyles. As I learn more and explore with him, submitting to him feels natural to me. And it's not because I'm a weak woman who gives in to a man, because I've never been that person. This is entirely different. I have a deep need and desire to give myself to him and trust him with my body, mind, and soul. Even at his dirtiest, I still feel adored—even cherished—by him.

Buried deep beneath his hard exterior, there's a man who wants to be loved but has been hurt badly. I know he's grieving his daughter, even though he refuses to talk about her. If my being here and giving him what he wants and needs helps him, then I'm totally fine with that. He's lived up to his promise of helping me move on from the depressed rut I was in. I still miss Nick and the life we had, but at least now I have hope that it's possible for me to find some kind of happiness again. Two weeks ago, I couldn't even imagine that.

While he checks his email, I make us pancakes and eggs and then wait at the table for him. When he comes in and takes his seat, I lean over and kiss him.

"Thank you for the ramming," I say, but for the first time, he doesn't laugh at our little joke. His face is hard and unsmiling. We eat in silence, and when he's finished he pushes his chair back and stands.

"I'm going out for a while. I left words in the book for you."

*Left words?*

"Okay. Is something wrong?"

He shakes his head, but his eyes are dark and troubled. "No. I'll see you later."

Confused, I watch him pull his boots on, grab his keys, and walk out the door, slamming it hard. A few minutes later, his motorcycle roars to life and pulls out of the driveway, the sound of the engine fading as he travels farther away. *Away from me. With no goodbye.*

After I clean up the kitchen and feed Sterling, I go to the guest room and open up the journal. There's also a box on the bed, but I'm not going to open it yet.

*Tabitha,*

*You'll know what to do with what's in the box. I'll be home at five. I'll eat while I'm out, so don't make dinner. Please be showered, dressed, and waiting in the dining room. Put on extra black eyeliner and dark lipstick for me.*

Hmm. His note sounds off to me, and not quite like his usual sexy or mysterious self.

I open the box and reveal a very short, slinky black dress with a plunging neckline, open back, and black pumps that have about a four-inch heel. If I don't break my ass in these shoes, it will be a miracle. I leave the items in the guest room and go about keeping myself busy for the day.

I call my best friend, Lara, whom I haven't spoken to in about a week. I know if I don't call her, she'll start to worry about me, and she'll start to blow up my phone with texts.

"It's about time. Where have you been?" she asks when she hears my voice.

"I'm still here in the mountains. I'm fine."

"You're still staying with Mystery Meat? Girl, what the hell is going on there? Please tell me you're not in the basement putting the lotion on."

I laugh, missing her and our crazy talks. "I'm totally fine. Actually, I feel better than I have in a long time."

"You definitely sound better. I can't remember the last time I heard you laugh. It's good to hear that again."

"Thank you. I miss you."

"We should get together. I could come there if you want? I'd like to meet the guy who has practically kidnapped my best friend."

I sigh uneasily. I don't know how Vandal would feel about Lara visiting. His own brother wants to visit, and Vandal keeps putting him off, so having someone he doesn't know come by is probably not something he's going to be keen on.

"He's kind of a recluse, Lara. I'm not sure that's a good idea. But I'll come see you soon. We'll have lunch."

"Are you sure you're okay? This guy seems a little bit creepy to me."

"I promise you, I'm fine. He's a really nice guy, just kind of a loner. He's going through a lot of shit, like I am." There's a long silence on the other end. "He's good to me. He's completely different than Nick, and that's what I need."

"So are you dating him, or is he like a friend with benefits?"

I can't explain any of the details to Lara because she won't understand and will likely lose her shit entirely. I would need hours to sit her down and really explain it to her, and I just don't have the patience right now.

"I guess like friends with benefits. Maybe more, but it's too soon. I'm just trying to find *me*. A me without Nick. It's not easy, Lara. I miss Nick like crazy, but I need to try to move on, like everyone has been telling me to. I just know I feel better, and I'm actually getting happier. That's all I want to think about."

"Okay, I understand, hon. I just worry about you. You're really fragile, and I don't want you to get hurt. Is he hot at least? Can't you text me a photo or something?" she jokes.

"Lara, he's hot as hell. You would die. He's over six feet tall, and built like a brick house. The guy is muscle on top of muscle. Total six-pack abs. And his hair is gorgeous; it's long and jet-black, like an Indian's. He's got tons of tattoos. Actually, I don't think I told you last time we talked—he's a tattoo artist."

"Get out, are you serious? I love me a tatted up man."

"Wait 'til you see the tattoo he did on me! He put angel wings on my back."

"What? *You?* I can't believe it."

"It hurt like crazy, but now that it's healing up, it's beautiful. The detail is incredible. I'll ask him to take a picture so I can text it to you. Oh, and he plays guitar. Or maybe it was a bass? I can't remember, but he's wicked talented. He's just yum, on so many levels. And he's romantic."

"Well, fuck. Does he have a brother?"

I laugh and pet Sterling who's just jumped up on my lap. "He does, but I haven't met him yet. I think he has a girlfriend though. What about Steve? Aren't you still dating him?"

"Ugh. I guess. He's kinda getting on my nerves."

I roll my eyes. Right around the three-month mark she always starts to get the itch for a new man.

"I'm not gonna say anything . . ." I tease.

"Good! I just want you to be happy, Tab. I'm sorry that I probably wasn't the best friend to you I could have been with everything that happened . . . I just really didn't know what to do to help you. I feel like I let you down."

"No, Lara. Please don't think that. I love you, and you're the best. No one could've helped me; trust me. I didn't want anyone near me—you know that. I just needed to get through this in my own way. And I'm getting better, I promise. Being here has been good for me, as crazy as that sounds. I'm in a beautiful house in the mountains with a lake, a hot guy, and an adorable blind kitten sitting on my lap."

"Blind kitten?" she repeats. "Are you serious?"

"Yes, he's got this cute little blind kitten that is just a total ball of love. Every day, I lie on the couch and read, and he curls up on me. I want to take him with me when I go home."

"Speaking of, when are you coming home?"

I sigh and flop back onto the couch. "I don't know. He said he's going back to his other house and back to his shop to work in two weeks. This was like a little vacation for him. I think I'll be going back home then, and then I'll have to figure out what I want to do next."

"So what happens to you then? Are you going to keep seeing him, or was this like a thirty-night stand?"

*Eep.* My heart pounds a little faster, thinking about this. I want to keep seeing him. "I'm not really sure. I'm going to cross that bridge when I get to it. I'm hoping we'll still see each other, but I don't know."

"Scandalous. I hope you figure it out." I hear Lara's other line ringing. "I gotta run; my break is over. You better call me in a few days. And send me some pictures."

"I will. Love ya."

"Love ya, too."

Staring at myself in the full-length mirror, I wonder where the pole is that should have come with this outfit. The dress is so short that it barely covers my lady bits, and it's tighter than any dress I would ever buy. Oh, and no panties were included. The shoes are like mini, slutty stilts. I don't know if we're doing stripper or hooker role-play or what. The requested dark makeup is just adding to the whorish look, which apparently is what he wants tonight.

I teeter out to the dining room at a quarter to five and wait. I'm not sure how he always comes home exactly when he says he will, but at five o'clock, his motorcycle idles in the driveway. He comes through the door wearing an old, beat-up leather jacket, his hair tied back, and dark sunglasses. My body immediately reacts to how sexy he looks, my heartbeat speeding up and dampness forming between my thighs. He washes his hands at the kitchen sink before approaching me in the dim dining room.

"Stand up," he says abruptly, his face still hard.

Standing, I try to balance myself on the shoes. "These shoes are insane, I never wear heels—"

He touches my lips with his finger. "I'll tell you when to talk," he practically growls.

Uh-oh. The bad mood is still very much here, and I have no idea why. What did I do? Should I use the safe word and end this now? No, that wouldn't be good. He hasn't done anything to hurt me or scare me. He's just in a mood. I can't use the safe word the first time I feel a tiny bit apprehensive.

He pulls the dining room chair I had been sitting on away from the table and sits on it, leaning back, legs spread, so he's facing down the hallway towards the bedroom.

"Crawl down to the bedroom on your hands and knees. Slowly. There's an envelope in the nightstand. Crawl back to me with it in your teeth."

*Crawl?* In this dress? I stare at him for a moment, trying to decipher what's going on here. He didn't shower, as he normally does before he engages in a scene with me. He had dinner without me. Where? With whom? Maybe he saw the girl he used to fuck but then didn't fuck, and fucked her?

My stomach turns with nerves. His eyes are locked onto mine, but they're dark and unreadable. Usually I can read them, but not tonight.

He breaks the silence. "Are we waiting for something? I could put a leash on you and walk you down there myself, if you prefer."

A *leash*?

"No," I reply, my voice shaking. I'm not scared of him, but I'm scared of what he's thinking. I'm ninety-nine percent sure he would never hurt me, but that single, tiny percentage point is enough to make the hair on my neck stand up. I get down on my hands and knees and crawl slowly down the hardwood floor of the hall. The short dress has ridden up, completely exposing half of my naked ass and my pussy. When I get to the bedroom, I kneel at the nightstand and retrieve the plain white envelope from the drawer, then crawl back to him with it in my mouth, stopping to kneel between his jean-clad legs. Sitting like a dog with the envelope in my mouth, I wait for him to take it. Finally he does, and removes a folded white piece of paper.

He hands it to me and says, "Read this aloud to me."

Fear grips me as I take the piece of paper from him, and I see a familiar picture on it. *My* picture. It's my social media page. I stare at it, utterly confused, and look back to him.

"Just read the first status post to me and then the replies to it," he instructs.

I swallow and begin reading.

"Jason posted yesterday, 'Hey Tabitha, what's up? I've been thinking about you a lot. I miss you.'

Then I replied, 'Hi Jason, I'm doing okay. I miss you, too.'

Then Jason wrote, 'We should have dinner and catch up. When will you be back in town?'

And I wrote, 'That sounds great. I'm staying with a friend right now, but I'll be back home in two weeks and would love to have dinner. I'll call you as soon as I get back.'

And then he wrote, 'Awesome, baby girl. See ya soon.'

And then I wrote, 'Can't wait.'"

Vandal snatches the paper out of my hand, glaring at me with a cold, menacing look.

Holy shit, is he *jealous*?

"Who's Jason?" he demands.

"He's an old friend. I've known him since grade school."

He nods slowly. "I see. And here you are, staying with a *friend*. Is that what we are?"

"No," I reply without much conviction. I don't know the right answer. "I don't know."

He raises an eyebrow at me. "Really? Do you fuck your friends? Do they tie you to the bed and lick every delicious inch of you until you scream?"

"No."

"Do you suck your friends?"

"No, of course not." Heat rises to my cheeks.

"Okay. I'm glad we have that clarified. Tell me, Tabitha, have you ever fucked Jason?"

My jaw clenches, and my chest tightens. "That's rude . . ."

"Referring to me as a *friend* to your friend was rude, Tabitha. I've given you expensive gifts, I've invaded every orifice of your body, you've swallowed gallons of my cum, you sleep in my arms, in my bed, every night. I've invited you to live in my home indefinitely, all expenses paid, yet you think of me as a *friend*? How the fuck am I supposed to feel about that?"

My body trembles. I've never seen him mad before, and he is clearly beyond pissed right now. "I didn't mean it, Vandal. Not like you're thinking."

"Then why did you say it?"

"Because he's my friend and it's a public page and my husband just died and it just seemed . . . easier. I didn't even think about it."

His jaw clenches, and I continue. "It's no one's business. What was I supposed to say? That I'm hanging out with my Dom? My boyfriend? My fuck-master?"

His eyes fly to meet mine, and now he's surpassed pissed. "Fuck-master?" he repeats. "Now that's a good one, Tabi. Actually, that's the first I've ever heard that term, so bravo."

"Vandal, I—"

"Answer me. Have you ever fucked Jason?"

"Excuse me?"

"You heard me. Don't make me repeat myself. You know I hate it, and I *will* spank you if you play stupid."

I let out a deep sigh and prepare myself. "Yes, I have had sex with Jason. A long time ago, in high school, we dated."

"Outstanding."

"He's just a friend now; he and Nick were really good friends. He was in our wedding party."

"He called you 'baby girl.' That's a little overly friendly, isn't it?"

Jason is a flirt, but that's just who he is. I would never sleep with him again.

"Not for him. You don't know him."

"That's right, I don't. But I thought it was safe to assume that the woman who agreed to be my sub, and begged me to fuck her awake every morning *forever*, would not be making plans with another fucking guy the minute she gets back home. And I thought maybe you were staying here, like we talked about." His voice rises. "I guess I was wrong. As fucking usual."

*Shit.* I didn't know he took all of that so seriously. Yes, of course I meant every word. I want to be his sub, and I've spent hours daydreaming about a forever with him, but I have no idea what's part of the scene and what's real. Or what *he* considers real.

"Do you want him?" he asks.

"God, no. Not at all. He's just a friend."

"So am I, apparently."

I shake my head. "No, you're not. You're much more than that."

"I know you've been reading, Tabitha. And I'm pretty sure you must have read the parts where it says that a sub is always, always, *always,* true to her fuck-master, as you think of me. That commitment is upheld at all times, no matter what. You don't skirt around it on fucking social media, or conveniently leave it out when making dinner plans with another man that you have a history of fucking."

"That's not fair. We've never talked about what we are to each other. I'm not sure what I'm supposed to say or how to act. I've asked you several times about us and what's going to happen, but you ignore me. And where have you been all day? Visiting another girl you used to fuck, like last time? Do you tell them you have a little fucked-up, depressed sub waiting in your house for you?"

"I don't discuss my personal life."

I scoff at him. "Oh, so that's okay? You're a hypocrite."

"It's different. I'm in the fucking public eye, and I don't want you to be part of that. And let me remind you, it's not your place to question me."

*What the fuck?* "Oh, please. How convenient. What public eye?"

"I'm in a band, Tabi. A pretty popular one. The fans and the press can be brutal."

"You couldn't have told me this sooner?" I ask. How could he not tell me all this?

"I just thought I meant more to you than this." He throws the paper into the air and looks away from me, shaking his head and clenching his fists. He *cares*. It's not just a game to him after all, and it's scaring him. It's clear as day to me now.

I gently put my hands on his legs and brace myself. I have to be honest with him, because I can't stand to see him so pissed off and upset like this. "Vandal, please. I'm falling in love with you..."

He looks at me as if I've poured acid on him, his face contorted with disbelief and pain. "Don't you dare fucking say that to me."

"Why? It's true."

He stares at me, his eyes dark and icy.

"You don't want to love me, Tabi. And you definitely don't want me to love you. Trust me." He whispers, "Love has no part in this."

My heart plummets. "You're lying," I say, tears running down my face. "I can tell you love me."

"You're fucking delusional."

I wince from his words. "Why are you doing this?"

"Because this is who I fucking am."

"No," I sob, "it's not. This is who you're telling yourself you are. If you don't love me, why do you care about Jason? You wouldn't be jealous if you didn't care."

He sneers at me. "Jealous? I don't get jealous. I just don't want some douchebag touching what's mine."

I almost fall back on my ass. "*Yours*? You don't own me."

"I guess you've learned nothing, then."

I shake my head in disbelief at him, more tears streaming down my cheeks. "Yeah. I guess you're right."

Standing, I pull the hem of the dress down, trying to cover myself, and kick off the stupid shoes.

"We're not done," he says, leaning forward.

"Yes, we are." I turn to walk away, and he grabs me around the waist, pulling me down on his lap, crushing my back against his muscled chest, his arm snaking around the front of my waist to keep me from getting up.

"Let me go," I try to push his arms off me, but he doesn't budge.

"Not until you stop crying and put your shoes back on."

I sniff and wipe my eyes, smearing the black eyeliner that just an hour ago I tried so hard to get perfect.

"You used to wipe my tears away," I remind him, heartbroken.

He leans his forehead against my back. "I'd take all your tears away if I could. Believe me."

Still with his arm wrapped around my waist, he leans down and grabs one of the shoes. "Slide your foot in."

"No. Go to hell."

"No means nothing to me, Tabitha. And I've been living in hell my entire life. Put the shoe on."

"I don't want to," I say childishly.

"You know what I do when I ride?" he asks. "I *think*. In fact, it's pretty much the only time I can clear my head enough to think at all. Sometimes I think about music, and write it in my head. Other times I think about my daughter and try to remember her smile. And sometimes, like today, I think about what I'm going to do to you."

Maybe I am just some kind of toy for him and I've misread what I thought were signs of care, and possibly love. It's possible that I've traded my grief for lust, and he's right, that love has no part in this at all. Is every touch, every word, every glimpse of affection between us just part of a game that I didn't realize I was playing?

Screwing my eyes closed to shut out more tears, I refuse to accept that. *I can't accept that.* I know I love him; I'm sure of it. I want his happiness. I hate his pain. I want to be the one to show him that he *can* have a good life, and that he can have a relationship with a woman that doesn't require being tied up to achieve a sense of control and mask his fear of being left. This isn't a whim for me anymore. I like the sensuality of the game, but I want the love, too. Can we have both?

"I read that shit online with Jason this morning and it really fucking pissed me off. I knew tonight would have to be different because I have to show you that what you did disrespects what we have and that I don't ever want to read words like that again," he continues, turning the shoe over in his hand. "As you know, there's a reason for the dress and the shoes. All day I've been thinking about how I can discipline you and how much I'm going to enjoy it." He lifts my foot and slides the shoe onto it. "You're going to enjoy it, too, aren't you?"

I don't say anything, but his words affect me in so many different, naughty ways.

I want to know what he wants to do to me and I shiver thinking of the ecstasy he has in store for me. I keep my other foot flat on the floor in defiance, knowing that it only ignites him. I know it's bad, but I enjoy taunting him and provoking him because the feeling of the unknown with him turns me on and sends tingles straight to my core.

"Now put this one on." He holds the other shoe up and I slide my foot in.

"They're really hard to walk in," I say, sniffling.

He moves my hair to the side and kisses my exposed neck. "You're not going to be walking," he whispers against my ear. "I think we need to have a little lesson." He reaches into his pocket, and I hear the jangling of something metal.

"Give me your hands, Tabitha."

I put my hands behind my back, and he wraps what feels like a thin, metal chain around my wrists. No silk ribbon tonight.

"Stand up."

I stand, wanting to pull the dress down that has ridden up to my ass, but I can't as now my hands are tied. I feel horribly slutty in this dress.

He runs his hands from my ankles, up my calves, over my thighs, tantalizing me slowly until he squeezes my ass. I feel his lips and then his teeth on my ass cheek as his hand slips between my thighs and his middle finger slides between my delicate, wet lips.

"You still want me, don't you?" he asks, pushing his finger up inside me.

"Yes."

He pushes another finger inside me. "You don't even hesitate to answer."

"Because I know what I want, unlike you." The words come out before I can stop myself, and his fingers tense up inside me, no longer caressing me.

"Is that right?" A hint of sarcastic amusement laces his deep voice.

He stands, his fingers still inside me, and pulls my head back to him by my hair with his other, causing my scalp to burn. "I know exactly what I want, darlin'. And I'm going to fucking show you. While I'm at it, you're going to learn how to behave so we don't have any more social media fuckery."

He lets go of my hair and pulls his fingers out of me, causing me to lose my balance a little. I wobble for a moment before he catches my arm to steady me. He pulls something else out of his pocket and holds it up in front of me.

"I bought you a present today. You know, while I was out meeting other women, as you so nicely accused."

I try to focus on the object and realize it's a small bullet vibrator. "Spread your legs a little more," he commands. When I do, I feel him slowly slide the vibrator into me, flipping the tiny switch. It buzzes and vibrates deep inside my pelvis.

"Turn around."

Once I'm facing him, he takes the sunglasses off the top of his head and places them on the table, then slowly takes off his faded leather jacket. My vintage leather fetish sparks up and the urge to feel and smell the leather rises.

"Do you want to know what I want?" he asks.

"Yes," I answer, trying to ignore the vibrator, how wet it's making me, and how my muscles are clenching involuntarily around it.

"I don't want you to leave. I want you to stay here, in my house, and be my sub. I want to come home to you waiting for me, dressed in lingerie or whatever other outfit I left for you. I want to tie you up and fuck your brains out all night and hear you whimper my name."

He pulls his shirt over his head and starts to unbuckle his belt, then continues. "I want you to fall asleep naked in my arms so I can take you whenever I want to." He pushes his jeans and boxers down, kicks his boots off, and steps out of his pants. "And I'd like to wake up with your lips around my cock."

*Please tell me you love me. Give me something to show me it's not a game.*

He reaches between my legs and gives the vibrator a push. "You better not come unless I tell you to." Kissing my lips softly, he pushes down on my shoulders. "Get on your knees and don't let that fall out."

I kneel awkwardly, trying not to fall on my ass while clenching the vibrator in my core. He leans back against the edge of the table in front of me. "I want you to suck my cock before I tell you what else I want."

I lick the head of his cock and swirl my tongue around him, slowly sliding my mouth down his hot shaft, gazing up at him. I love watching his breathing change and seeing his eyes get drowsy and lusty. He touches my face as I go down on him, and he watches me intently. He pulls his cock out of my mouth and slides his thumb into my mouth in its place.

"Come up here," his voice is low and tinged with a hint of urgency. I carefully stand up, and he reaches behind me and unwinds the chain, letting it fall to the floor, and takes the vibrator out next. He holds my face in his hands and looks into my eyes for a few moments, staring straight into my soul like he does, and looking back into his, I see the many broken parts of him.

"What's wrong? Talk to me." I coax, placing my hands on his chest.

He leans his forehead against mine and closes his eyes, inhaling me, and us, deep into his lungs before he answers.

"No one's ever said they love me before."

My heart clenches. My God, this man needs to be loved so badly, and I want to be the one to give it to him, but doing so will put my already broken heart in jeopardy of being further shattered. Am I strong enough to risk that? Could he ever love me back? And more importantly, can I let go of the past?

"Well . . ." I whisper, my heart pounding. "I guess I'm the first, and hopefully, the last."

His hands go to my waist and grip me tighter, pulling me even closer against his body, as if he's afraid I'm going to run. I place a soft kiss directly over his heart, and then tilt my head up to meet his dark eyes. "I love you," I say, my voice small and shaky.

"You shouldn't . . . I don't want to hurt you."

"Then don't."

He shakes his head. "Easier said than done."

"Hey," I say softly, "I believe in you, Vandal. Whatever happened in the past . . . that doesn't have to make you who you are now. That's not the man I know today. If you don't like who you are, you can change the parts you don't like . . . I'll help you."

"There's so much you don't know about me." He pushes my hair away from my face, his eyes full of pain and regret.

I pull his head down to mine and kiss his lips. "I don't want to know. I love who you are right now. I love the man you've been since you brought me here." I slowly brainwash myself with my own delusions. I want it all to go away. I just want to be with him, now and forever. "You have to learn to let some walls down."

He nods. "I'm so tired of holding the walls up, Tabi."

Sliding my hands up his chest, I clasp them behind his neck. "We can do it together."

"I don't deserve you," he whispers, and a lone tear slowly slides down his face, the sight of it stopping my heart.

In that moment, everything changes. There is a shift, deep and permanent, as if the hand of a monstrous clock just ticked to the next moment, and then stayed there.

*It wasn't supposed to happen like this.*

This isn't just about me anymore.

VANDAL

This fucking chick is killing me. *Killing me.*

She's got my head so twisted up, I don't know if I want to stand here and hug her or bend her over this table and slam her ass while she's got that vibrator in her.

*I'm falling in love with you.*

Words I've never heard once in my thirty years on this fucking planet, and now I hear them from a girl whose life I wrecked and is destined to hate me. This twisted irony can only happen to me.

The evil little voices in me are telling me to hurt her now before she hurts me. Cut her down, rip her heart out. Bring another woman home. Get drunk off my ass. Get high as a kite. Stomp all ideas of love and happiness out of her fast and hard. Tell her the truth about the accident and watch the love in her eyes wither away and die.

"Don't shut me out," she says in her sweet voice, her hands tangled in my hair at the back of my neck. She looks so sexy in this dress, and when she crawled down the hall, I could have blown a nut just looking at her. My brain swirls with the endless possibilities of keeping her as my sub *and* having her love me.

*Say it back.*

It's what she wants to hear. Of course even I know that I'm supposed to say it back to her. I know how much it's hurting her right now that I didn't. But once I say those words, there's no coming back. I'll always be the one who loved her and lied right to her face.

"I'm not shutting you out," I say, regaining my composure. "I'm thinking."

"About?" She asks, a slight shake to her voice.

I have to give her something if I want her to stay. She's giving me everything – her trust, her body, and now her heart. If I don't attempt to give her something back, she's gonna bolt.

"I want you to stay with me. Indefinitely. We'll figure out the details of the hows and wheres later." I slide my finger down the front of the plunging neckline of her dress, between her breasts. "Is that what you want, too? This isn't a game for me. We need to clarify some parameters and expectations if you're going to stay." I stroke the swell of her breasts beneath the thin, tight dress while I wait for her to answer.

"Yes. I want to stay."

"Good. I'll take care of you. I'll give you everything you need and want. I don't want you to work outside the house for someone else. I want you to focus on your photography, and make that your career if that's what you want. If you need some equipment, I'll get it for you. If you need a studio, we'll either find you one in town or we can have one built here or at my other house—we'll decide that later."

Her hand flutters to her mouth in surprise. "Oh my God, Vandal . . . you would let me do that? You would do all of that for me? Can you afford that?"

"Yes, but it's in return for what you are giving me. Which is *you*. Twenty-four seven. Exclusively. I don't want you dating or having lunch with other men. I don't share well, on any level. Call me an asshole, but that's who I am. What's mine is mine, and there is no gray area on that." I hold her gaze, hoping she understands how serious I am. "And yes, I can afford it. Believe it or not, I've been very responsible with my money, thanks to Gram's help. I get income from the tattoo shop and from the band, in addition to my inheritance. Okay?"

"Of course . . . I don't want anyone else, but why can't we just be in a normal relationship then?"

"Because I'm not normal. We're not getting engaged, Tabitha. Don't confuse this with some conventional relationship. This is an agreement. I want you; I care about you. I like you a lot. Don't think you can throw emotions and words at me to break me down." She already has broken me down, but I'm not ready to give in yet. I need more time. "We'll agree on a sum of money that I'll deposit into your bank account. I don't want you to ever feel trapped here. You can leave whenever you want and you'll have enough money to take care of yourself for a while."

"Wait . . . you can't pay me for being with you. I don't want that."

"I can and I will. And don't make it sound like prostitution. I'm not paying you to fuck me, Tabitha. It's an equal arrangement. You're giving me everything I need in the way that I need it, and I'm making sure you have everything you need."

"Okay . . . I guess. I don't want your money though. That's not what I need or want at all . . ." Her voice trails off and I know exactly what she's hinting at.

I slide my hand up to her throat and squeeze gently, because I love how it makes her eyes go so big and her breath quicken. "I know you don't want my money. I trust you."

"I trust you, too."

"The band I'm in is pretty popular. I expect one hundred percent discretion and commitment from you about what I do with my business and personal life. I don't want you posting pictures or updates about me on your social media page."

"Okay. Are you famous or something?"

I let out a little laugh and stroke her cheek. "Or something."

She shifts on her feet. I'm sure the shoes are starting to hurt. "I don't care about who you are, or any of that," she replies.

"Ya know, I actually believe you when you say that."

"Because it's true. What band are you in? Maybe I've heard your music or have you saved in my playlist and don't even know it."

"I doubt it."

"Stop being so difficult and just tell me. You don't have to be so secretive. I'm going to find out eventually."

"I don't want to talk anymore," I say, growing impatient. "The short version is I want you to be mine, and I'll treat you like a fucking princess as long as you do the things I ask and don't fuck with me. I don't deal with shit well. I also don't know how to fucking date. What you see here is what you get. And, in case you haven't noticed, I have some abandonment issues."

"I did notice. In case *you* haven't noticed, I'm not going anywhere."

"Why is that, exactly?" I slowly push the sleeves of her dress down until her breasts spill out. I cup her firm flesh in my hands and caress her, her nipples hardening against my palms.

"I don't know," she breathes. "I like how you make me feel. You make me forget everything else exists."

"You make me feel the same." I press my lips down hard on hers and suck her bottom lip between my teeth. "I want you to forget everything." *Everything. Even what you don't know yet.*

As she kisses me, her hands move from my neck and slowly slide down my arms.

With her wearing heels I can kiss her without having to bend down, and I take advantage of that fully, devouring her lips and reaching behind her to grab her ass.

I turn her away from me and then spin us both around, bending her over the table as she gasps in surprise with the sudden change in position. I push my leather jacket across the table next to her head. "You can use that to muffle your screams," I say, admiring her body bent over the hard surface, her lean leg muscles taut, her perfect, round, naked ass peeking out from under the short, tight dress.

"Keep your hands flat on the table," I say, giving her ass a quick slap, loving how her tight flesh bounces. "You look hot as fucking hell dressed like a slut, but you aren't one, are you?"

"No."

"And you're not going to act like one, are you?"

"Only with you."

I'm glad she can't see the smile that crosses my face. "Ah. So you *are* learning." I stroke her ass and push her dress up further until it's around her waist.

"Tell me how many men you've been with."

"Excuse me?" Her head turns towards me.

I stroke her inner thigh, my hand inching closer to her pussy. "How many men have you fucked?" I raise my voice slightly and tighten my grip on her thigh. "If you make me repeat myself I'll spank you. How many times do we have to go over that?"

"Three."

"Ever?" I ask, surprised. I pull my hand away and rest it gently on her back. *Damn.* I don't think I know any women that have only been with three men.

"No, yesterday," she says sarcastically. "Yes, ever. Geez."

I smack her butt hard. "Don't be a smart-ass."

"Then don't act shocked that I'm not one of the whores you're used to."

"Am I the third?"

"Yes."

Well, shit. This bit of news musters up the animal in me. She's the closest thing to a virgin I've ever been near.

"So, just Jason and Nick? That's it?"

"And you."

"How many times with Jason?"

"Seriously? Are we sixteen?"

I spank her again. "This is important to me, so just fucking answer."

She lets out a sigh. "Once."

"Wow."

"How many women have you been with?" she asks, turning her head in my direction.

"You don't really want me to answer that, do you?"

"No."

"Does it make you jealous?" Standing behind her, I continue caressing her thighs, the head of my dick pressing against the crevice of her ass.

"Yes. Very much."

I lay over her, my chest against her back, my cock shoved further against her ass.

"How does it feel knowing you're the only one I'll be fucking from now on?"

"Scary."

I kiss her shoulder quickly and pull away a bit, not expecting that answer. "Scary?"

"What happens when you get bored of me?"

Pushing her hair to the side, I trail kisses to her neck, sucking on her flesh as I go, leaving red marks. I wedge my cock deeper between her ass cheeks.

"That will never happen." I reach down between us and guide my cock into her dripping wet pussy. I think my words turn her on. Or maybe it's just my voice. Either way, she responds exactly as I want her to and melts for me. Pushing myself off her back, I stand straight and pull my cock all the way out, then slowly glide it all the way in again to the hilt, my balls pressed against her lips. I stroke in and out of her slowly, her pussy milking my cock with faint, wet suction sounds.

Pulling out, I dip my finger into her wet cave and spread her juices up between her ass cheeks around her puckered flesh, gently pushing the tip of my finger inside. She arches up quickly but I'm faster than her, and quickly push her back down.

"No!" There's fear in her voice and her entire body tenses up beneath me.

I rub a gentle circle around her quivering hole. "'No' doesn't work here," I growl. "I want you."

"Please, I don't want to do that."

I press the glistening head of my cock against her ass and push a tiny bit, my heart racing with desire for her.

"Vandal, please . . ." she begs, her voice cracking.

"You'll love it if you let me." I push a little harder, spreading her more.

Before I can react, she's straightening up, knocking me backwards, and scuttles over to the other side of the table.

No one ever says no to me. Containing my anger, I stare her down. She could have just used the safe word if she really wanted me to stop, so I think she's testing me to find out what she can get away with.

"Get back over here," I say pointing down to the spot in front of me that she just vacated.

"No."

I run my hand through my hair, annoyed. "If I have to chase and catch you, you're not going to like it, Tabi."

"Are you going to force me?" She looks beautiful, her hair rumpled, her makeup smeared across her teary face, her dress hanging off her body. I love how she looks ruined just as much as when she is perfect. Maybe even more, because pretty is smoke and mirrors. Destroyed is real.

"Force is a gray word in this world, darlin'. You know that. You gave yourself to me, right?"

She nods and licks her lips, her eyes locking onto mine. "Yes."

"You can use the safe word if it's a hard line for you. I'm not a rapist."

"I know."

"Come here, then."

She slowly comes back to stand in front of me, wobbling on the high heels like a little girl playing dress-up. I pick her up effortlessly and sit on her on the table in front of me, spreading her legs so I can stand between her thighs.

"I guess you've never done that with the two before me?"

She shakes her head. "No. Obviously."

"You're scared of it?"

"Yes. You're too big." She glances down uneasily at my still-hard dick. Which is huge, by the way.

I suppress my laugh because I can see that she's legit petrified.

"Why didn't you just use your word? You know I can force you if you don't use it. If you're really mine, I can take what I want and you give it. That's how it works."

She touches my chest hesitantly. "I know that, and I agreed to it. I want to make you happy. I don't want you to be disappointed in me. I'm just scared. Lara said it hurts. A lot." She gulps. "But if you really want it, then I'll do it for you."

*Fuck*. What can I say to that?

If she were anyone else, I would slam her down on the floor and do what I want, like I always have. I would take what I want and not give two fucks how she felt or if it hurt her and split her apart. I would prove that I was in control and that her feelings didn't matter to me. But I can't do that to her, because she's willing to let me do anything to her, just to make me happy, even if it means she has to endure pain and fear to give me what I want. Because she loves me.

*And I love her.*

"You're changing everything for me," I say slowly, my voice husky.

"Is that really such a bad thing, Vandal?"

I look into her eyes and wrap her legs around my waist. "I have no fucking idea anymore." I pull her head to me and crush my lips against hers, ramming my cock into her at the same time. She tightens her thighs around me and snakes her arms around my neck. She's rattling my cage so fucking hard. She doesn't just take down my walls, she picks my locks and pulls a massive break-and-enter on me.

# chapter twenty

TABITHA

*Tabi,*

*My brother is coming today. Ya-fucking-hoo.*

*I've never been with a girl in front of my friends or family before.*

*I want a relationship with my brother. This is important to him. He's bringing his new girlfriend.*

*I really don't want them to know what kind of relationship we have or how we met. I don't think they would understand, so let's keep that between us.*

*Help me do this right.*

*I promise not to fuck you on the table until they leave.*

I cover my mouth and giggle. I love when his cute side shows up.

I open the gift box and find an outfit that makes me squeal. Skinny jeans, little black boots, a black leather belt, white lace tank top and a flowy black top. In a small gift bag is a necklace with a pendant that looks as if it's made of stained glass, in the shape of a heart. It's gorgeous.

Normal girl clothes! Squee!

I pick up the journal and the pen.

*Vandal,*

*I will always help you do what's right and I am honored to meet your brother.*

*These clothes are amazing! And this necklace is wow!*

*Today, I love you more.*

*Tabi*

I give him a big hug when I find him out on the back deck cleaning the barbecue grill.

"I love everything," I say, beaming. "Everything fits perfectly. How do you manage to buy clothes for me that fit so well? It's baffling. I can't go shopping without trying a million things on, and I'll end up buying two things that actually fit."

He grins, obviously proud of himself. "I know every inch of you, inside and out." Looking me up and down in my new outfit, he raises his eyebrows in approval. "You look sweet. I can't wait to rip it all off you later."

I check him out when he goes back to cleaning the grill with a big, gnarly brush. He's wearing dark jeans, a gray thermal shirt that outlines his chiseled chest, back, shoulders, and arms, and black motorcycle boots. His jet-black hair is straight and shiny in the sun. He's nervous about Lukas coming, but I'm really not quite sure why. There must be more to it than just him not being comfortable around people with a woman he's in a relationship with.

"What can I do to help?" I ask, rubbing my hand on his back. "I could dice up some of that fresh fruit we have."

"Yeah, that would be nice. Lukas is bringing steaks and teriyaki chicken kabobs and some other stuff. We have soda, beer, wine, juice, and water. It's just two of them; she's not bringing her son."

I look at him, surprised at the mention of her having a son. "I didn't know his girlfriend had a kid."

He nods. "Yeah, two kids, actually. She's much older than him. Older than me, actually. Like, upper thirties. A cougar." He laughs, shaking his head, and I wonder how old he is. He looks to be about early thirties. "I think her kids are seven and eighteen. She's a good person . . . like you, but she's kinda in a mess right now with her husband, and Lukas is all fucking crazy about her. They're still trying to figure shit out. I told Lukas I didn't have a problem with her bringing her son but he thinks having a kid around is going to upset me. Especially Tommy. Katie was all gaga about him."

He looks off out at the lake and takes a deep breath. "Some days I almost feel normal," he admits, glancing back over to me. "I can get through the day without wanting to drink to numb the pain. Some days I can think about her without fuckin' losing it. A few times, I've been able to remember something cute she did and I can actually smile about it."

I touch his hand. "I know, Vandal. I feel the same. I still have some really hard days, but they are lessening. And that doesn't mean we're forgetting them. Our hearts are healing. One day while I was at the cemetery, right after Nick died, an old woman came up to me, and she said something I've been trying so hard to hold on to. She said, 'You're not dead. You get to live. You get to love. And it won't be easy, but it's our gift in this world to be able to feel again.'"

Narrowing his eyes at me, he leans against the wood railing of the deck. "I get that. And I *do* want to live my life." He looks down at his boots, his jaw clenching tightly. "I just don't want to ever forget her, ya know?"

I do know, because I struggle with that too, but it's different for me. I lost my husband, and now I'm trying to move on with another man. The guilt is hard to get over. I don't want to ever forget Nick, but it's hard to move on without feeling as if I'm replacing him, and it's hard to try to keep his memory alive without feeling as if I can't let go of him, and let myself having feelings for Vandal.

"You won't ever forget her, Vandal. You're allowed to be happy, and still remember her. You can have both."

He pulls me against his chest and wraps his arms around my waist. "So can you," he replies.

I go up on my toes and kiss his cheek. "I'm trying," I say. "And I'm really proud of you for not drinking again. You're stronger than you think you are. I'm going to go cut up that fruit now."

Just as I'm putting all the fruit into a pretty glass bowl the doorbell rings, my stomach fluttering with nerves as Vandal goes to the front door. I'm overcome with a bit of a surreal feeling. Meeting another man's family is not something I ever thought I would be doing. At one time I was very close to Nick's parents and his brother, and I considered them family. Since the accident, I've pulled away from them because being around them hurts too much and reminds me of all the family holidays and good times we spent together that I'll never experience again.

From the kitchen, I see Vandal open the front door and a very good-looking, young guy comes in with a pretty girl. They both hug Vandal, which catches me off-guard. I was expecting fist bumps or back-slaps between him and Lukas, not a long hug.

They make their way into the kitchen where Vandal takes the shopping bag away from his brother and sets it on the counter.

"Hey, guys, I want you to meet Tabitha." He moves to stand next to me. "Tabi, this is my brother, Lukas, and his girlfriend, Ivy."

Lukas extends his hand out to me, which is covered in tattoos, even his fingers. "Hey, it's great to finally meet you," he says. I smile at him and take his hand, and I have to admit I'm a little enthralled.

He looks a lot like Vandal, only with shorter, black hair that reaches to his shoulders. They both have the same dark eyes, and are both muscular and covered in tattoos, but Vandal is a few inches taller. Vandal also has a dark sexuality about him, whereas Lukas has an adorable boyish charm that is a lethal combination with his bad boy, sexy look.

"It's nice to meet you," I reply, and then turn to Ivy quickly because I feel Vandal's eyes on me, watching me look at his brother. "It's great to meet you," I say. She smiles warmly at me and gives me a hug, immediately making me feel comfortable with her. She's pretty, in a sweet, unassuming way. She's about my height, her long cherry-brown hair parted on the side and pulled over one shoulder, and she's dressed casually in jeans and a pink cashmere sweater. I have that feeling you get around certain people where you just know you are going to become friends.

"You, too. We've heard so many great things about you. We bought a ton of food. These guys eat like mad," she says with a teasing smile and bright eyes.

We all go out onto the back deck and make ourselves comfortable around the table, while Vandal puts some music on that pipes through the outdoor speakers and then unwraps the food and places assorted steaks and chicken kabobs on the grill.

"I have my violin in the car. If I can talk my bro into it, we'll jam a little after dinner," Lukas says, cracking open a soda.

Vandal grins and shakes his head while he pokes at the food on the grill. "I knew you were gonna corner me."

"I would absolutely love to hear you guys play. Vandal says you're amazing," I say to Lukas.

Ivy's face lights up. "Wait 'til you hear them play, Tabitha. I could listen to Lukas play the violin for hours. The first time I heard him perform, my mouth about hit the floor. And I didn't even know he played." She slaps his arm playfully. "He took me to hear the band, telling me his cousins and brother were in the band, but he didn't tell me that he plays guest cameos on some of their songs. So we're sitting in the club listening to them perform, and Lukas gets up to use the men's room, or so I thought, and next thing I know, he's on stage."

"Oh, wow!" I exclaim. "What an awesome surprise!"

Ivy leans against Lukas and he kisses her head. "It really was so cool," she says. "That's the first night I met all of them, and Evie, too. That was before she and Storm were together, and Asher was making fun of her on stage about the blizzard, and I thought she was gonna die because she was there with her boyfriend."

"Asher's an asshole," Vandal interjects, still standing over the grill.

Lukas rolls his eyes behind Vandal's back. "No, he's not, he was just joking around."

"What happened with a blizzard?" I ask, confused. If my memory is right, Evie is the girl that was here the first morning I stayed here, and she's the one who gave Sterling to Vandal. I shake my head, remembering how jealous I'd felt, thinking they were involved. I guess she really is Vandal's cousin's fiancée, from the sounds of it.

Ivy leans towards me and touches my arm. "It's kind of a long story, but Evie was driving in a snow storm and her car got stuck, and Storm, who's Lukas's and Vandal's cousin, came along and offered her a ride, and then he crashed *his* truck." She takes a bite of fruit and chews before continuing. "They were stuck on the side of a mountain road in the blizzard for an entire weekend together, and they fell in love, even though Evie had a boyfriend already."

"They didn't fall in love, they fucked like rabbits in the back of that truck," Vandal yells over his shoulder.

"Vandal!" Ivy scolds. "They did not! Evie isn't like that! She told me they didn't have sex until months later."

Lukas and Vandal start to crack up. "Poor fuckin' Storm finally meets a chick and it takes him months to hook up with her," Lukas jokes.

"They did fool around though," Ivy says, grinning knowingly at me. "She was crazy about him, but she was living with her boyfriend and they'd been together since high school. He was a jerk though, and treated her like crap. She finally left him for Storm."

"Evie is annoying as fuck," Vandal spouts, turning around to smile at us. It's nice to see him joking around and having fun.

"Vandal!" Ivy scolds again, shaking her head. "She is not." She looks at me. "Vandal hates everyone."

"Everyone is hated until proven likable," Vandal advises. "Did you see the cat she gave me? He has no eyes."

Lukas chokes on his soda. "What the fuck?"

"He's adorable. He's inside," I tell them. "Vandal loves him. I do, too, he's such a cuddle bunny."

"No eyes?" Lukas repeats. "For real?"

Vandal walks over to the table and stands behind me, putting his hands on my shoulders. His fingers are warm from standing over the grill. "Fuck yeah, no eyes," Vandal says. "Apparently some kids hurt him. He's awesome though; he plays and acts like a normal cat. I love that little fucker. He eats like a pig. Good thing we're eating out here or he'd be trying to steal the food right off our plates."

"We have to check him out after we eat," Lukas says.

I touch Vandal's hand on my shoulder and he gives me a gentle squeeze.

"So how did you two meet?" Ivy inquires, smiling at us.

I open my mouth to answer but Vandal beats me to it. "We bumped into each other at a cafe and she spilled coffee on me. I thought she was cute so I asked her to go for a ride on the bike, and I brought her here."

"And you never left?" Lukas questions me with a skeptical glint in his eye.

I squirm in my seat. "Um . . . no. I kinda needed a vacation and he asked me if I wanted to stay here with him, so I did."

Ivy gapes at us. "Wow! I think that's great. Sometimes we just *know*."

"Van, I have to say I've never seen you look so un-miserable. You actually seem happy. It's about time."

"Tabi's just what I needed, I guess." He squeezes my shoulders again and goes back to the grill to check on the food, but Lukas's eyes stay on me for a few moments, and I get the feeling he's trying to piece our story together and figure us out.

"Tabi, go get some plates, please?" Vandal says. "The food is ready."

"I'll help." Ivy jumps up and follows me into the house. "Can I see the cat?" she asks once inside. "I'm a cat-lover myself."

"Sure, let's go find him. He's probably asleep on the bed. It's his favorite place."

I head down the hall and she follows me into the bedroom, and sure enough, Sterling is sprawled out at the foot of the comforter. I gently pick him up, kiss his forehead and he purrs instantly. I've never met a cat that just loves to be held so much.

"Here . . . he likes to be cuddled." I hand him to her and she holds him like a baby, and he just flops in her arms, purring.

The smile on her face warms my heart. "My God . . . he is so cute. I could just eat him up. The poor little baby, how could someone hurt him?" She snuggles him against her.

"I know; it's terrible. But he's got a great life now. We spoil him rotten."

She smiles at the cat and then turns to me, lowering her voice. "Vandal seems to really like you. It's nice to see him smile."

"He's kinda closed about his feelings sometimes, but I'm pretty head over heels for him."

"He's been through so much . . . Give him time. I know he can be difficult, but I really don't think he would let you stay here if he weren't serious. Vandal doesn't do relationships, from what I've heard, so he must really be interested."

I take a deep breath. "I've been through a lot, too . . . My husband passed away recently."

She touches my arm. "Oh, Tabitha, I'm so sorry. I didn't know."

"It's okay, really. I'm doing much better. Vandal has helped me so much. I'm just taking it one day at a time."

"Trust me, I know the feeling. I've had my share of shit lately, too. My life is pretty much upside-down." She lays Sterling gently on the bed. "Let's go get those plates before the guys think we ran away."

When Ivy and I join the guys outside again, Vandal eyes me like a hawk and lifts his chin up at me, which I take as a gesture for me to go to him.

"Did you get lost?" he asks. His eyes are dark and his Dom tone is in full force.

I hand him a plate. "No. Ivy wanted to see Sterling."

"What did you tell her?" he asks softly, so his brother and Ivy can't hear.

"About what?"

"Us."

"Nothing. She said we look happy and they're happy for us."

"I don't want them to know about the D/s."

My heart skips. "I wouldn't tell them about that. Do you really think I would talk about that casually to people I just met?"

"No. I'm just making sure, because it's very private."

"Agreed. Now stop it. You're surrounded by people that care about you. No one is out to get you or pry into your life."

He leans down and whispers in my ear, "I'm going to fuck you so hard later." He kisses my cheek and I grab two plates piled with food and bring them over to the table.

"I'm starving," Lukas says.

"You are *always* hungry. You're worse than my kids," Ivy replies.

Vandal brings the rest of the food over and takes his seat next to me, then pulls my plate closer to his.

"You'll love this teriyaki chicken," he says to me, cutting it up into small pieces for me, as he does every night when we have dinner. I honestly don't know why he does it, and I feel as if it's one of those things that I just shouldn't question. We ignore Ivy and Lukas's odd sideways glances at us.

"So, Van, I had to fire Dana," Lukas says between bites of steak.

"Who the hell is Dana?" Vandal slides my plate back over to me, my food now cut into tiny pieces and arranged neatly around the plate.

Lukas glares at his brother with slight annoyance. "The receptionist at the tat parlor? The girl that makes all the appointments and makes people pay us?"

"Oh. Why'd you fire her?"

"She was sleeping with the customers."

"So?"

"Vandal," Ivy says, "You guys have one of the best reputations in the state for having not only two of the most talented artists, but also being the cleanest and most professional parlor. You can't have someone that unprofessional at the forefront."

Vandal raises a suspicious eye at Lukas. "Did you bang her?"

Lukas slams his fork down. "Fuck no."

"Neither did I. Hire someone else then who's not going to blow our clients."

"Great plan," Ivy says, and we smile across the table at each other. I don't think either one of us wants a slutty girl working where our men are all day.

After dinner, Lukas goes out to his car to get his violin and Vandal grabs his acoustic bass and we sit out back with tiki torches lit. It's hard not to swoon at the sight of these two brothers sitting side by side, the torches casting a warm glow over their muscled, tattooed arms, with their silky black hair falling over their eyes. Lukas raises the bow and slowly glides it down the strings, his eyes closed as a haunting sound floats from his violin. I hold my breath listening to him, completely captivated, the way he sways slowly as he plays, so fluid in his motion, as if he is one with the beautiful wooden instrument. He pauses for a moment and Vandal strums his bass, the deep sound resonating straight through me, his hands moving up and down the strings seductively, occasionally tapping the side of the wood. I watch his hands, the way they move so confidently, slow then fast, much like they touch and play my body. Lukas comes in again and they play together in perfect unison, a dark duet that is half metal and half classical.

Ivy and I are both entranced, watching them play, the raw sexuality and talent of these men sucking us both in like a vacuum. I'm sure Ivy is under the same trance with Lukas as I am with Vandal, powerless to fight it. I cross my legs as the familiar tingling manifests between my thighs while I watch the man I'm in love with, his head slightly bent towards the guitar, long hair hanging down his chest, fingers stepping up and down the strings. Everything about him pulls me and makes me want him more and more, like an undeniable magnet.

I cannot imagine the insane effect these guys must have on the female fans. The girls must be literally drooling over them, ovaries exploding with a mere glance from either brother. Vandal never talks about the band or his future plans, so I'm left to wonder if we stay in a relationship, how much of his life is dedicated to the band and the tattoo parlor, and how that will affect us. I'm not quite sure how I'll feel knowing that hordes of women will be gawking at him, getting wet over him, offering themselves to him, wanting nothing in return except to be able to say they hooked up with him. Will he resist them and remain committed to me? Or will he eventually end up cheating and want to be free to have a variety of women? I could never share him or accept him being with another woman.

Night comes, and I catch Vandal eyeing me with that lustful gaze he gets when he wants me. I'm sure I must have the same look in my own eyes after watching him play because I feel incredibly turned on and woozy, almost drunk from the music, mixed with the sexiness the brothers ooze.

Lukas puts his violin down. "We should get going," he says. "It's getting late."

"You guys can crash here if you want," Vandal suggests, surprising me. "You could stay in the guest room."

Lukas closes up his violin case. "I wish we could, but we can't, man. Ivy has a sitter at the house with Tommy."

"Ah. Gotcha."

Ivy helps me clean up the table, and the guys extinguish the torches and grab their instruments, then we all go inside to say goodbye. I'm glad the guys had a good day together, and I hope this is the start of them strengthening their bond.

"I'm just gonna use the restroom," Ivy says.

"Sure. It's down the hall to the right," I tell her, not sure if she's ever been here before. Vandal disappears down the hall to put his bass away, and Lukas turns to me in the living room and grabs my hand, turning my wrist over. I have slight red marks on my wrists from the ribbons that Vandal ties me with, which fade but come back again since he ties my wrists several nights per week.

"Is he tying you?" he asks, his voice lowered.

I pull my hand away. "That's none of your business."

He shakes his head. "Yeah, you're right. But you seem like a sweet girl. Just be careful what you're getting into. I don't want to see either of you get hurt. If he's got you living here, doing this with you, he's not going to just let you go."

"I don't want to go."

He stares at me and then tilts his head slowly, his brow furrowing. "What's your last name?" he asks.

"What?" I ask, confused. "It's Bennett. Why?"

His face pales. "I thought you looked familiar. Do you know who I am? Do you remember me?"

"Um . . . Vandal's brother? Have we met before?" He doesn't look at all familiar to me. I would never forget a man that looked like him.

He opens his mouth and then clams up when Vandal and Ivy come into the room.

"What's going on?" Vandal asks, eyeing us.

"Vandal, can I talk to you real quick?" Lukas asks. "I need to talk to you about the shop."

"So call me tomorrow." He yawns. "I'm tired."

Lukas's face is hard. "No. We have to talk about it now." He turns to Ivy. "I'll be right back, babe."

Ivy and I watch as they walk through the kitchen and out the back sliding doors, Lukas with his hand gripping Vandal's arm. Something is definitely up.

"Is everything all right?" she asks me, looking just as confused as I feel.

"Yeah, I hope so."

# chapter twenty-one

VANDAL

Lukas is tripping out, practically dragging me through the house. As soon as we get outside, I pull my arm from his death grip.

"Dude, what's going on?" I ask him.

He points to the house. "Do you know who that is?"

"Who? What are we talking about?"

"Tabitha. Tabitha *Bennett*?"

He knows.

*He fucking knows.*

I stare him down, my breathing getting deeper as my heart thumps harder, like a drum.

"Leave it alone, Lukas. Go home," I say, my voice like ice.

He looks at me with wide eyes. "Leave it alone? Vandal, what are you doing? Have you lost your fucking mind?"

"How do you know who she is?" I demand, fear growing in me at the notion that he may have said something to her while I was out of the room. She could be in the car with Ivy right now, waiting to get far away from me.

He crosses his arms and stares up at the moonlit sky, and then turns to me slowly. "I was there the night of the accident. I saw her, at the hospital. I think she was in shock; the nurse left her in the hallway on a gurney, all bloody and banged up, right next to me. I was waiting for someone to tell me what was going on with you. It was total chaos."

"You didn't tell her, did you?" I ask, stepping closer to him. "Just now, when you were with her?"

"So, she really doesn't know who you are?"

"No. She has no idea," I admit.

He paces across the deck, shaking his head, and comes back to stand in front of me again. "You can't do this. *Why* would you do this?"

"It wasn't planned. I met her by accident at the cemetery. She was a fucking mess, just like me. She was falling apart at her husband's grave. I saw her there a few times, and the last time, I couldn't stay away from her. Everything after that just kinda happened."

"Kinda happened?" he repeats. "I can't believe this. I thought you were getting better. I thought you were happy and finally found someone normal to be with, and that you were going to just not be so . . . fucking dysfunctional. And now I find out *this*. You really do create your own disasters, Van."

"I *am* happy, Lukas. And so is she. And look who's talking. You're no better than me. You're just as fucked up as I am."

"She's happy because she doesn't know you were part of the fucking accident that killed her husband. Vandal, come on." I look towards the house to make sure the girls aren't watching us from a window. "You can't do this shit," Lukas continues. "And for the record, I *am* better than you. I would never deceive someone like this. It's cruel."

"She loves me," I say, but I know it's a weak excuse because Lukas is right—I shouldn't be treating her this way.

"You're fucking tying her up with your sick shit. I saw her wrists; they're all red."

I grab his throat and push him up against the house. "I am *not* sick," I seethe, and quickly let him go before I hurt him. "You don't know anything about it or what we have. She's here willingly. She doesn't judge me. She wants it. She wants *me*."

He shakes his head and lowers his eyes away from me as he rubs his throat.

"Lukas, don't fuck with me. You don't understand. I can't lose her. I've never cared about any woman like I do for her. She's everything I've always wanted. She gets me. She really loves me." He sighs and backs up a few steps. "I'll tell her someday, but not now. She's not ready yet, and neither am I. Just let us be fucking happy for a little while."

"Vandal, this will never work. When she finds out, she's going to freak the fuck out. You can't lie to people like that."

"I *will* tell her, just not today. I need more time."

"Time to do what?" he questions, throwing his hands up in the air.

"To make her happy, and show her who I really am, so maybe she can forgive me."

He shakes his head angrily. "I don't know, man. This is so fucking wrong. She's a nice girl, and you're fucking with her mind and her heart. Do you even love her?"

Grinding my teeth, I take my time answering him. "Yeah, I think I do."

He runs his hand through his hair, just like I do when I'm distraught. "Okay, look, I want you to be happy. You know that. You've had a shit fucking life and I think you need someone like her to love you and fucking help you get your shit together, like Ivy has done for me. I know what that feels like. But you cannot hurt Tabitha, Vandal." He grabs my shoulders and gives me a little shake, forcing me to meet his eyes. "Promise me you'll tell her soon. If you really care about her and love her, you have to come clean. Sooner or later, she's gonna find out. You can't hide her here forever."

"I know." *But I want to.*

"You could tell her now, while we're here," he suggests. "It might help, make it easier to have us here as a buffer or whatever. And if she freaks out, I'll take her home."

Rage rises up in me again at the thought of him taking her away from me, taking her home to a dark, lonely house that is just going to depress her. "No. Fuck no. Not today."

He sighs with exasperation. "Fine. I'm not going to fight with you. We had a nice day today. I noticed you didn't have one drink and I'm proud of you for that. I'd like to have some more days like this. Just think about what you're doing, okay? Think about *her.* Lies lead to more lies. You'll never dig yourself out. If she really loves you, she'll be able to forgive you. Maybe not right away, but eventually. You have to let that be *her* choice, not yours."

I rub my temples as my head starts to throb. "I know, I know. Please, no more."

"Are you still getting headaches from the accident?" he asks, concerned.

"Sometimes, when I get stressed out like this."

"You should see the doctor. Don't fuck around with a head injury."

I wave him away. "I'm fine. You should go. The girls are probably having fits about us hiding out here."

"It would be good for Ivy and Tabitha to become friends. Ivy is really sweet and she lost a lot of friends after the split with her husband because they're married to friends of her husband and all that shit, and they don't like me. She would be a good friend to Tabitha, especially if shit goes down and she needs someone to talk to."

*Shit goes down.*

As in when Tabi freaks out when she learns that I crashed my car into hers and killed the one man she loved more than anything.

I can't get to Tabi fast enough after Lukas and Ivy leave. I pull her to me and kiss her roughly, raping her mouth with mine, my tongue twisting around hers as I pull her blouse off and tug the white tank top down to expose her naked chest. I cup her breast in my hand and squeeze her hard, her nipple immediately stiffening against my palm. Dipping my head down, I suck her into my mouth, swirling my tongue around her nipple before biting it between my teeth while my hands work on removing her belt and then her jeans. I tug them down with her panties and force her out of her shoes, pulling her pants off. Fisting her hair, I twist her around and bend her over the credenza next to the front door, kicking her legs apart with my foot. I lick my fingers and slide them across her pussy, moistening them before I plunge into her, accidentally slamming her head into the wall. I pull her head up by her hair and bend down over her body, turning her head to kiss her.

"Sorry, sweetness," I rasp in her ear.

"Don't be," she comes back, breathless and panting. "Don't stop."

A wave of carnal desire floods me hearing her words and I pound into her wet slit harder and deeper. I want to fuck her apart, crawl inside of her and own every single inch of her. I pull her up off the credenza and turn her around, lifting her up and shoving her against the wall. Her legs wrap tight around my waist and she whimpers like a kitten as my cock slides back into her swollen, waiting folds. Linking her hands in mine, I stretch them above her head against the wall and seek out her baby-doll lips, kissing her long and deep, our teeth gnashing against each other.

"Can I . . ." she gasps against my mouth.

"Can you what?" I let her body slide down a few inches, so I can stroke into her with more force.

"Can I come?" Her voice is sweet, an angel's voice saying a whore's words. *I love it.*

"Yes, darlin'. You should come right now."

And she does, because she does everything I want and need and ask for. And all of that fuels me and drowns out Lukas's accusations and his visible disgust in my mind. She clenches and grips my shaft, her juices drenching me. Releasing her hands, I slide mine down her sinewy body to grip her ass, pulling her away from the wall and holding her body up with my arms as I bounce her up and down on my rock-hard cock. Her hands grip my shoulders and she kisses and bites my neck as I shoot inside of her.

"Don't stop biting me. I fucking love that."

Of course she does as she's told. I carry her to the couch and fall on top of her, spreading her legs and driving back in. I fuck her for hours, and soon the sun is coming up, and she's raw and exhausted and almost incoherent from orgasm overload, but I still don't want to stop. I can keep going for hours more if I want to.

"Vandal . . . please . . ." she breathes, pushing me away. "I can't anymore."

"Do *not* push me away from you. Ever." I pull her leg up, wrapping it around my waist as I roll onto my side next to her.

"You've been fucking me non-stop since your brother left. Are you okay? Did you have a fight or something?"

"No."

"He asked me if I recognized him."

My heart jumps into my fucking throat. "Do you?"

"No. I would remember him."

"What do you mean by that exactly, Tabitha?"

She swallows nervously, and I enjoy the glimmer of fear I see in her eyes. "He's different looking, with the hair and all the tattoos. Like you. I would remember him."

I stare down at her and run my hand slowly up her thigh. "You think my little brother is hot?"

"Vandal, he looks so much like you there is no way I can answer that without it coming out wrong. If I think you're hot, then he would have to be hot, too." Jealousy kicks in but I tamp it down. At least she's being honest. If she had denied being attracted to him I would have known she was lying, and that would bother me even more.

"He's nicer than I am. He doesn't tie up Ivy and fuck her raw."

Rubbing her foot slowly up my naked leg, she locks her gaze onto mine and takes a moment to answer me.

"Poor Ivy," she says, her voice sultry. "She doesn't know what she's missing." She pulls my head down to her and kisses me in that soft, teasing way that drives me wild.

My phone rings late that night, but I'm still awake. *Thinking.* I check the screen and see that it's Sydni.

I slide my finger across the screen and answer. "Yeah?" I lean up a little, keeping my other arm around Tabi, who's sleeping beside me.

"Hey, you asleep?"

"No worries. You okay?"

"Yeah, just crazy busy and I figured if I didn't call you now I'd keep forgetting."

I laugh at her. "I get it. What's going on?"

"Next Saturday night, Sugar Kiss is playing at the Rabbit Hole. We want you to play some A&E songs with us, to get you back on stage a little bit. It'll be fun, like old times."

Excitement floods through my veins thinking about performing again. "Shit, that would be cool."

"So do it."

"Yeah, Syd. That would be fucking great. Text me the details and I'll be there."

"Well, that was easy. The girls will be stoked."

"I'll see ya there."

I end the call and lie awake for a while thinking about how cool my life would be if I could play with Ashes & Embers again *and* have Tabitha in my life. Lukas is right; I can't keep lying to her. Every day is another nail in the coffin. I make up my mind right there that I'm going to take Tabi to the gig next week, slowly get her introduced to my life, and then tell her the truth.

I leave the bed without waking her, pull on some pants, and go downstairs into the basement. I find what I'm looking for in the far corner. Kneeling on the floor, I open the box and suck in a deep breath. I pull out her blanket and a teddy bear and hold them to me, inhaling her scent.

*Fuck, I miss her. So much.*

# chapter twenty-two

TABITHA

"Sugar Kiss?" I repeat, my head in the refrigerator. "I've never heard of them." Closing the door, I pop a grape in my mouth. He's standing across the room, arms crossed, leaning against the wall.

"Are you serious? You're a chick; you should love them. They're an all-girl rock band."

"I told you I mostly listen to new-age music, like harps and flutes."

"Well, hopefully you'll enjoy it if you come. They're good friends of mine. I've known Sydni the longest. She's a bass player, too, and in a few weeks, when my band goes on tour, she's going to be filling in for me. Her band has opened for us a few times, and we've played a lot of gigs together over the years, so we know each other's songs," he explains.

"So, what band are *you* in? I don't think you ever told me." He follows me into the living room and watches me hunt for my e-reader, which I can never find when I want it.

"That doesn't matter," he replies. "I'm on a break from them."

"It matters to *me*. I want to know so I can fan-girl."

"Sit," he says, pointing to the couch. "Now."

I do as he says and look up at him, not understanding why he's all jittery.

"We talked about this, remember? If you're going to come with me, I need you to be discreet. Please don't be telling your friends or posting it on social media or any of that shit."

"I'm not. I was just curious," I reply, pouting a little. "I'm proud of you, that's all. You're in a sorta famous rock band. Well, supposedly." I smile at him playfully. "Do you have groupies and fans?"

"Maybe," he says with a sexy smirk. "You know what the female fans do when they meet me?" He reaches down and strokes my hair.

"What do they do?"

"Anything I ask them to." His eyes are dark and lusty. I don't want to think about fans and groupies and all sorts of women touching him.

"Is that right?"

His hand slides down to caress my neck. "Yes. How do you feel about that? About me fucking other women?"

"It makes me feel sick and jealous," I admit.

"So you think I should give that part of my career up? The benefit of having as many women as I want?"

I nod and answer with confidence. "Yes."

"That seems awfully greedy of you, Tabi. To keep me all for yourself. Doesn't it?"

"Yes."

He strokes his thumb across my lips and I suck it into my mouth, my eyes on his, watching as he sways a little. He pushes his thumb further into my mouth and I suck harder.

"You're my naughty girl, aren't you?"

I nod, and he slowly pulls his finger out of my mouth and licks it.

"Get in your position. I need to go get something."

I go to the floor and kneel, palms down, and wait for him to come back. The anticipation of not knowing what he's going to do makes my pulse quicken and my skin flush.

Thankfully he's not gone long. I watch his feet cross the room, and he sits on the couch.

He taps my shoulder. "Kneel in front of me, Tabicat."

I rise and turn, positioning myself to kneel in front of him, between his legs, keeping my eyes averted as I was taught. I know he loves this, and it doesn't bother me at all to do it.

"I have something very special for you. Look up at me."

I raise my eyes to see him holding a small black box. "I had these custom made for you; I just wasn't sure when I should give them to you. Now seems like a good time."

He pulls what looks like a silver bracelet with little bells hanging off of it out of the box.

"These are slave bells, and this is an ankle cuff. I want you to wear this, I really like the sound they make." He kneels down and fastens it around my ankle. I shake my foot and a faint tinkling sound comes from them, like tiny fairy bells. I love it.

"Vandal, thank you." I lean to kiss him, but he puts his hands up to stop me.

"I have something else for you, but it's very important to me. I need you to think about it before you accept it."

"All right. I promise I will." My curiosity is running rampant. What else could he have in that little box?

His hands are shaking slightly as he lifts the next object out of the purple velvet-lined box. I stare at it, taking in its beauty but also the intense meaning behind it. It's a silver necklace adorned with red crystals embedded in the chain, with a locking silver heart pendant at the center of the chain.

He turns the heart over. "It's inscribed," he tells me, his voice deep with emotion. I squint at the tiny words.

*You are my heart. I am your armor.*

My heart flip-flops. I cannot even speak as he lifts out a tiny key, showing me that it's a real lock. I now know what this is. It's a submissive collar. It's a symbol of commitment and ownership between a Dom and a sub. I know for him this type of commitment is huge.

I can't stop the tears that pool in my eyes and slowly fall down my cheeks. "Vandal . . ." I whisper. I don't know what to say, and even more so, I'm afraid to speak.

"If you accept this, we take things to a deeper level. I want this with you, Tabi, only you. I have no desire to be with someone else, and I want you to feel confident in that. I want you to give yourself to me in every way, and I'll always take care of you and cherish you. I have no doubt in my feelings for you and what I want. The length of time we've known each other doesn't mean shit to me." He fingers the necklace in his hands. "I've been thinking about it, and I want to sell my other house so I can buy a house that you help pick out and feel at home in, if you're open to that. I'd like a dedicated scene room for us, and a studio for you. I don't know how you feel about selling your house—we can talk about all that later. I just want you to know that even though I probably don't show it all in the right ways, I'm serious about this. About us and our someday."

There is a fine line to be walked where we are right now. This is not to be confused with an engagement ring. This is not a marriage proposal. I'm pretty sure there is no hope of having children together. This is a deep sexual and emotional arrangement. And while those other things could possibly be mixed in, I don't think they are in the cards with him.

However, he's offering his own version of forever, that, if I'm honest with myself, I could probably be quite happy with. He's gorgeous, sexy, intelligent, incredibly talented, caring, funny, and knows how to please me. And he can be very loving in his own way. I know in my heart that he would take care of me, and I want to do the same for him now.

Maybe we are just meant to be together, and this is the way it had to happen. I remember what the old woman at the cemetery said to me that day a few months ago: *"Sometimes falling in love can hurt. It's a stumble off a cliff, with a lot of bumps and bruises on the way down, until you land with a heart-stopping crash, not sure if you lived or if it killed you. If you're lucky, that other person is lying on the ground next to you, just as battered and beaten, and you pick each other up and walk off together."*

How did she know?

"Tabi?" He touches my cheek and I slowly come out of the daydream state I was in, my eyes focusing on him. "Is this what you want?" he asks, still waiting for my answer.

"You're not giving me much time to think, Vandal."

"Do you really need to think about it? Or did you know the answer before I even asked?"

"I think *you* knew the answer before you asked," I say back to him. "But just so we're on the same page, the answer is yes."

He places the chain around my neck and uses the tiny key to lock it in place with the heart. I reach up to my throat and touch it lightly while he puts the tiny key in his pocket.

"Thank you, Vandal. It's beautiful."

"*You're* beautiful." He puts his hands on my face, his dark eyes so close to mine, swimming with hope and desire. "Now I'm going to fuck you like I've never fucked anyone else before." My heart lurches and gallops in response.

Swooping me up into his muscular inked arms, he carries me into the bedroom and lays me gently on the plush comforter of his bed. The electric fireplace is burning, making the room warm and amber. He takes my clothes off slowly, kissing each inch of me that he reveals as he goes, tantalizing me with his warm lips. When I'm finally naked, he stands and undresses while I watch him hungrily. I let my eyes wander over his broad chest, down his flat, chiseled abs, to his long, thick cock.

I could stare at him for hours. For a man, he is incredibly beautiful. The way his long hair brushes over his perfect, smooth, dark skin and how his tattoos move with his muscles is mesmerizing. Kneeling on the bed, he climbs on top of me and slowly lowers his body between my parted thighs. His kisses are soft and lingering, dancing on my lips while his hand moves down my body, gentle and caressing. I slide one hand around his waist and up to his shoulder, while my other hand moves down his body to rest on his rock-hard curved ass, pulling him into me. I want to feel him inside of me so badly.

He pushes my hair out of my face and cups my cheek. “Look at me,” he whispers. Opening my eyes, I lock my gaze onto his. “Don’t close your eyes . . . Stay with me.” He slowly eases his cock into me, gentler and slower than I could have ever thought possible for him. My eyes flutter from the sheer ecstasy of feeling him deep inside of me and he rubs his thumb across my eyelid. “Eyes open, Tabicat.”

His kisses grow deeper, his tongue licking mine as he strokes in and out of me, slowly and carefully—every inch felt. I raise my leg and wind it around his waist, locking us together as he moves inside of me, making me drowsy with his gentle, deep rhythm. More and more, he leaves my hands free to touch him when we have sex, and I’ve grown to love it both tied and untied.

He makes love to me for hours, shattering me bit by bit with this new gentle side of him. I have never felt so loved or so adored by a man just from the passion in his kiss or the softness of his touch. This is what I have always longed for and never had, not even with Nick. Vandal has completely touched my soul and captured my heart.

After he falls asleep, I quietly climb out of bed and use the bathroom, then go down the hall to the guest room. Grabbing the journal and pen, I sit on the bed and open it to the next page. I haven’t had a chance to write in it for a few days.

*Vandal,*

*I don't know where this path will lead us or what the future holds for us. But I know that today, in this moment, that I am yours and you are mine. You made a promise and you kept it, and I will be forever grateful to you.*

*I am your heart and you are my armor, always.*

*Love,*

*Tabi*

I pick up Sterling and carry him to the bedroom, crawling into bed next to Vandal. Sterling curls up against me, purring like a little motor. I wish I could sleep, but I am tormented by buried secrets, broken promises, and twisted lies.

# chapter twenty-three

VANDAL

"You're quiet."

She's barely said a word during the drive to the gig. I glance at her in the passenger seat and she looks sexy-as-hell in the outfit I got her of tight jeans, black boots, white sweater, and black silk scarf with white roses embroidered on it. First I had a dress picked out, but I knew I'd never keep my hands or the attention of the other guys at the show off her, so jeans seemed safer. As usual she is completely oblivious as to how sexy and cute she looks.

Reaching across the console, I grab her hand and realize her wedding band and engagement ring aren't on. She's worn them every day since we met, and even though it bugged the shit out of me, I obviously wasn't douche enough to say something about it. Taking them off had to be her decision, not mine. I can't help but wonder if she took them off because of a commitment to me, or if she is just being respectful to me by not looking married while we're out in public. Not that it would be the first time I'd be seen with a married woman, but this is different. *She's* different.

She smiles over at me in the dim light of the car. "I feel kinda nervous. Will it be a big crowd?"

"No, this is a small, private venue. I'm only playing three songs, so I won't be on stage too long. Lukas is gonna stop by, too; he'll hang out with you."

"Ivy, too?"

"No, they had a fight."

"Oh no. They didn't break up, did they?"

I shrug. "I don't think so. I'm sure they'll figure it out; they have some issues to work on. Lukas isn't the type to give up."

"Are you?" she asks, squeezing my hand.

"No. I'm not a quitter at anything."

When we get to the Rabbit Hole, I grab my bass out of the back seat and a bouncer lets us in through the private side door to avoid the crowd.

"Hey, Van, been a long time. Good to see you," the bouncer says, nodding his head in greeting at us. I don't recognize the guy at all, but I fist bump him anyway and pretend I remember him as we head down the hall.

I stop in the hallway before we go any further and pull Tabi into me. "You should know, I've fucked every girl in Sugar Kiss at some point."

Her mouth falls open in total shock mixed with disgust. "What? You could have warned me, and maybe worded that a little nicer."

"It was just party stuff; I wasn't involved with them. But we're all friends. I told Sydni that I was in a relationship last time I saw her. So if the girls are kinda flirty, just ignore it, okay? They're used to me being a certain way, and it's going to take a while for people to get used to me not being like that."

"You really could have told me this before. Won't this be awkward?"

"No."

"It is for me. They're probably all gorgeous and sexy and perfect, right?"

I probably shouldn't have told her the truth. So much for me trying to be honest and open. She literally looks green with jealousy. Or nausea. Or both, most likely.

"Hey, you're my Tabicat, right? Who's got the collar on?"

Her eyes go soft and she smiles shyly. "Me," she murmurs.

"That's right. You're mine. I'm yours. End of story." I kiss her lips. "And *you* are gorgeous and sexy and perfect. And sweet. You have nothing to be jealous about. I don't like jealousy."

She quirks an accusing eyebrow at me. "Really? Since when?"

I grab her hand, ignoring her innuendo about my own jealousy issues. "Let's go."

The VIP room is pretty packed, but we make our way through the crowd to the far corner where the girls are hanging out. I'm stopped a few times along the way to say hey, but I hold on to Tabi's hand and keep moving after a few seconds of talking. She seems even smaller to me in my own element, her five-foot, one-hundred-and-ten pound body almost lost amongst all these people.

"And he made it!" Sydni yells when she sees me. She jumps up and gives me a hug, a drink in her hand.

"Hey, Syd."

"Hey, buddy. And who do we have here?" She smiles at Tabitha. I know that Sydni is genuinely happy for me to have a girlfriend and isn't jealous. She might flirt with me, but I know our friendship will always come first.

"This is Tabitha. Tabi, this is Sydni. She's one of my oldest friends, and a fucking great bass player."

"Nice to meet you," Tabi says, blushing. She's fucking adorable.

"I'm glad you came. I wouldn't believe Vandal had a girlfriend unless I saw her with my own damn eyes. You're absolutely beautiful." Sydni nudges me. "Awesome catch, Van. Hang on to her."

I put my arm around Tabi and pull her closer. "I plan to."

Sydni turns to the other girls and yells over at them. "Hey, ladies, look who's here! Our man, Vandal, with his girlfriend."

There's nothing like having eight eyes of those you've fucked staring at you while you stand next to the woman you're falling in love with. It's not exactly a warm and fuzzy feeling, and for once, I'm not proud of some of the things I've done. Or *whom* I've done, in this case.

All the girls look a little shocked, two of them definitely look a little crazy jealous, but at least they're all friendly and polite to Tabitha, who looks like a baby deer in the headlights. I'm going to have to do something to make up this awkwardness to her, to show her I appreciate how strong she is. I sure as shit wouldn't want to be in a room with a bunch of guys she'd slept with, and would be pretty murderous by the time the night was over if I was.

I pull Tabitha to a couch along the wall and we sit next to Piper, who's got long, razor-edged purple hair, and is probably the cutest and nicest of all these girls in the band. She used to follow me around like a lost puppy when we were going through our thing of screwing on the road.

"I'm Piper," she says to Tabi.

"That's a pretty name. I love your hair!"

Piper beams. "Thanks!"

"Piper is the guitarist," I tell Tabitha, and she nods above the loud voices around us.

"Are you a musician, too?" Piper questions, and Tabitha looks away, biting her lip.

"No, not at all," she finally answers.

"She's a photographer," I say for her.

"Hey, maybe you can take some pictures of me and the girls. We need some for our PR stuff, like the website, or online profiles, all that stuff. We were just talking about this, like a week ago."

"I'd love that. Would that be okay?" she asks me, and yes, it turns me on that she asked me permission.

"Sure, baby. We can talk about that. I think it would be great."

They start to talk about the dynamics of dying hair, and I relax a little with the idea that this might really work out. Maybe there won't be any trauma or crisis to tear my life apart again.

The girls play a few songs before I have to join them, so I lead Tabi to a small table that is off to the side of the stage, hidden from the audience, where she can watch us play without being exposed. She seems less nervous now and excited to be so close to everything that is going on.

"I think you photographing the girls is a great idea," I say. "I think you should pursue that. I'll get you Piper and Sydni's contact info. Actually, I'll talk to Asher about you taking some pictures for us, too."

"Who's Asher again?"

"He's my cousin, and he's like the founder of the band, so he's supposedly our fearless leader. We don't exactly like each other, but I think he'll dig the picture idea."

A smile lights up her face. "Vandal, do you know how exciting that would be? You have no idea how long I've wanted to really focus on my photography."

Seeing her so happy is an awesome feeling. I've seen her photos, and they are really good. Her sitting behind a desk answering a phone is a waste of her talent, so if I can help her achieve her dream, I'm going to do whatever I can to make that happen for her.

"Well, now it's a reality. I know a ton of models and musicians that I'm sure would love to work with you."

She stares at me for a minute and shakes her head slightly in disbelief. "I really am happy, Vandal. I never thought I would be again."

"Neither did I. And this is just the beginning. I've never believed in that meeting-the-right-person shit to change your life, but I feel like the motherfuckin' poster child of it right now."

She throws her head back and laughs, her eyes shining under the lights, her hair bouncing around her face. *I love this chick.*

*I should tell her.*

"What's so funny?" We both turn at the sound of Lukas's voice.

"Hey, man," I say. "Glad you came."

"This place is a zoo. The girls are really getting popular."

"They wicked are. Be careful, if they see you, they may drag you on stage, too."

He takes a sip of his beer. "No fuckin' way. Not tonight. I'm just here to listen." He turns to Tabi. "You havin' fun? You look beautiful."

"I am, and thank you. The girls seem nice, and I'm really liking their music."

"She likes new-age music," I say, nudging her with my arm.

"Nothing wrong with that." Lukas comes to her defense. "I listen to that when I'm just chilling out."

"See?" she says. "You might like it, too, Vandal. I'll play some nice harp music for you later that I have saved on my phone."

"Play him some Native American flute and bring out his inner Indian," Lukas teases.

"Yeah, you're funny," I muse.

Sydni has taken over the mic on stage. "We have a special guest tonight who's going to play a few songs with us!" she yells. The crowd screams. I grab my bass and give Tabitha a quick kiss.

"Stay here with Lukas, okay? Don't wander off. There are a lot of drunk idiots around."

Sydni lets out a woop. "It's my good friend, Vandal fuckin' Valentine, from Ashes & Embers!" The crowd roars as I head onto the stage and it feels great to be in front of an audience again. Sydni greets me with a big kiss on the cheek, which makes the crowd scream even more. I do a mock bow.

"We're gonna do some covers of our favorite Ashes & Embers songs for you guys tonight!"

I start playing the intro to one of our heaviest songs and the girls come in perfectly. Sydni plays by my side in exact time with me. I gotta say, she's good. She's gonna do great on the A&E tour when it starts in a few weeks, and I can't even be pissed about it. Truth is, I could tour now because I haven't been drunk or wasted in weeks, but right now, I'd rather let things be as they are and skip the tour, and focus on getting Tabi settled into a life with me. I never thought I'd ever feel that way about a woman, but fuck it, I do.

The girls prance around the stage in their sexy clothes, flirting with me for the crowd's enjoyment, and I just grin. I've never been a crowd teaser, like Storm, who loves to play with the crowd and get them involved. I just want to play my bass and get lost in the music and the movement of the sea of people. I've been called the quiet, brooding, dark member of A&E, but I don't care. I like it that way.

I glance over to the side of the stage and see Jill talking to Tabitha and Lukas. Jill is like a fucking groupie on steroids that has ingratiated herself into Ashes & Embers and kinda tries to keep us organized at concerts. She's also a big fan of Sugar Kiss. We're all guilty of fucking her at some point, but her main obsession has always been Storm. She started drinking heavily when Storm hooked up with Evie, and she looks pretty wasted tonight, even from where I'm standing. I don't like her near Tabitha when she's intoxicated because Jill is a ruthless bitch who likes to hurt people and cause trouble.

Sure enough, next time I look over, Tabi appears upset and Lukas looks as if he's arguing with Jill. *Fuck*.

I try to ignore whatever is going on with them and focus on enjoying my time on stage with these girls that I've watched grow from a garage band to superstars. Not to mention I don't know when I'm going to get on stage again, and I want to savor this time and not be worried about what kind of shit Jill is starting.

After a few more songs, Sydni drags me to the mic at the center of the stage. "Can I get a huge thank you for the amazing Vandal Valentine for joining us tonight?"

The audience roars and jumps up and down. I flash the peace sign and walk off stage to find Lukas sitting alone to the side.

I hand my bass to one of the roadies I recognize as I turn to Lukas. "Where's Tabi? Did Jill say something to her?"

Lukas shifts his gaze around nervously. "I think Tabi's in the bathroom. Jill came over here drunk and was asking her dumb questions about how she met you and telling her you were an asshole that fucked everything that moved."

I bang my fist on the table. "That fucking whore. What the hell?"

"She also brought up the accident—"

"What? Does she know who Tabitha is?"

"No, she was just saying you crashed into a car a few months ago and killed your daughter, a friend, and a guy in the other car, and that you've been a fucked up mess ever since. Tabi got really upset, and I kept trying to diffuse Jill, but you know how she is. Once she starts, you can't shut her the hell up."

"Fucking bitch!" My mood instantly turns to fury, and I want to wring Jill's neck. I run my hand through my hair. "I need to find Tabitha. Why did you let her go?"

Lukas looks at me as if I'm crazy. "What did you want me to

do? I can't stop her from going to the bathroom. I offered to walk her there but she said no, I didn't want to creep her out."

"Did Jill follow her? Where the hell is she?"

"I don't know. This is what I'm talking about, Van. You can't be lying to her about everything and live like this. You can't keep everyone quiet. Aria paid off as many people as she could to keep quiet—obviously Jill wasn't one of them. Now she's drunk and running her mouth. This is the first time you've been out with Tabitha, and in under an hour, you've got a mess on your hands. Tell her the fucking truth."

"I know, all right? I have to go find Tabi. I don't want her wandering around here upset."

I go off to look for her and find her in the hallway by the restrooms with Jill. I pick up the pace and close the space between us quickly.

"What the fuck is going on?" I demand, my eyes locked on Jill.

"I'm telling your little girlfriend all about you. Someone has to warn her."

"Really? You think because you sucked my dick a few times that you know me?" I ask her, my voice rising. "You're a whore and a drunk. You don't even know what the hell you're talking about."

Tabi touches my arm. "Vandal, please . . ."

"Renee was one of my best friends. You didn't know that, did you, *Alex*?" Jill slurs.

My gut sinks. I had no idea that Renee was friends with Jill. Could the world get any smaller?

I lean closer to Jill. "No, I didn't think you had any friends at all because you're a spiteful bitch," I bark in her ear.

"At least I'm not a murderer," she throws in my face.

I slam my fist against the door next to Jill's head and she jumps. "You better shut your fucking mouth and stay out of my life and away from anyone I'm associated with. You've fucked your way through the band—go find some new victims. You'll be hearing from my lawyer tomorrow about harassing us."

I grab Tabi's hand and drag her down the hall.

"You better run while you can, little girl!" Jill yells after us.

I'm so furious I can't even speak. Tabi is dead quiet as she hangs on to my hand, not saying a word as we grab my stuff and head out to the parking lot. I open the passenger side door and let her in, then go around and get in the driver's seat. I'm afraid to ask her what else Jill told her.

"Are you okay?" I finally ask when we've driven a few miles away and I can't stand the silence any more. She nods but still won't speak. *Shit.*

"Other than that fiasco, did you enjoy the concert?"

She still says nothing.

I try a different angle. "Answer me, Tabi. I won't be ignored by you."

She swallows as she stares out the windshield. "Yes. I thought Sugar Kiss was great. And you . . ." She pauses and I glance over at her. Her eyes are closed tight. "You were amazing. So perfect up there on the stage, like you were born to be there. Your presence is just so . . . intense."

She opens her eyes again and I see a tear shimmering in the corner of her eye. "I really like the hard stuff you played with the girls, but when you played the soft acoustic songs with Lukas that night, that was just so soulful. I loved it. It's like there are two sides of you." Her voice cracks a little at the end.

*She knows.*

Neither one of us talks during the rest of the drive to the house, and the silence is maddening to me. I want to force her to talk, but I'm afraid of what she's going to say. My mind is racing, not knowing what she's thinking, not knowing what she's pieced together. Whatever she says when she finally talks, whatever she does, I deserve it and I'll have to accept it no matter how bad it is.

Once inside the house, she sits on the chair in the living room. Not the couch where I can sit with her, as she usually does, but the lone chair. Actually, I don't think I've ever sat in that chair, and I know from this day forward I will hate the sight of it.

"She called you Alex," she finally says, piercing the long, bloated silence.

"I know. I was adopted when I was five and they changed my name. They didn't like my real name of Vandal. They thought it was strange."

Her voice comes out strained with emotion as she stares at her hands in her lap. "Please tell me it's all just a coincidence. Our accidents happening in the same month. The driver of the other car was named Alex. The little girl crying. You losing your daughter. Us meeting in a cemetery. All your secrecy." She looks at me with pleading eyes. "Tell me you didn't know."

I sit on the couch and take my leather jacket off, the pain in my chest and my head coming on hard from the mention of the little girl crying. *My Katie.*

"Come here," I finally say.

"No."

"Tabi . . ."

With a deep sigh she crosses the room and kneels in front of me, as she's done a hundred times or more, and will probably never do again.

Taking a deep breath, I lift her chin so I can look into her blue eyes that are no longer as bright as they were earlier today. "It was me," I say softly. "I was the driver of the car. It was my fault."

Her entire body starts to tremble and tears spring from her eyes, spilling down her cheeks. "How long have you known?" she chokes out.

"I've known from the day I met you in the cemetery. Actually, before that."

She puts her head into her hands. "The accident killed my

husband, Vandal. It almost killed me. You let me sit here and cry and never said a word."

"I know. I should have told you."

"You made me talk about Nick. Christ, you even questioned me about sex with him. How could you do that, knowing you were part of the accident that caused his death? You touched me. Do you know how sick that is? Didn't you feel any guilt at all for what you were doing?" She shakes her head and a teardrop falls to the floor and disintegrates. *Just like us.*

I hang my head down, knowing she's right. "Yes, I did. You're right, it was a horrible thing for me to do, and I'm sorry."

"Is that all you can say? You're *sorry*?" She slaps me, and I'm stunned for a moment, rubbing my cheek. After a few seconds I lift my eyes to meet hers.

"Yes. I *am* sorry. You don't know how fucking sorry I am. I had no idea what I was doing. I saw you at the cemetery and then I couldn't stop thinking about you. I hated myself for ruining so many lives, including yours. You were happy and loved. And I ruined it." I search for the right words, but they're not coming to me. "I thought I could give it back to you, and make it better."

"Better for who? For you?"

"Better for both of us. To move past it, to not be alone. I wanted you to smile like I saw in your pictures. I wanted to know what it felt like to be the reason for the smile and not the agony."

I hate myself right now more than I ever have, and that's saying a lot. I don't know how to fight or explain myself. I've never had to before; I've never had a reason to. I don't know how to make logical sense of what I do or did, because usually, there isn't any logic in anything I do. I just *do*. There is no way for me to make her understand my behavior when I don't even understand it myself.

She stares at me, unblinking for a long time. She looks as if she's in shock. I know I'm losing her, but I don't know the words to fix this. I only know how to express myself physically, and that's not going to work with what's happening between us right now.

"My husband is dead. You caused the accident? What were you doing when you crashed into us, then? Were you drunk? Screwing around with that girl? I have to know what happened. Did your daughter distract you somehow? Tell me! How did it happen? Why do you think it's your fault?" she demands, her voice rising with every word.

"No . . . none of that. I fell asleep. I was exhausted and shouldn't have been driving. My daughters mother was being a bitch and threatening me if I didn't bring Katie home. I swear that's the truth, Tabitha. I would never drink and drive with Katie, or fool around while I'm driving."

She's staring at me, unblinking, tears still falling from her eyes. "You *fell asleep*? You're sure?" she repeats.

"Yes, I'm sure. I'm sorry. There's nothing else I can say. I'm sorry for all of it. I'm sorry about Nick, and Renee, and Katie." I lift her chin, forcing her to look at me. "I'm sorry I hurt you."

Fresh tears well from her red, puffy eyes. "I told you I loved you, Vandal. I meant that. You've never *once* said it to me. How do you think that feels, on top of everything else? I feel guilty and more alone than I did before."

"You're not alone, Tabi. I'm still here." I pull her against my chest, hoping I can somehow comfort her again.

"I'm so confused right now, I don't even know what to feel. My head is spinning." She twists herself away from me. "I don't want you touching me."

"I'm supposed to be able to touch you whenever I want. You agreed to that. Let me just hold you. You'll feel better. We both will. Please."

"No," she says, backing farther away. "How is it that you can touch me but you can't say the words I need to hear? What's wrong with you?"

*If I only knew the answer to that question.*

I shake my head slowly. "I don't know," I admit. "But whatever is wrong with me, you were making it better. That much I *do* know."

The look in her eyes says it all though. I can't see love or desire or care there at all anymore.

All I see is pain, confusion and regret.

TABITHA

He looks shattered and I have to admit, a part of me likes it. I want to see him suffer. Maybe not a lot, but a little. He can't walk away from this unscathed. I can't let him. I won't get out of this without scars, so neither should he.

"Just because I haven't said it, doesn't mean I don't feel it, Tabi. It matters to *me* that I feel it, because I've never loved a woman before. They've always just been objects for me, and I couldn't control that about myself. It was just who I was and how I felt." Taking a deep breath, he moves in front of me so I have to look at him. "Love came easy for you; you told me that yourself. You and Nick had a happy, easy relationship with rainbows and unicorns without any fucking pain and lies and struggles." He swallows hard. "I've never had that, and I never will. I'm not an easy person. And you're not either, anymore, whether you like it or not. We changed each other. You made me better, and I guess I made you worse, but I *do* love you in the only way that I know how to right now." He lowers his voice and touches my cheek. "I've never said that to anyone except Katie. Please don't take it away from me."

My God, I hate how he can just turn me upside-down. As fast as I put the walls around my heart to protect myself against him, he's already breaking through, baring his soul to me, forcing me to see the man I love, ugly flaws and all. *But if he knew everything about me, would he still be standing here loving me? Or would he feel like I do right now—torn to shreds?*

My entire body sighs and I touch his hand at my cheek and let it stay there for a moment before pulling his hand away. I can't be close to him right now. I need to get far away from him and be alone with the turmoil that's in my head and heart and figure this out.

"I don't know what you did to me, Vandal," I say, my voice softer, void of the fury it held earlier. "How can I even separate this all in my head and figure out what was love and what was control? That's what you do: you control and manipulate and dominate, and it's all wrapped up in this . . . this matrix that is you. You controlled my body and my thoughts. You made me want you, and you made me need you. I don't know if all of that made me love you, too." My voice cracks and I choke back the lump in my throat. "How do I know if it's real love? Maybe my head is just fucked up from being your sub. I gave every part of myself to you and was totally focused on you in every way. I'm not denying that I didn't want it, or that I didn't enjoy it. I went into this willingly," I say, looking up into his pained gaze. "Somehow you took the pain away, just like you said you could, and that's what I needed. But now I'm questioning if I really love you or not. Don't you see that? I don't know if I can trust my feelings."

He looks panicked, eyes wide, grabbing my hands. "Of course you can trust your feelings. Your heart never lies. Gram told me that and she's right about every-fucking-thing. I never manipulated your heart, Tabi. You know that. If anything, I tried to keep that out of it."

"I know, and that hurts even more. You didn't want my love. You didn't want to love me."

He shakes his head, his hair falling into his face. "You're right. And that should tell you something right fucking there. We loved each other, even though neither one of us wanted it. That's real, Tabi. We can't deny that."

I cross my arms, holding myself. "I was depressed and hopeless when I met you in that cemetery. My life was a mess and I didn't care about anything anymore," I'm embarrassed now, admitting how low I had sunk at that point in my depression. "Then you showed up and I just said fuck it, maybe this scary-looking guy will murder me and save me the trouble."

"Tabi . . ."

"But then I became fascinated with you, and I liked how you made me feel. I loved how dangerous you felt. When you touched me, you woke something up inside me. I don't know how to explain it. It all just happened so quickly, like a switch being flipped, and it seemed better than being dead, or wallowing in depression and misery. You were a welcome distraction."

He puts his hands on my shoulders, forcing me to look at him. I don't want to, but I have no choice but to gaze up into his eyes.

"Baby, I didn't plan on any of that. I just wanted to hear your voice, see your smile, feel your touch. And when I brought you here, I could feel that you would be everything I wanted, and I knew I could make you forget all that shit and make you happy, even if only for a little while." He bends down a little to make sure I'm looking him in the eye. "I never meant to hurt you. All I've wanted was for you to be happy and safe and to fucking love me just a little."

I'm falling into his eyes again, being swept into him with his words, but I don't want it now. *I don't deserve it.* I push his hands off me and put space between us again. *What have I gotten myself into? How am I ever going to get out of this without a broken heart? Or without breaking his, too?*

"Let me ask you something, Vandal. Was it all out of guilt? Because now I can't stop thinking that. Like being with me was just something to make you feel better."

He follows me across the room, cornering me so there's nowhere else for me to go.

"Tabi . . . no." He shakes his head and slams his fist against the wall. "I felt guilty, yeah, but you want to know the honest truth? I felt more jealous than anything else. I told you that. I could see how much you loved him. I saw your profile online, the happy posts, the pictures, all that shit . . . and then I saw you agonizing over his grave and I felt awful for you, and I felt like it was all my fucking fault and I wanted to make it better for you somehow, but yeah, I felt jealous, too. And if that makes me sick, then I don't fucking care." He puts his hands on my face, forcing me to look at him. "But most of all, I just wanted *you*. Just for me. That's all. I just wanted you and me together." Tears form in his eyes, his face so full of defiant pain that it physically hurts me to see him this way. My heart is cracking, breaking open with every word, and I don't know if it will ever go back together again. "I still want that, Tabi," he whispers. "I want us."

"I don't know what us is." Saying those words to him cracks what's left of my heart into a million pieces, but it's true. I'm more lost and confused now than I was when I met him. I can't deal with the games or the guilt anymore. It all just keeps getting worse. Every piece of this puzzle is creating a picture I don't want to see.

"We're what we always were. Nothing has to change. You're still you and I'm still me. I want everything we talked about."

I pull his hands off my face. "You're the one that killed my husband," I say, hating myself for adding to his pain. "That's who you are to me. How the hell am I supposed to live with that? How can I look at you?"

More pain clouds his eyes. I want to comfort him, but I'm rooted where I am. I can't move or touch him. I can't even meet his eyes. I have to hold on to some tiny shred of my devotion to Nick.

"I know I did. I killed my friend, too, and I killed my daughter. The most precious thing ever to be in my life. I live with that every day. I can barely look at myself." He closes his eyes and hangs his head. "I can't apologize enough, Tabitha. They're gone. If I could take it back or change it, or let them live and let myself die, I would do it in a heartbeat."

I blink back the tears that threaten to come again. I don't want to cry or feel pain anymore. I'm overwhelmed once again with grief, and now regret on top of that, and I'm not sure I can get through this a second time. Not without him: my rock.

"Vandal . . ."

"Without you, I wouldn't want to live, Tabitha. That's where I was when we met. I wanted to self destruct, just like you did. I was slowly trying to kill myself. I was drinking all the time, and taking pills, cutting myself, torturing myself. I got kicked out of the band. My life was destroyed, and I didn't give a shit about any of it. I just wanted it all to be over."

He puts his finger under my chin, forcing me to look into his eyes again. "My daughter was the sun in my life. She brightened my days. And I lost her. But you . . . you became the moon and stars in my dark nights. Your love is like a fire that burns into my soul. I can't lose you, too."

I reach for his hand and link our fingers together. "I do love you, Vandal. I just can't deal with all this right now. I need some time to think. Please." I look around the room frantically. "I really need to get out of here. I'm taking your car so I can get myself home. You can come get it tomorrow, or whenever you want." I drop his hand and quickly move away from him.

"What? No." He grabs my arm. "Don't leave."

I pull away from him and grab my purse, his car keys, and my cell phone. Everything has gotten out of control and gone too far, and I know that it's my fault just as much as it is his.

"Tabitha, this is your home," he says desperately. "You don't leave. We have an agreement. Did you forget?"

I stare up at him, knowing full well what card he's trying to play. "You always said I could leave whenever I wanted if I had to," I remind him. "Do you need the safe word to get this through to you? *Red*. Okay?" I say, my voice controlled. "Everything stops now. All of this."

His eyes wince. "Don't do this." He stands and paces the room, eyes wild like a caged animal, pushing his hands through his hair. "You don't know what you're doing. Just stay here and calm down, and we'll talk."

"No. I can't do this. I'm leaving. Do you want the necklace back? Give me the key and I'll take it off."

He looks horrified at the mention of me doing such a thing. "Tabi, this isn't like a regular break-up. A lot of emotional damage can be done when a Dom/sub relationship is severed. You know that, right? We have a responsibility to each other and the commitment we made when we started this." He halts pacing and stops in front of me. "Please don't take the necklace off. You have to understand how much you wearing it means to me. Once you take that off, you're telling me we're over for good."

"Just stop!" I yell, startling both of us. "I'm leaving. Please, if you really do love me, let me go. I have to get away from you. You don't understand what this is doing to me. I need to go think." I rub my forehead, which is throbbing with emotion overload. I need to be alone to piece this all together.

He falls onto the couch and puts his head in his hands in defeat. "If you need to leave, then go. Just fucking go."

I head for the door with Sterling chasing after me, and my heart snaps again as he stops next to me and tilts his head up. I bend down and rub the soft fur under his chin. "Goodbye, little guy. I'll miss you and your cuddles so much." He rubs his head into my palm, his purr echoing right through me.

"Then don't leave us," Vandal mumbles from the couch, his head still down.

"I'm sorry. I'm so sorry." I run out the door, slamming it behind me. I don't look back. I *can't* look back and see the damage I've done.

I throw open the garage door and get into the car, the tears in full force streaming down my cheeks. As I throttle the car down the street, I know that Vandal is still sitting on the couch, fighting the urge to drink.

I've lost everything. *Again.*

# chapter twenty-five

VANDAL

My heart's pounding double time, my head is throbbing, and my hands are shaking as I stumble to the bathroom and find my bottle of Valium and down a few before taking out the pack of razor blades I bought a while back when I wasn't sure which way this was gonna go. Biting the blade between my teeth I yank my jeans off and then start the slow slice on my thigh. My eyes close and I exhale slowly as the blood drips down my leg and onto the tiled floor. The lingering scent of her perfume and shampoo seep into me as I revel in the release of the emotions that are assaulting me.

I dig my cellphone out of my jeans pocket and call her. I've never called her before, but I'm glad I took her phone when she was sleeping weeks ago so I could get her number and program mine into her phone. Just in case something like this happened.

It rings and rings. Voicemail.

I redial.

*Rings. Rings. Rings. Rings.* Voicemail.

*Fuck!*

I send a text:

***Me: Answer your phone. You're still mine.***

I bandage my leg and clean the blood off the floor before going back to the living room. Crashing back on the couch, I redial again. *Rings. Rings. Rings. Rings.* Voicemail.

Fuck! I need to hear her voice. Her *real* voice, not this fake, happy voicemail voice shit.

I hit redial nonstop for an hour. I'm drowsy from the Valium, but I fight falling asleep. I should go after her, but she's got my car, and I can't ride my bike on these dark roads, especially all fucked up on Valium. I could have Lukas drive me to her house though. I quickly call Lukas.

"Hey," he answers.

"Lukas . . . she left. You have to drive me to her house. She took my car."

"What? You're talking too fast. Start over."

"That fucking whore Jill told her, she knows everything. Tabi got upset and left me. She took my car and she won't answer her phone. I've been calling her for an hour."

He sighs on the other end. "Vandal, listen to me. You have to give her some time. You going over there and forcing her to talk to you more is only going to make things worse."

"I have to fucking talk to her!"

"I know, but you have to let her calm down first. Trust me on this; I have way more experience with this than you do. You gotta let her calm down. Women don't like to be rushed or cornered when they're pissed. They're like cats. They'll scratch your eyes out."

"We were so fucking happy, Lukas. Now she hates me. She wouldn't even look at me." I press my fingers into my forehead, my mind spinning. I just want her back here *now*.

"Van, I'm sure she doesn't hate you. She's upset. Think about how hard this is for her to deal with. Just give her some time to process it all. Chasing her down will only make her run more."

"Fuck!" I yell, frustrated. I hate him for being so calm and rational all the time. Why couldn't I have some of those traits?

"Vandal, calm down. There's nothing you can do but just let her be for a little while. Trust me. Don't make it worse or you're going to regret it."

"I can't deal with any of this. She took my car," I repeat. "I'm going to need a ride over there at some point to get it."

"That's fine. Don't worry. When she's ready, we'll go get it. I'll drive you. Just watch a movie or listen to some music and go to bed for now. Okay?"

*Watch a movie? Is he fucking crazy?*

"Do you think she'll come back? Or do you think I fucked up way too bad?"

He hesitates before answering me. "This was a pretty big fuck-up, but if she really loves you, which I think she does, she'll come around. *If* you give her some time."

"Fine," I mutter drowsily.

"Call me tomorrow. In the meantime, stop calling her."

I end the call with Lukas.

*Shit. Fuck.*

I send another text to Tabi:

***Me: Plz just let me know u r ok***

A few seconds later, my phone beeps.

***Tabitha: I'm home and I'm fine. Very upset though. Please stop calling.***

***Me: Come back. Let me hold you. Let me fix this.***

***Tabitha: Please stop.***

***Me: I can't. I need you. You need me.***

***Tabitha: I'll txt you 2moro and you can come get your car. Goodnight.***

"Please don't make a scene at her house, all right?" Lukas says as he drives me to get my car. I'm completely hungover from all the Valium and I feel as if a truck ran me over.

"What the fuck ever."

"Maybe you should put this off until you're in a better mood."

"No. I need my car and I want to see her."

"You don't need your car. You have another one at the other house we could go get."

"She's got my hot rod."

He laughs, his jaw dropping. "Shit, you let her drive your favorite car?"

"I didn't *let* her, she took it. I don't care about the car anyway. I just want her back."

We drive the rest of the way in silence except for me directing Lukas which streets to turn down.

I sit up in my seat as we drive down her street. "It's the blue house on the right." I point to her house and he pulls in front and throws the car in park.

"I'm going to wait here, just in case," he says. "If she wants you to leave her alone, just leave, okay? Don't make things worse."

Ignoring him, I jog up to the front steps. I ring the doorbell and wait impatiently. A few seconds go by and she opens the door, leaving the screen door between us.

"Can I come in?" I ask her.

"No. This is the house I shared with my husband. You don't belong in here." She opens the screen door a few inches and passes my keychain through to me, pulling the screen door shut again.

"Really?" I ask in disbelief. "This is what you're going to do?"

"Vandal, please don't make this harder. I'm exhausted, and I'm sure you are, too. You look terrible."

"We can't even talk about this? It's just over? Just like that?"

She looks at me tearfully, and all I want to do is wrap my arms around her and hold her forever.

"I don't know," she replies. "I need some time away from you to figure things out in my head. I can't think when you're around."

She's still wearing the necklace. If she wanted it off she could have easily removed it with pliers or picked the tiny lock. I hope it means something that she hasn't taken it off.

"I miss you," I say. "So does Sterling."

"Please don't do that. I'm upset enough."

"Just come back home with me then. Don't throw everything away. I'll leave you alone; you can have the guest room. Just come back with me."

She bites her lip and looks up at me through the screen, and for a moment I think I've broken through her walls.

"I'm sorry I didn't tell you about the accident. I just didn't know how, and then with each day that went by I was afraid to lose you if I told you. I wasn't trying to hurt you." I plead with my eyes for her to give me another chance to make this right.

She stares past me at Lukas waiting, and then flicks her attention back to me. "But you *did* hurt me. A lot. When I was already hurting."

I put my hand flat on the screen door, wishing I could touch her. "Tabi, I've never been in a relationship before. Ever. I'm not trying to make excuses, just telling the truth. I know I'm not good at this and I fucked up royally, but I never meant to hurt you. I can be better—just give me a chance. Didn't I make you happy at all?" Emotion wells up in me and I'm not used to it at all. *Fuck.*

She places her hand against mine, the meshy screen between us. "You made me very happy, Vandal. More than you know."

I swallow hard. "Then let me keep doing it."

She pulls her hand away, tears sliding down her cheeks.

"Please, just give me some time. Can you give me that? My head is really messed up right now."

*No.*

"Fine. I'll be waiting for you; you know that, right? And you're getting a spanking when you come back," I tease, trying to make her smile. She does, but it's a sad smile that doesn't reach her eyes, and it breaks me.

"Be good, Vandal. Don't get all destructive and do things you'll regret, okay? And give Sterling lots of love for me. I have to go now." More tears spill from her eyes and she quickly closes the door before I can say anything else.

*Fuck.*

I don't want to leave. I want to stand by her door until she comes out and lets me take her back home. Closing my eyes, I will her to come back, but she doesn't.

"Vandal. Come on," Lukas yells from the street.

I wave my hand at him in annoyance and head to my car, but I break down as soon as I try to get behind the wheel because she's got the seat shoved so far forward I have to shove it back before I can get in. I can't face the thought of her never standing on her tiptoes to kiss me again or never feeling her small body tucked up against mine while she sleeps. I can't face the thought of never again seeing how beautiful she looks kneeling for me and how adorable she looks sitting on the floor playing with Sterling.

*I have to fix this. Somehow, I have to get her back.*

It's been six months, and I'm still waiting.

Two months after Tabi left, Sterling and I moved into a new house closer to the tattoo shop, and I sold the one that I lived in with Katie. It was bittersweet to sell it, but the memories were too painful for me to stay there.

Every day I send Tabitha a text to tell her I miss her, or to say hello, or to say good night. Sometimes she replies, but it's always short. I'll take what I can get, though. At least she's not telling me to go fuck myself.

Aria told me that if you picture something in your mind enough, you can manifest it into your life. I have a picture in my mind of me, Tabi, and Sterling living in a beautiful home, with a photography studio for her and a sex room filled with lots of toys, a nice yard with lots of little whimsical statues, a koi pond, candlelit dinners, lots of laughter, and no more secrets. The house I bought is everything I wanted and everything I know she would love. It's pretty barren inside for now, because I want to wait for her to decorate and furnish it with me so it's her home, too. I don't care though, I can sit around without a lot of furniture. Years ago I slept on the floor for months, so I can do this — no sweat. My hope is someday, she'll live here with me. Until then, we'll wait.

Asher let me and Sydni split the tour so I could play some of the concerts, and it worked out great for everyone. Being on stage was like therapy for me, and so is working at the tattoo shop with Lukas again. I feel like I belong for once and have spent a little more time with my cousins getting to know them. Much to Asher and Storm's dismay, the *Get Vandalized!* T-shirts have way outsold any of the other band T-shirts. I like to rub this in their faces every chance I get.

When Tabi left, I realized once again that I was at a fork in the road of my life. I could choose the road of self-destruction, which is the road I've always taken, or I could take the road that is smoother, straighter, and well-lit.

*If you keep doing what you've been doing, you'll keep getting what you've been getting.*

Lukas said those words to me not long ago, urging me to choose the smooth road for once. Staying straight and sober, focusing on putting my life back together again, has definitely turned out much better than hacking my flesh and getting wasted every day.

I miss Tabitha so much it literally hurts, but I'm giving her the space she asked for. I didn't think it would stretch out to six fucking months so far, but I'm doing the best I can, dealing with it.

I've turned down all sexual advances from the Sugar Kiss chicks and other random hook-ups, staying true to my commitment to her. I've never jerked off so much in my entire friggin' life, but I refuse to break the commitment we made to each other. Until she can look me in the eye and tell me goodbye forever, I consider myself hers.

I hope she's doing the same.

I stalk her new photography website and social media page more than I should, hoping I don't turn into a raging lunatic if I ever see her mention another guy or see any flirting, but thankfully, I haven't. Ivy told me that Tabi opened a photography studio in town and purchased some new equipment, and I hope she used some of the money that I had sent to her a few months ago. We had a text fight over that, but I promised her when we first met that if she ever had to leave, I would make sure she was okay financially. She takes some amazing photographs and I couldn't be more proud of her for following her dreams. Even if she doesn't come back to me, I still want her to be happy.

All I can do is wait. And hope. And wait.

And wait some more.

# chapter twenty-six

TABITHA

Its strange how when you're hurt, you think nothing could ever hurt this much again. But that's not true. When Nick died, I couldn't imagine ever feeling a pain like that again. But leaving Vandal not only ripped my heart out, but ripped half my soul out, too. It was a different type of pain than I felt when I lost Nick, but it was just as bad. In some ways I had a deeper connection with Vandal. Maybe because he made me feel like he needed me. While I know Nick loved me, he never really made me feel *needed*. He wasn't the damaged, tortured man that Vandal is, and in a lot of ways, that tugged at my heart.

Maybe it was the pain of all of it combined that did me in. Losing Nick. The fight with Vandal. Struggling with my own guilt. Falling in love with Vandal. Leaving Vandal. Trying to figure out who the hell I was and what I wanted, and what kind of person I had become.

I cracked like an egg.

I was off the grid so long my mother came looking for me. And then promptly had me meeting with a psychologist twice per week, who I finally talked about the accident to. I told her how Nick and Renee died instantly, Vandal was unconscious, but while we waited for the ambulance to come, I was conscious, and so was Katie. I crawled out of the car, bleeding and confused. I saw things no one should ever see. I heard the crying. *I will never not hear the crying*. I tried to crawl to the crying and came across artwork in the road. I wondered why artwork was in the road, and why it was bumpy. Only it wasn't the road at all -- it was Vandal lying in the road, and I was staring at his tattooed arm and chest. Then the crying stopped, and I was left alone with the bloody artwork, and I was scared until his hand slowly moved and touched mine and didn't let go until the ambulance came and the paramedics pulled us apart. I think he became mine right then.

I can never tell him what I remember, but I will never, ever forget.

I didn't tell the therapist about the D/s part of my relationship with Vandal. I know she would think it was abusive, but mostly, I just wanted to keep that part of my life private. I also didn't tell her all of my secrets, because I'm still too scared to admit them.

I sold the house and found a small apartment near my new studio. I couldn't bring myself to buy a house, because a certain long-haired, sexy man that refused to give up had texted me photos of my dream house, with a cute little blind cat curled up on a cushioned window seat overlooking a pond. *Come home to us,* he texted with the photos, and I wanted to jump in my car and drive right over, but I held back. I wasn't ready yet.

Lara asked me if I could possibly forgive him. And after much thinking and soul searching, I realized I didn't have to forgive him. The accident changed us. He was a victim, just like the rest of us. He should have told me who he was, but now I understand his reasons for not telling me all too well. None of us are perfect, and we all do things we're not proud of when we're scared, hurt, and upset. I know that better than anyone else.

No matter how hard I try, I can't stop thinking of him. Every morning, I want to kiss him. I miss him bathing me. I miss having breakfast with him. I miss the sex, the submission, and the control. I miss his voice. I miss his eyes and his smile. I miss Sterling. I miss hearing his music and the way it floated into me. I miss feeling loved, cherished, and desired. I miss *us*, and what we could have been with more time.

I tried to distract myself, but my thoughts always went back to him. I always wanted to call him to share my day with him, and hear him tell me about his.

Lara and I went to one of his concerts, and it was amazing watching him on stage. I enjoyed seeing girls flirt with him and watching him walk away from them, even though he didn't know I was there. *He still loves me*. After that, I finally came to terms with the fact that I was truly in love with this guy and I wanted him in my life, no matter what. I just didn't know how to fix all the wrongs we created.

He texts me, once every day. I save them all so I can keep reading them.

*Good morning, sunshine*

*I fucking miss you*

*Hope you're having a great day*

*Sterling just barfed. I stepped in it. I know you're laughing.*

*I miss waking up to you*

*Good night, Tabicat*

*I wish you were here*

*You will love this house.*

*Come home*

*Lukas says hi*

*Migraine all day :(*

*Piper showed me the pix. So proud of you.*

*My cock misses you*

*Do you ever think of me?*

*I miss your eyes*

*I hope you're eating*

*Sweet dreams, Tabicat*

*I hope you call me someday*

*I hardly smile without you*

*You were the best part of my day*

*Are you getting these?*

*You're still mine. I will spank you again.*

One day, Asher saunters into my photography studio as I'm looking through a catalog of backdrops I want to order. I'd met him once before when I took some photos for the band website, but it was brief and we didn't really talk, so I'm not sure why he's here today.

"Hi . . ." I say. "What's up?"

He's tall and muscular, wearing an old tattered leather cowboy hat over his long wavy brown hair.

"Time's up," he says, studying the various photos on the wall, not looking at me.

I furrow my brow at him. "Excuse me?"

"We wait for love to come to us when the time is right; we don't make love wait for us to decide."

"Um, what?"

He walks towards the front window of the studio and then spins on his heel to look at me, the sun catching the gem that's embedded in a skeleton key around his neck, shooting a ray of light directly in my face. I hold my hand up to shield my eyes from it.

"Stop wasting time. You've got his love, go get it," he says.

I blink the sunspots from my vision, but he's gone.

*Don't make love wait.*

As odd as that encounter was, his words burn into my brain, and I know he's right.

*It's time.*

I need to get Vandal back before I lose him forever.

# chapter twenty-seven

VANDAL

“I’m here again,” I say, placing a teddy bear on the headstone. Most of the bears I’ve left are gone. I’m not sure if they blow away, or if the caretaker takes them after a while and trashes them. I try not to think about where they go.

“Happy birthday, baby girl.”

I wipe my eyes and lie on the ground in front of the headstone. What I wouldn’t do to have her here, to see her dressed up in a special birthday dress, blowing out candles like little girls should.

I come here about once a month now. I’m learning to feel close to her in other places, but still feel the pull to come here, too. She’s helped me be the man I should have been a long time ago.

I haven’t cut myself or had a drink in a long time. If Gram is right and Katie’s watching over me, I want her to see a good man that deserves her. No matter what, I’ll always be her father, and I want Katie’s dad to be someone she would look up to, not be ashamed of. *And I want to be a man that Tabi could spend her life with.*

The sun is warm on my face and birds are chirping in the trees, and I hope that wherever my little girl is, it’s as pretty as it is here today.

“Hey.”

Looking around, disoriented, I see her leaning against the big oak tree. My tree.

*Oh, God.*

She's here.

I stand and brush the leaves off my legs, blinking to make sure I'm not daydreaming. She's still there. Slowly I walk over to her, trying to think of something to say to break the ice, but my mind is a total blank. I stop in front of her and just look at her, taking her in. Her eyes are bright and happy, and she's not as boney. She's wearing jeans and a black T-shirt with the sleeves and neck cut, and my heart stops when I see the red slashy writing on it.

***Got Vandalized!***

I let out a little laugh. "You're wearing one of my shirts, but it's got a typo."

"Evie had it made for me. I felt it was appropriate." She smiles shyly up at me, the sun dazzling in her eyes. If she's been talking to Evie and Ivy, that means she's still staying close and she hasn't cut ties with the people in my life. I have to believe she's staying close to them for a reason. My pulse quickens when I see she's also still wearing the necklace I gave her.

"You never took it off?" I ask, my eyes on her throat.

She tilts her head. "How could I? You've got the key."

"It's in my pocket. I always have it with me." I meet her blue gaze. *Shit. Please don't ask for it.* "You could have taken it off yourself."

"No, I couldn't. And I won't. Only you can do that."

"Did you track me down to take it off?"

"Nope," she says simply.

"Why are you here, then?"

"For closure," she answers, making my heart sink.

I swallow hard. "With me?"

She shakes her head no, and I nod, understanding. Hope rises in my chest and spreads a foreign smile across my lips.

"This isn't going to be easy, Vandal," she says softly. "We have a lot of baggage." I nod in agreement. "It's going to take a lot of work for us to clean up the mess we made . . . but it's our mess. I'm okay with there still being some D/s in our relationship, but I need a little more from you. A little less caveman, okay?" she asks, and I nod again. "I need you to show me your emotions. You can't just use sex and control all the time."

"I can work on that." I take a deep breath. "I miss you so fucking much, Tabi. But I've been good while you've been gone. If you came back, I wanted you to come back to something better, something you deserve."

She reaches for my hand, but a hint of sadness fills her eyes. "I want you to have someone you deserve, too. I want you back in my life, but-"

"I want you, too," I interrupt, pulling her closer. "That's all that fucking matters. We'll take it slow. You can teach me how to date, and I'll teach you how to cook." Her hand squeezes mine tighter and she nods slowly, a smile spreading across her face. "I'm in this for the long haul, baby. Good and bad, up and down, and everything in between," I take a deep breath. "I love you."

Her breath catches. "You used to have a real hard time saying that. That hurt me a lot."

"I've never said it to anyone before. I guess it took me a while to trust that it was real. But now I know it is; it just keeps getting stronger."

She goes up on her toes and kisses my lips very softy. "It's about time. I want to forget about the past and what happened to us, Vandal. Can we really do that?"

"I don't think we can ever forget. But maybe we can move forward from it together?"

She stares into my eyes, but hesitates before answering. "Yes. Let's just move forward and be happy."

"You wanna go for a ride?" I whisper, stroking my thumb across her cheek.

"Yes," her voice cracks a little. "Take me away from here."

That's all I need to hear.

*She's mine.*

I lean down and kiss her lips, loving the taste of her again, and pull her against me where she fits perfectly. She wraps her arms around my neck tight, as if she never wants to let go, and nothing has ever felt so good to me. I kiss her deeper, our tongues dancing, breath quickening. Pulling away from her mouth, I look into the eyes I'm going to be looking at for a very long time.

"I love you, Tabicat. For fuckin' ever. No more of this leaving shit, okay?"

Her smile is brighter than the sun. "I love you, too. *So* much. I'm not going anywhere ever again."

# epilogue

*Two weeks later*

*Vandal Valentine.* Just his name makes my heart flutter and my body tingle. Our relationship was born in lies, deceit, and guilt. He thinks meeting me was *his* plan, *his* deceit, born of *his* guilt.

But it wasn't just his plan. It was mine, too.

It was irony at it's best.

My eyes drift over to a box in the corner of my bedroom that I couldn't throw away when I packed up my things earlier this week to prepare to move into Vandal's new house this coming weekend. It pulls me to it like a magnet, and I go to it, kneeling in front of it like an altar to be prayed upon.

Slowly opening the box, I stare down into the pile of bent folders that led me to the man that was never supposed to own my heart. I finger the papers that I spent hours printing on my little inkjet printer and then poured over during sleepless nights.

Analyzing the words.

Studying the pictures.

Trying to figure out what kind of man he was, and what made him tick.

Months ago, these sheets of paper and the words and pictures on them fueled an insane hatred inside me that made me do the unthinkable: plot revenge.

My husband was a great man with morals, respect and a heart of gold. The man that took his life was none of those things. His dirty laundry was aired all over the internet. Drugs. Alcohol. Devious sexual behavior. Rehab. Lewd photos of him with women.

Fights in bars and backstage. The list seemed endless and the more I read, the madder I became. What higher power decided that this man should be allowed to live while three innocent people—one of those a child—lost their life?

I wanted to hurt him like he hurt me. *But how?*

It was like fate handed him to me that day in the cemetery when we met. I knew exactly who he was. My brain scrambled as he loomed over me at my husbands grave and one look in his eyes revealed something startling that even I could recognize: *he wanted me.* I could feel it emanating from him like fire. So when he asked me to go with him, I went. I knew what he wanted, and I could use that to get inside him and then destroy any part of him I was able to. Of course I was petrified, but I was so messed up in the head, I just didn't care. My grief and anger had unhinged me.

My feeble plan turned into a big fail. This man was not a man who loved. He was not one to be easily seduced. He took the control that I thought I had and soon I was spiraling into a dark, sensual hole with him. I fell into those black eyes of his, and I couldn't crawl back out. The truth is, I didn't want to, because I fell in love with him. I saw layers of him I never expected to uncover. I felt his care, his love, his intense desire, his sadness, and his regret. He wasn't the monster I thought he was.

He was just a man who made a terrible mistake.

And then I saw the glimmer of hope in his eyes, and I felt it in the way his touch changed. The power shifted. He fell in love with me, too.

I absolutely hated lying to him, because my feelings for him were very real. I can't deny any of that, as much as I struggled with it. I just wanted him to tell the truth. I *needed* to hear it.

But when his truth finally came out, I couldn't handle any of it anymore. I should have told him my truth that same night, and let all the cards fall, but I was paralyzed with fear and shame. He and I were a mess in every sense of the word. We both set out to get to each other for our own twisted reasons, and somewhere in that tangled mess, we found love, and that wasn't supposed to happen.

It hurt like hell to leave him but I had to get away from him and give us both time and space to think about what we had done not only to each other, but to ourselves as well.

I spent most of that time beating myself up for being so weak. I fell in love with Vandal way too fast. I submitted to him way too willingly. I found happiness much too soon. I didn't deserve to start over and have a new life when Nick's was ripped away from him. How could I let the man that took him away give me everything? Wouldn't that make me an even worse person? Could I live with that?

I realized Vandal's intentions, although deceptive, were not to hurt me, but to give me something back—and all he had to offer was himself. How could I hate him for that? Wasn't he loving me in his own way the entire time? Everyone makes mistakes, even horrible ones. But that doesn't mean they don't deserve to be loved.

*My* intentions, however, were to try to hurt him and that makes me worse than him. Now all I can do is love him and hope that I can forgive myself for my own deceptive behavior and not let it slowly eat at me.

I close the lid on the box and shove it back to the pile with my other belongings. Maybe someday, when we're stronger, I can tell him the truth.

For now, I just want to focus on the new life I'm starting with the man I love.

They say a relationship can't last if its built on lies, but I refuse to believe that. Maybe the truth doesn't always matter, and protecting someone from heartache is more important. I believe that fate brought us together, so we could love and heal each other in the way we each needed the most, and to me, that's all that matters.

Our love will never be pretty. It will always be tarnished by the past. Those ghosts will always haunt us. We are both so damaged by our pasts, by ourselves, by our lies, and by each other. It's who we are, and it's bound us together forever.

# sterling *the cat*

Sterling is the cat who inspired the kitty in the book. He resides at Blind Cat Rescue (at the time of publication of this book), and a portion of this book's sales will be donated to his care.

If you would like to make your own donation, please visit Blind Cat Rescue:
www.blindcatrescue.com

# acknowledgments


To everyone who has read my books, *Thank You! You have helped my dreams come true!*

Thank you to my husband, Eddie, who has consistently supported my dreams, let me have all the furry pets I want, listened to my incessant babbling, brought me many latte's and cute gifts, hugged me when I needed it, and has just always loved me for *me*. I love you.

Heartfelt thanks to Laramie Briscoe and Aimie Grey for being there for me every step of the way and having faith in me no matter what while I wrote this. I love you both!

Endless thanks to Caroline Richards for being my rock, keeping my head together, being the anal freak that she is to keep me on track, and for reminding me to sleep. I would be lost without you.

Andrea, I am so grateful for your friendship and our mutual love of furbabies! Thank you for all of your advice and input while beta reading and for supporting me!

Melony, thank you for reaching out to me to be a beta reader! Your input is invaluable and you kept me straight with the facts many times! #timemachine

Sue B.! You are amazing! I appreciate your input immensely!

Jaimie, thank you for cleaning my messes and being awesome in every way possible.

Laurie Fisher, I just love you, girl! Thank you for all of your help! xo.

Thank you to Invicta's Art & Photography for the beautiful photo of Ash that I stalked you for. I'll be back!

Ash Armand, thank you for bringing Vandal to life visually for my cover. You are beautiful inside and out.

Thank you Mandy Hollis and Rainey Wilson for the gorgeous photos of my Tabitha.

Millions of hugs to Lauren McKellar who has taught me so much and really helped me tell this story tons better. I love you hard!

Thank you Max at Max Effect for making my pages so pretty for the first edition of this book.

Thank you Perfectly Publishable for re-formatting for me after I rewrote some chapters. You do amazing work!

I cannot thank Lisa at Adept Edits enough for helping me fix up this story when I wasn't quite happy with it. I'm sure I drove you insane and you were so incredibly patient and helpful. I love you bunches!

Jane Mortensen!! Thank you for the awesome trailer! You rock!

Kari at Cover to Cover Designs – thank you for another gorgeous cover! You always capture my vision, it's like we share a brain.

Faye, thank you so much for your endless support and for always going above and beyond to help me and be there for me. You are an amazing friend and I am so glad to have met you! I don't know what I would do without you and your gentle, yet much needed guidance.

Toni, I'm so glad I was stalking reviews on Goodreads and met you. You always give it to me straight, Jersey style! I love how you push me to do better and not settle.

Danielle, you are such a valuable friend to me. Your input and feedback always helps me look at the bigger picture.

Jesiree, I just want to adopt you, I think. Can that happen?

I am overwhelmed with the amount of support I have received by so many people, it would be impossible to thank them all individually, but please know that you are all wonderful and I appreciate you so much. Extra hugs and thank you to Mary Orr, Angel Dust, Debs Cameron, Ing at As the Pages Turn, Book Fancy,

InkSlingers, and the gals at Bare Naked Words. Also, thank you to all the blogs and friends that helped promote this book!

Thank you to my mom in Heaven, who saved all my notebooks of scribbled writing that I started so many years ago and thought I threw away. Who knew my writing about hot rock stars over twenty years ago would be popular now?

# SNEAK PEEK OF LUKAS

## ASHES & EMBERS 3

# LUKAS - CHAPTER 1

## IVY

"Baby, I miss you so much," his voice is raspy with strained desire.

I press the phone to my ear, my heart pounding, a thin sheen of sweat spreading over my skin.

"I miss you, too, more than ever." My fingers tighten around the phone.

"Just wait 'til I get my hands on you tomorrow night. You'd better get a lot of rest tonight because you're going to need it. I'm gonna fuck you so hard you're not gonna be able to walk 'til Monday."

My breath catches and I cover my mouth with my hand. *Tomorrow night. Friday night.*

"Oooh . . . let's just forget dinner and spend the night in bed."

"Mmm, baby, I like the way you think," he sighs into the phone. "I better go now. I'll see you tomorrow."

"I love you." My stomach twists into a knot.

"I love you, too, babe," he says back.

The words are so familiar to me; he's said them to me thousands of times. But this time, he's not saying them to me, and that's not my voice saying it back. I have said them, many times. But not this time.

This time, there's someone else hearing and saying those words with *my* husband.

I wait for him to hang up before I gently press the end button and put the phone back in its charger next to the bed, my hand trembling so violently that I almost drop it. Hot tears burn in my eyes and spill down my cheeks. Grabbing a tissue from the nightstand, I dab my eyes and run for the master bathroom as I hear him coming down the hall toward our bedroom.

I sit on the edge of the bathtub, trembling, my mind racing, trying to somehow make sense of what I just heard. It must be some sort of mistake. Or a joke. I did *not* just hear my husband on our telephone, at midnight, telling another woman he loves her and he's going to see her tomorrow night.

*He misses her.*

*He loves her.*

*She loves him.*

*He's going to fuck her hard.*

I lurch toward the toilet and vomit up eighteen years of trust, devotion, commitment, and love.

Now all that's left is lies.

"Ivy . . . are you alright?" The doorknob rattles. "Babe, why is the door locked?"

I wipe my face with a cold, damp washcloth and take a deep shaky breath. "I'm not feeling well. Go to bed."

"Can I get you anything? Unlock the door. I don't want you locked in the bathroom while you're sick."

Still sitting on the floor in front of the toilet, I reach over to unlock the door, and he immediately comes in, standing over me.

"What's wrong?" He squints at me in the bright light of the bathroom. "You were fine a little while ago. Did you eat something bad?"

*No. I married something bad.*

Concern is all over his face, and it looks sincere, causing my stomach to turn again at the thought of how long he's been lying to me. Right to my face. As I kneel on the floor, I vomit again, and he takes a step backward. My head spins round and round. *He loves her. He misses her. She loves him. Friday night. He's supposed to love me. Only me.*

Earlier, he mentioned having to work late tomorrow night. He's been working nights and weekends for a long time, leaving me and the kids here alone.

*He was with her.*

*Of course.*

As I continue to wretch, more signs flood through my mind like evil flash cards.

Strange expenses on our credit cards.

Long nights at the office.

A short temper with the children.

Avoiding family outings.

Lack of interest in sex. *Only with me, apparently.*

My stomach heaves again.

"Ivy, you're worrying me. You never get sick." He fills a small paper bathroom cup with water and hands it to me. "Try to drink a little water."

Taking the cup, I peer up at him and start to sob. I've loved Paul for eighteen years, and never once in all that time have I ever doubted him in any way. *Not once.*

Confusion shrouds his face. "Are you crying? What's wrong?"

"I heard you." My voice is a scratchy whisper, my throat raw from dry heaving. I take a few sips of water, my hand shaking as I hold the tiny cup and wait for him to say something.

"Heard me what?"

"You, while you were downstairs on the phone." I swallow back the acid in my mouth. "With another woman."

His skin pales, and his hand goes to clutch the back of his head like he does when he's mad or upset. "Fuck." He closes his eyes for a moment and then opens them slowly to meet mine. "You were eavesdropping on me?"

I stare at him in disbelief. "Are you serious? That's all you can say? No, I wasn't eavesdropping. I saw the phone light up and thought one of the kids was calling somebody."

He blows out a deep breath. "I'm sorry. I'm so sorry, Ivy." He paces the small room. "We have to talk. I didn't want you to find out like this." *Oh, God. He's not even denying it.*

I stand up and wobble on my legs for a second before pushing past him into the bedroom. The bathroom is suddenly a way too personal space to be sharing with him. I sit on the edge of the bed, stunned that he hasn't denied anything. *Why isn't he denying it? This is the part where I find out it was some kind of misunderstanding.*

"Paul, what's going on?" More tears stream down my face. "Please tell me I'm hallucinating or something, or that this is some kind of misunderstanding."

He sits on the bed about three feet away from me. "Ivy, I'm so sorry—"

"You're sleeping with another woman? You love her?" I demand, crying harder.

He rubs his forehead. "I don't think we should talk about this when you just got sick."

"I just got sick *because* of this."

He looks at me and then quickly looks down at the floor like he can't stand to see the sight of me. "I'm sorry. I didn't want you to find out this way," he says again, his voice low.

My stomach pitches, and new tears spill from my eyes.

"Did you want me to find out at all? Or were you just going to keep seeing her behind my back?"

Still staring at the floor, he shakes his head. "I really don't know."

"So it's true?" My body trembles uncontrollably as reality starts to edge back in.

The man I've loved since high school looks me in the eyes and nods his head. "Yes, I've been having an affair."

My heart and stomach both sink, and then rage boils up inside me.

"Are you kidding me?" I hiss, trying not to yell. "I've been having a physical relationship with the detachable showerhead for a year now while you've been with another woman?" All this time, I assumed that his lack of sexual interest in me was due to him working too hard and dealing with too much stress. I never once even considered he was having an affair.

"Please don't yell. I don't want the kids to hear this." He glances toward the hallway. "I didn't plan any of this. You know how I feel about infidelity. I hate it . . . but it just happened."

I let out a half-hysterical laugh. "Really? How exactly did it just happen, Paul? Who is she?"

"The hygienist at the dentist office," he admits quietly, not meeting my eyes.

I cannot even fathom how anyone could be attracted to someone while they are scraping plaque and other ickiness from their gum line. The visual of it almost makes me laugh.

"I can't believe this. The hygienist?" Despite the fact that she's had her fingers in his mouth, as well as mine and my children's, I have to admit she's young, thin, gorgeous, and bubbly. She's the kind of woman that all men want and all women hate but secretly want to be.

"She's like twenty-two years old, Paul. What's happened to you? Cheating on me for a year? Leaving me and the kids every weekend while you spend time with her?! Lying to all of us? What the hell is wrong with you?"

He sits there staring at the floor and doesn't say a word. I want him to give me some kind of answer, some kind of explanation. But he gives me nothing.

I grab another tissue and blow my nose, hating that I'm crying in front of him because I am not a pretty crier, and now I suddenly feel ashamed to look like a mess in front of him.

"So now what?" I ask, even though I don't want to hear the answer at all, because I already know what's coming. "What do we do now?"

"We don't have to talk about that right now. I think you've had enough for today. Why don't you—"

I slam my hand on the nightstand, making him jump. "Don't coddle me, Paul! Just say it. I don't want to drag this on. This is killing me inside. Do you even see that? Do you even care?"

"Of course I care, Ivy. I care about you and the kids more than anything in the world."

"Apparently not, or we wouldn't be sitting here discussing your affair."

He ignores my sarcasm. "You know I care about you and the kids. I always will. But I think we've grown apart over the past few years. You've said it yourself a few times. We barely see each other. We argue-"

"We barely see each other? Paul, you're never home. I'm always here with the kids! You're either working, or I guess, lately, you've been out dating, having wild sex, and having a fun life with someone else while you forget you have a family at home. The only reason we argue is because you're never here! Don't you dare try to blame this on 'us'. I've been a good wife and mother. I've never strayed. I take care of everything around here."

He closes his eyes for a long time and nods. "You're right. You are, and I know that. You've always been a great wife, and you're a terrific mom." He shakes his head slowly, still looking at the floor, which seems to be the only place his eyes can focus on now. "I guess I just started to want something more, or different, than that."

I stare at this stranger who has taken over my husband's body. "More? What does that even mean? We have two beautiful children and a nice house. Both of us have good jobs. We've been in a relationship for twenty years, eighteen of which we've been married! We have everything you've said you always wanted. What more do you want?"

His face contorts with exasperation and confusion. "I don't know, Ivy. This is hard for me, too. I love you and the kids. I'm very torn. I just . . . I don't even know how to explain it. I guess I just want something different. When I met Charlene, it's like everything I thought I wanted...changed. I don't know how to explain it."

"That's just great. I'm glad to hear that Charlene has led you to the path of true happiness and saved you from your boring, torturous life here with your family. I'm sure her sexy body had absolutely nothing to do with any of it." I hurl my tissue into the small garbage pail next to the nightstand.

"That's not true, and I didn't mean it like that. Maybe because I've only ever been with you, I got restless. Don't you ever wonder what it would be like to be with someone else?"

I turn to stare at him. "So you got bored sleeping with me and had to have some twenty year old? Someone you could fuck so hard they couldn't walk? Is that what you said to her? When did you become a pig? And no, I've never thought about being with another man. Unlike you, I've always been more than happy with exactly what I have, even though you've never fucked me so hard I couldn't walk. In fact, most times, you can barely stay awake to finish the job."

He winces at my comment but reaches for my hand. I quickly pull away. "Don't touch me, Paul."

"I'm trying to apologize."

"Don't. That's not even possible. What are you going to do now? What do you want?" I repeat.

He sighs and looks around our bedroom like he's never been here before. "I don't think it's right for me to stay here anymore with all this going on. I'm going to leave and come back tomorrow to pack some things, and if it's okay with you, I'll come back with a truck next weekend for the rest of my stuff. We should probably talk to a lawyer. I promise I'll take care of you and the kids. You don't have to worry." I can tell by the way he's talking that he's thought about all of this before. He's mulled it around in his mind, trying to figure out what to say and what to do, and now he's just reciting it.

Divorce. He's divorcing me. *And I don't have to worry.* He doesn't even want to try to make our marriage work. I am floored that he can throw eighteen years of marriage away over some girl he barely knows, who is only a few years older than his own daughter.

I shake my reeling head slowly. "Just like that? We're over? You don't even want to try to fix this? We could try couples therapy. Lots of people do that. It's nothing to be ashamed of, and they're very discrete—"

"Ivy, I've been sleeping with another woman for a year. How do we fix that?"

The brutality of his words stuns me. I lost a year of my marriage without even knowing it. How did I not know? How did I miss all the signs?

"I thought you loved me." My voice cracks. "I thought we loved each other." I realize I sound pathetic, but I can't stop the words that shoot from my heart to my mouth, no matter how much I don't want to say them right now.

"I *do* love you, but I somehow fell in love with her, too." He walks slowly to the closet that we share and throws some clothes into his gym bag. "This has been a mess for me, too, Ivy. It's been destroying me inside to lie to you for so long. I know you don't deserve it, and I hate hurting you."

"Then why did you? Why couldn't you just stay committed to us? Why would you let someone come between us?"

He approaches me with his overstuffed bag in his hand. "I don't know. I wish I had a better answer, but I don't. I never wanted to hurt you. Ever. One thing just kept leading to another. You're right —I should have stopped it. I'm an asshole. I know that."

"So you want to leave me and the kids? For her?" I demand.

"Not *for* her. But for now, I think I need to leave. And I'm not leaving the kids. I'm still their father."

My heart cracks and shatters into a million little isolated memories of our life together, splattering like blood at a brutal crime scene. This will never be able to be cleaned up or put back together again. He's obliterated it.

His eyes are on me as I fall apart. I know he can't see it, but all my hopes and dreams of growing old together with the man I love are climbing into that bag with him to be given to someone else.

"Is it because I'm not as thin as I was?" I ask him, my voice shaking. "I can join a gym, buy new clothes—"

"Ivy, God . . . no. You're beautiful, and I still love you. It's not that at all."

I shake my head slowly back and forth as I try to grasp what's happening to us. "I just don't understand what I did wrong."

He takes a few steps closer to me. "You didn't do anything wrong, I swear to you. I didn't plan it, and I wasn't looking for it. Actually, she kinda reminds me of you when we were young. She's happy and carefree. I like being with her and not having kids screaming and fighting, or on the other side of the bedroom wall, blasting video games and music. I'm sorry."

"You wanted kids, Paul. They make noise."

"I know that. But come on, Ivy. We had Macy when you were eighteen and I was nineteen. We were way too young to have a baby. We never got to enjoy ourselves or each other. And as soon as she was able to be by herself a little bit and not need one-hundred percent of your attention, Tommy came along. I guess I want to have fun for a little while, while I'm still young."

"You should leave now." My voice is dull, lifeless. I refuse to look at him. I've had enough. His resentment toward his own family is making me hate him, and I want to inflict some sort of bodily harm on him.

He hesitates for a moment and then just turns and leaves. His footsteps pound down the stairs, and the front door squeaks opens, then closes. His car door slams and then backs out of our driveway, the headlights flashing across the bedroom windows.

And he's gone. Just like that.

I sit on the bed, staring at the wall in a daze, until the sun comes up, wondering what the heck just happened.

# LUKAS - CHAPTER 2

## LUKAS

Insomnia is a bully of the worst kind. Pushing me. Shoving me. Laughing in my face. Waiting 'til I feel safe and then kicking me in the skull. I fight back, but we all know how this story goes—the bully wins.

So I lay awake, staring at my cathedral ceiling and feeling uncomfortable in my own bed. Not just because I can't sleep, but because there's a chick next to me that I know I'm never going to sleep with again. I want to love her. I *should* love her. She's cute with a banging body and long silky black hair with blue highlights. Her eyes are like fucking sapphires, and she has a giggle that sounds like a demented elf. She's a musician, like me, so she gets me. She knows when to stay and when to go away, and she sucks me like I'm a cherry lollipop.

There's just one thing that's wrong.

Rolling over toward me, her lips press against my cheek. "You're so much nicer in bed than Vandal ever was." I feel her lips turn into a smile as she snuggles against my shoulder.

Yup. That's the thing that's wrong—she slept with my older brother a few times. Actually, I'm pretty sure sleeping wasn't involved at all while he had her tied to his bed being *vandal*ized, as he so nicely puts it. Even though I've tried, I just can't get that out of my head. I don't want to be second choice, or get my brother's leftovers. Who would want to always be compared to his brother? I don't want to be with a woman that Vandal has seen naked and violated. I want someone that's just . . . mine.

I sit up, slowly untangling myself from her, and try to find my clothes in the dark room.

"Where you going?" Her hand lands on my back, her voice drowsy as she fights off sleep.

I turn toward her, dreading that I'm going to upset her, but I feel like the band-aid ripping approach is probably best.

"Rio, I can't do this anymore," I say softly.

"Do what?"

"This. Us."

Bolting up, she holds the sheet against her naked chest. "Why?" Her bright blue eyes darken.

"I really like you. You're one of my best friends . . . it's just not going past that for me. I wish it was."

Her usually pretty face falls into a sad frown. "Lukas . . . I love being with you. Maybe we just need some more time. Don't think about it going any further, just let it happen."

I slowly shake my head. "I won't do that to you." Standing, I pull on my jeans. "I'm sorry. The last thing I want to do is hurt you."

"That's what I love most about you," she says wistfully. "You're the only one that actually cares and doesn't treat me like a toy."

I hate that my brother has boned every chick within a hundred mile radius, and I hate myself even more for not being able to move past it.

She crawls across the bed toward me, her long dark hair forming a silk curtain over her tits. "Lukas, it's all right if you don't love me. I can deal with that. Really." Hope and desperation taint her voice, and it upsets me to hear that in her. She's so much better than that; she just doesn't know it yet.

Picking her clothes up off my bedroom floor, I place them next to her so she can get dressed. "It's not all right with me," I say. "And you deserve more. Don't settle, okay? You don't have to. The right guy will come, trust me. And he's going to be lucky as hell."

"I doubt it," she replies, slipping her shirt over her head.

"I'll wait in the living room for you, and I'll take you home."

"Lukas?" Her soft voice stops me before I get to the bedroom door. "There might not be a right one for any of us. Maybe that's just a myth, ya know?"

Maybe so, but I believe in the mythical and have faith in the legends of time. Fantasy drips through my veins. It's what's kept me alive.

**ASHES & EMBERS ROCK STAR ROMANCE SERIES:**

Storm - Ashes & Embers book 1

Vandal - Ashes & Embers book 2

Lukas - Ashes & Embers book 3

Talon - Ashes & Embers book 4

Loving Storm (sequel) - Ashes & Embers book 5

**ALL TORN UP SERIES (Ashes & Embers Spin Off Series, Contemporary Romance):**

Torn - All Torn Up series book 1

Tied - All Torn Up series book 2

**STANDALONE BOOKS:**

No Tomorrow

Visit my web site at www.cariancolewrites.com for more info on upcoming books!

Carian Cole has a passion for the bad boys, those covered in tattoos, sexy smirks, ripped jeans, fast cars, motorcycles and of course, the sweet girls who try to tame them and win their hearts.

Born and raised a Jersey girl, Carian now resides in beautiful New Hampshire with her husband and their multitude of furry pets. She spends most of her time writing, reading, and vacuuming.

Carian loves to hear from readers and interacts daily on her social media accounts.

*Stalk me!*

www.cariancolewrites.com
carrie@cariancole.com

Made in the USA
Columbia, SC
25 October 2024